Alexina Mackay Harrison

The Story of the Life of MacKay of Uganda Told for Boys by his Sister

Alexina Mackay Harrison

The Story of the Life of MacKay of Uganda Told for Boys by his Sister

ISBN/EAN: 9783337415488

Printed in Europe, USA, Canada, Australia, Japan

Cover: Foto ©Andreas Hilbeck / pixelio.de

More available books at **www.hansebooks.com**

THE

STORY OF THE LIFE

OF

MACKAY OF UGANDA

TOLD FOR BOYS

BY

HIS SISTER

With Portrait and Twelve Illustrations

NINTH THOUSAND

London
HODDER AND STOUGHTON
27, PATERNOSTER ROW

MDCCCXCII

PREFACE.

THIS book is written especially for boys, in the hope that Mackay's example may lead many of them to think of Africa, and devote their lives to its moral and spiritual regeneration.

They will please to remember that, like Livingstone and Krapf, Mackay was a pioneer, and that every year in Africa the difficulties become less and the dangers fewer. In a little while will—

> "The palpitating engines
> Snort in steam across her acres."

Then missionaries and traders will be borne speedily away from the fever-stricken coast ; over flooded rivers, the weary jungles and the waterless plains, right up to the noble lake, where a commodious and comfortable steamer will be available to transport them and their goods to any port they choose.

I desire to tender my thanks to Mr. Eugene Stock for his permission to incorporate in this book Bishop

Tucker's account of his visit to Uganda ; also to record my obligation to the Rev. John Stewart, Edderton, N.B., for his trouble in collecting from old friends several incidents of my brother's early life.

The whole of the matter in this volume is fresh, and is not found in the larger book, " Mackay of Uganda."   If it confirm and increase the good already done by that volume, I shall be richly recompensed.

J. W. H.

September, 1891.

CONTENTS.

CHAPTER VIII.

CHAPTER IX.

CHAPTER X.

CHAPTER XI.

CHAPTER XII.

CHAPTER XIII.

CHAPTER XIV.

CHAPTER XV.

CHAPTER XVI.

CHAPTER I,

A DISCOVERY.

> " And Afric, sunny Afric,—
>   Where the sand has drunk hot tears,
> From the brimming eyes of millions,
>   Through the long ungracious years,—
> Go, call her children brothers,
>   Bid their dark eyes flash with glee,
> As they list the wondrous story
>   Christ hath made them men and free."
>
> W. WRIGHT HAY.

IT was the year 1849, in Aberdeenshire. Summer and autumn had gone, the birch and the rowan were stripped of their leaves ; the gowan was no longer under the foot ; and the yellow broom and the purple heather were looked for in vain. True, Tap o' Noth still towered his majestic head above Rhynie village, but this morning he seemed to have wrapped himself in his ermine mantle, for with the exception of here and there a rough-walled, low-thatched cottage, or a crag or two projecting from his side, from summit to base he was white, snowy white. In the village too all was bleak and desolate and still, save for the eerie sough of the wind blowing across the moor, sighing and moaning among the stiffened branches of the trees, and improvising æolian harps in the draughty windows of the cottages. Already lines of white marked the thresholds, and thistles of frost garnished the window-panes.

It was the first cold of the season, and seemed to have arrived too early and to be regarded as an intruder. The suddenness of the invasion had rendered work a little more difficult, and heightened the demand for courage and industry. So evidently thought a minister as he gazed on the dreary scene from his study window ; for, with the scarcely audible reflection that a storm was at hand and that probably there would neither be letters nor the *Witness* that day, he threw out some crumbs to a golden robin who was pleading hard for shelter on the sill, and resumed his chair and his book.·

A cosy enough study it looked, as the ruddy fire lightened the dim atmosphere and shone out on two large book-cases, the glass doors of which revealed the names of the best thinkers of the day. A profusion of gazetteers, blue-books, atlases, and books of travel littered the table and floor. A picture of the Disruption worthies overhung the mantel, and engravings of the old Reformers filled niches in the walls. Presently the minister rose, and suspended a large map of Africa from a nail on the top of one of the book-cases, in near proximity to the window. A quaint-looking map it was.

Certainly no ships sailed on its waters ; neither did rhinoceroses, hippopotami, or ostriches disport themselves on its shores, nor yet had the engraver

> " O'er uninhabitable downs
> Placed elephants for want of towns ";

and yet strange it seemed, the greater part being delineated as an immense featureless blank, near the middle of which a solitary caterpillar crawled, with the label " Mountains of the Moon " distinctly printed on its back. For up to this time the continent of Africa had been, as it were, hidden, and its myriad peoples almost unknown. The Scottish traveller Mungo Park had, in 1796, explored the Niger, and corroborated the statement of Herodotus, which few geographers then believed, that the great river flows from west to east before it turns in a south-easterly direction towards the Bight of Benin.

Another Scotchman, James Bruce, had as early as 1770 traced the *Blue* Nile to its source, and although at the time many ridiculed his wonderful stories, more recent travellers have confirmed his re-searches ; but the origin of the *White*, or main stream of the Nile, was still shrouded in mystery. The eminent travellers Burton, Speke, Baker, Grant, Cameron, and Stanley had not yet even dreamed of the honours that awaited them, to say nothing of another Scotchman, David Livingstone, who had been quietly pursuing his missionary labours at Kuruman and Kolobeng.

Events, however, had now begun to move apace, for on the 1st of August of this year (1849) Livingstone sighted Lake Ngami, which was the first of a long chain of remarkable discoveries by that celebrated missionary which have led to the opening up of the "Dark Continent" to European enterprise and to the messengers of the Gospel of Peace.

But the first explorers who penetrated the interior from the *east* coast of the continent were Johann Ludwig Krapf, and John Rebmann, pioneer missionaries of the Church Missionary Society. At the risk of their lives, and enduring untold privations —for they could not even enjoy the luxury of oxen, which Livingstone did—they traversed countries never before visited by civilised man ; and although their object was simply to commence missionary labours among the heathen, the results of their geographical researches have been truly wonderful.

The minister's attention seemed riveted on this *terra incognita* of Eastern Africa ; for, repeating to himself " Lat. 3° 30′ S., long. 37° E.," he proceeded, with pencil in one hand and magnifying-glass in the other, to note something on the map.

Presently a tap came to the door, and a very tall, spare old woman entered with a soft, stately step. This was Ann McWilliam, or "the minister's Annie," as she was called in the parish. She was quite a character in her way, and, as was the wont with better-class servants in those old-fashioned days, was on familiar terms with her employers and had much of her own way with people and things in general. She had been housekeeper to the minister in his bachelor days, and although she had vowed that if he ever married she would quit the house, and really did adhere to her resolution, she very speedily re-appeared on the scene ; for, although Annie was no gossip, she liked to be considered as an authority on all matters that concerned her pastor, and found it gall and wormwood to be unable to answer the many questions that were asked her concerning the young wife, what " providin' " she had brought, and especi-ally about the *piano*, for hitherto the fiddle and the bagpipes were the only musical instruments known in the village.

Annie had never laid claim to beauty, but, what was better, she was good and true ; and this morning a tender smile brightened and warmed the kind old face and made her heart glow with joy. The minister had neither heard the knock nor seen her enter, but as the firelight leaped up more ruddily as she threw on another log he gave her a passing glance, and she seized the opportunity to say, " I've brocht ye a present, sir." He took no notice of the remark, however, but said, " Do you see this pear-shaped continent, Annie? This is Africa ; you see that, unlike all the other continents, it has few inlets, no great gulfs nor great river estuaries ; in other words, although it is a mighty mass it has comparatively little coast-line, and as a necessary consequence it has made very little progress in civilisation. Though it is three times the size of Europe, it has far less coast-line than our continent, which fact explains more than anything else its past history and its backward condition. While Europe has surrendered herself to the ocean, as if aware of future prosperity through her navies, Africa has on the other hand shut herself up from the sea, and has ever remained isolated and uninfluenced by the pulse-beats of the world. But should any navigable rivers be discovered, so that missionaries and Christian traders could get with ease into the interior, then no doubt progress would be rapid.

"Till now, Annie, the east *coast* even has been quite unknown to us, but there has been a wonderful discovery. Two German missionaries in connection with the Church Missionary Society have made several journeys inland from Mombasa, and have discovered a great mountain mass of volcanic origin, the culminating peak of which is nearly 20,000 feet high, and covered with perpetual snow. *Kilimanjaro*, it is called.* The results of this discovery will be far-

---

* The actual height of the "great ice dome," which was first seen by Rebmann in 1848, has since been ascertained by Dr. Hans Meyer to be 19,700 ft. high. He declares it to be the loftiest mountain in Africa, and in the German Empire, and has named it "Kaiser Wilhelm's Peak." Mount Kenia, to the north of it, discovered by Krapf, in 1849, is said to be 18,000 ft. high. Dr. Carl Peters, however, estimates the height to be 23,000 ft. !

reaching, for the information will give a zest to geographical exploration, and will probably lead to · the Church Missionary Society sending inland a great host of missionaries before long, and that will be the first real check to the terrible slave trade which has been carried on for ages between this coast and the ports on the Red Sea and Persian Gulf. The cruelty which takes place daily in carrying off these poor people from their homes and transporting them beyond the seas is frightful and beyond description. The slave-traders are chiefly Arabs. They buy or take captive the natives of the far interior, where no white man has as yet ventured to penetrate, and burn their villages. Thousands die on the march down to the coast, from the wounds and bad treatment they receive; the old and the infants are left to die from exhaustion and starvation, and of course only the strong and the hardy survive, to suffer still greater cruelty on the sea voyage. They are packed like herrings in a barrel, in the holds of wretched dhows, where the half of them perish from foul air and hunger, and then, if a British cruiser gives chase to these vessels and is likely to run them in, the slavers kill their victims by a knock on the head, or throw them into the sea and escape themselves."

" Ay, sir! it is dreadful; and I aften think we owe a debt o' gratitude to Africa, for it sheltered baith the law and the Gospel; for the Nile cradled the infant Moses, and our blessed Lord Himsel' learned to lisp and to walk by its banks ; and the Spirit o' the Lord seems to have recognised the obligation, for in the early days o' the Kirk, Philip was ta'en awa frae a great revival in Samaria to send a missionary to the court o' an African queen, although we dinna read o' ony results."

" There must have been results, Annie, for we know that Christianity was *established* in the fourth century in Abyssinia, and prevails there still, although in a very corrupt form, and to this day the sovereign of that country traces his descent to King David, styles himself ' King of Zion, King of Kings of Ethiopia,' and confers the order of Solomon on his favourite chiefs. Yes, Annie: ' He shall speak peace unto the heathen ; and His dominion shall be from sea to sea, and from the river unto the ends of the earth.' The Gospel banner will yet be planted at the very heart of this continent, altho' not likely in your day nor mine, Annie."

" But maybe it'll be in your *son's*, sir ! and wha will say he'll nae hae a han' in it ? "

Something in her tone made the minister look round, and for the first time he noticed that she was gazing with reverent love at an infant on her arm. The minister drew his hand through his hair : it took him some seconds to transport his thoughts from tropical Africa to his own fireside, but after some explanations, he said, " A boy ! Bring him near the window, and let me see him."

"Sic a day, sir! It's awfu' unlucky to come on sic a day! He'll hae the win' in his teeth a' his life!"

"Annie! such superstitions are unworthy a Christian woman! Besides, you know what Samuel Rutherford says, 'Grace groweth best in *winter.*' He will be a better man for adversity;" and as his eye lighted on an old picture on the opposite wall, he added, "May he be another John Knox, Annie! may he defend the faith of his fathers before priestly antagonists! and may his tongue never quail before the sceptre of a queen!"

"I hope he'll hae mair tact and prudence, and hae a safter tongue and a gentler hand, sir, than John Knox; though nae doot he was raised up for his time. Na! he is nae gaen to be a John Knox; he'll gang his ain gait and jest be himsel', jest Alexander Mackay!"

"Oh! and so you have settled the name, too, have you, Annie?"

"Of course, sir. Fat ither than hae the name o' his father named upon him?" And Annie retired in her dignified way from the room.

She did not quite get her own way in this matter, however, for when the christening took place the name of a Celtic ancestor was revived. This legacy the boy never appreciated, for although he used the initial "M." to distinguish him from his father, no amount of teasing would tempt him to divulge what it stood for.

CHAPTER II.

EARLY DAYS.

" 'Tis strange how thought upon a child
    Will, like a presence, sometimes press,
And when his pulse is beating wild,
    And life itself is in excess—
When foot and hand, and ear and eye,
    Are all with ardour straining high,—

" How in his heart will spring
A feeling whose mysterious thrall
Is stronger, sweeter far than all ;
    And on its silent wing,
How with the clouds he'll float away,
As wandering and as lost as they ! "

N. P. WILLIS.

RHYNIE is for the most part a high-lying, pastoral, and sparsely peopled district. The inhabitants are believed to be of Pictish origin, and are a sturdy, shrewd, independent, and hospitable class of people. Their history has predisposed them to religion, for the Seceders and the Independents have been in the district for several generations. The Disruption conflict of 1843, which agitated Scotland from the Orkneys to the Solway Firth, reached a climax here, for Rhynie formed part of the famous Presbytery of Strathbogie, and its minister was one of the seven deposed by the Evangelical majority of the Church of Scotland ; and no doubt this contest had a large share in quickening both the spiritual and intellectual life of the people. Even forty years ago many were wont to walk six miles to church every Sunday and six back. Weather never deterred them ; indeed, their struggle with the elements on the way seemed to harden their frames and develop their brain-power, so that by the time they reached the house of God their appetite was whetted for a good doctrinal discourse and plenty of it. Short measure did not take in those days. They desired a good meal, and on their way home the little companies beguiled the weary miles by recalling the heads of the sermon, the observations on these, and the inferences drawn by the preacher ; while the children were appealed to for the illustrations.

The dress of the women was primitive in the extreme. Many went to church in the mob-caps with a plain band of riband which fastened below the chin ; while the better class wore bonnets made of pasteboard covered with black silk, close-fitting to the face. When these wore out they were replaced by others of the same style and pattern. Linsey-woolsey dresses, spun from a mixture of white and black fleeces, to save the expense of dyeing, and tartan shawls, completed the costume. Each woman carried her Bible neatly tied up in a white handkerchief, together with a sprig of southernwood or a bouquet of roses if it was summer, while the other hand invariably held a gingham umbrella! This fashion is now, however, quite obsolete, for with the smoke of the railway engine there came a wonderful change in the manners and dress of the inhabitants.

Looking back over the forty years of Alexander Mackay's life, it is evident that from the day almost that he emerged from the cradle God was preparing him in His own way and building him a pioneer missionary. Godly parents, a pious nurse who doted on him, the Bible-loving women of the parish, the intelligent workmen in the neighbourhood, each and all, unknown to themselves, and equally hidden from him, contributed a share in his equipment for the special work which the Master needed him to do.

In 1851 the new Free Church was erected close by the Manse; and as the stones were dressed in the garden, a golden opportunity presented itself to the boy to acquire practical knowledge and to use his dexterous fingers. His beauty and extraordinary gentleness, together with his wonderful aptitude for picking up all kinds of handicraft, speedily ingratiated him with the workmen, who took a delight in supplying him with the necessary tools to enable him to imagine that he was giving important assistance. When he appeared on the scene he was accosted with the question, " Weel, laddie, gaen to gie 's a sermon the day?" and the invariable reply (in which there was something like prophetic instinct) was,

" Please give me trowel ; can preach and build, same time ! "

He was full of questions, and was never satisfied until he thoroughly understood the reason of everything. One day he saw a man repairing a fence, and he asked how the fence came to be so broken down. The man replied that the snow had done it. The boy was incredulous, and after reflection he went back to the man and asked if snow was very heavy. "No, not very," was the reply. "Well, then, how could it break down a fence in that way?" But when it was explained to him that it was the great accumulation of snow lying against the fence that caused it to fall, he went away quite satisfied.

He was a very meditative boy, and very impressible to the moods of nature. A hot August day was his delight, and as the sunbeams played on the heathery slopes of Noth, and glanced on the silvery streaks of the burns as they rippled down its brow, he would tell Annie that " the mountain had donned the regal purple in honour of the visitors who had appeared in the neighbourhood. You know he must be old, for the Roman fort and the giant's footprints tell of other days.* Still he is neither blind nor deaf. He can

---

* According to tradition, the Noth was guarded! by a giant of extraordinary dimensions—

> "Between his een there was a yaird,
> Between his shou'ders three."

But he required all his enormous proportions to combat his foes,

see the unusual number of carriages in the lanes, and feel the tread of the horsemen on his side, and no doubt connects them with the sudden surprises of the red grouse. Hark to his long sigh accompanying that echo of firing in the glen and the merry laughter of the sportsmen as they bag their game, never thinking that the birds will no more breakfast off the leaves of the heather nor peck the cranberries which hide among its roots! But, as many of these Southerners have attired themselves, for the nonce, in the kilt and sporan and Glengarry bonnet, he takes it as a compliment to himself, and returns it by putting on his brightest smile and looking his very best. You know you like to look nice too, Annie. But why do you not iron your neck and take out all the creases, and smooth the furrows out of your brow?"

Then Annie's heart experienced a pang which only the aged know, and, yearning for the society of her contemporaries, she replied, "If it's fine the morn, we'll gang to Blackhills for a day or twa."

especially the rival giant who guarded the hill of Bennachie, some thirteen miles distant. A frequent exchange of compliments took place between the two, in the shape of huge boulders thrown by the one against the other. On the Tap o' Noth may yet be seen (?) one of these, with the marks of five gigantic fingers thereon. On the occasion on which it was hurled, the giant of Noth retaliated by raising a huge mass of rock with the intention of hurling it at his adversary, who put out his foot and touched the boulder, with the result that it remains still on Noth with the impress of the giant's toe on it to this day!—See "Legendary Ballad Lore," by A. I. M'Connochie.

"Oh, that will be delightful! But why do you look so sad, Annie?"

"Only because ye didna ken me when I was young, laddie."

" I am glad I did not, for then you would not be *old Annie,* and you could not tell me all I want to know."

On the morrow the pair set out on their excursion to the farm. It was six miles from the village, and situated in a lonely glen at the foot of the Buck,* amidst wild and rugged scenery. Untamed nature on every side, and nothing to disturb the silence but the birr of the moor-cock, the bleating of the sheep, and the song of the burns intersecting the peat-moss. Every now and again a bell-shaped foxglove or a curious-looking rock attracted the boy's attention, and off he darted and forgot to return :

> "And heedless of his shouted name
>   As of the carol of a bird,
>   Stood gazing on the empty air,
>   As if some dream were passing there."

At length they pursued their way along the sheep-track amid the brushwood and heather, until they reached the hospitable home of Mrs. Smith, where fresh milk, new-laid eggs, and heather honey regaled the weary-footed travellers.

* The "Buck o' the Cabrach" is mentioned by Elspeth Mucklebackit in "The Antiquary," in her account of the coronach or Highland lament for the dead, after the "Battle o' the Harlaw.'

The repast over, they drew round the blazing fire of wood and peat, for the sun had gone down and a chilly breeze blew from " the Buck." The chimney was open to the heavens, and in the settle hung legs and shoulders of smoked mutton. The busy knitting-needles glanced in the firelight as the two old friends entertained each other with cherished stories which they had learned in childhood of the Brothers Erskine and of their father, the sainted Henry Erskine, who had been condemned to imprisonment for preaching at " conventicles," and how through the intercession of friends the sentence was commuted to banishment from the kingdom. The boy, seated on a low stool, listened appreciatively until Mrs. Smith produced her wheel and began to spin the wool yielded by the previous clipping. He then became oblivious to his friends and their conversation,—

> "While flashes of intelligence dart from his pale-blue eyes,
> Broad beams of golden humour, and long looks of surprise,
> And laughter ripples o'er his lips, and joy like sunshine lies
> Upon the fair fields of his cheeks, and danceth in his eyes."

The friends exchanged glances, and in private afterwards talked of the peculiar look in his face, which spoke of a future, and wondered what that future would be.

> " Yet evermore the mystery which rang him round did press
> Upon their larger sense, and set their riper wits to guess,—
> To guess, but ever miss the mark, to flounder and to fall,
> To wonder quite as much at him, as he, sweet child, at all."

For even their love for him did not foresee that the impression which he took and photographed in his mind of that spinning-wheel would be reproduced thirty-five years afterwards for Mwanga, King of Uganda!

The following summer, when he was nearly four years of age, he spent a month at Blackhills; and this visit did him much good, for Mrs. Smith would allow him no lessons except to read a chapter from the Bible aloud to her, morning and evening. She was so proud of his attainments, however, that when a distant neighbour from some lonely cottage among the hills dropped in, she would put her hand in the "crap" in the wall beside the "saut poke" in the "ingle neuk" for the big Bible, and calling the boy, would tell him to read aloud the tenth chapter of Nehemiah. He did this, pronouncing with accuracy the names of those who sealed the covenant, and preserving the inflections so as to read gracefully.

Mr. Smith, the present tenant of the farm, tells how, on this visit, the boy followed him wherever he went at his work:

"Whether the farmer swung the scythe or turned the hay,"

or

'Merrily, with oft-repeated stroke,
  Sounds from the threshing-floor the busy flail,"

there the child was, inquiring the reason for everything he saw done, and understanding the explanation as easily as a grown-up person.

2

"One day," Mr. Smith says, "I was taking up some small stones out of the ground, and I asked him to fetch me a small pick. He went, but as he did not return, I knew that something was preventing him from doing what he undertook. So I went to see what was the matter, and found that he had not fully understood the kind of tool I wanted, but having found a large *pinch lever*, which he had seen used for taking up stones, he was bringing it. It was six feet long, and by far too heavy for him to carry; still, he had succeeded in bringing it fifty yards or so. The way he accomplished it was by lifting one end at a time, and going round with it, and then going to the other end and doing the same thing, and every turn brought it six feet on! This shows his readiness of resource, and his determination to accomplish whatever he took in hand, even at four years of age."

In order to draw him out, the farmer amused himself by arguing occasionally with him on different subjects; but the boy got tired of arguments, and said, one day, quite gravely, " Now, Mr. Smith, we must not have any more disputes in this way, but, as ' the law is open,' we will settle everything there where it ought to be settled, and let us live in peace henceforward." Another time he went to the byre while the cows were being milked, and expatiated on the difference between the higher and lower animals, taking himself as an example of the higher and the cows of the lower. When some one remarked that "the brute creation know more than they get credit for," he replied, " Oh, yes, I allow the lower animals have *instinct*, but that is different from the power of reason in man, although it is very useful to them. It helps them to preserve their lives, and sometimes it helps them to preserve the lives of their masters too."

A niece of Mr. Smith says, " When my sister and I were children, nothing was such a treat to us as to get our mother to tell us sayings and doings of Mackay when he was a child. She was so happy in recalling them, and invariably concluded her stories with the remark, " I did like that laddie ! "

When he was five years of age, the *régime* of his old nurse came to rather a sudden end. One morning a heavy fall awoke him, and as the curly head raised itself from the pillow, the blue eyes opened wider and wider, as he saw his friend lying prostrate on the nursery hearth, with her head in close proximity to the fire. In a minute he was up, dragging and pulling her out of danger ; but, failing in his efforts to move her, with wonderful foresight he returned to his cot, and seizing his quilt, tucked it well over her head, lest a blazing log should fall on her. He then sped like lightning to his parents' room, exclaiming, " Annie is dead ! I am sure she is dead ! "

Annie, however, recovered, and in a few days was herself again. But it was thought advisable that she should have some lighter occupation, so she invested her savings in furnishing a small house in Old Aberdeen, conveniently situated for letting lodgings to students attending King's College.

The prospect of her departure was the boy's first real grief. When the day came for their last walk Annie said, " Cheer up, laddie ! I'm comin' back to see ye ilka summer ; but we'll gang the noo to the Brig o' Bogie. I want to show ye something afore I gae awa'."

When they reached the bridge, Annie sat down to rest on the stone coping of the low wall, while the boy leaned idly over, wondering what was to be seen. After a little Annie said, " I'm gaen awa' the morn !" but he was already absorbed in the click-clack of the mill-wheel, and he heard her not.

After repeated efforts to gain his attention, she pulled his sleeve, saying, " I'm nae gaen to let onybody whip my bairn when I'm awa' ; " and producing a little leather " tawse " out of her pocket, she dropped it into the stream.

It took the boy a minute to forget the wheel and to realise the situation, but when he did so he darted to the other side of the bridge, screamed, and then rushed down the bank and into the Bogie. Annie was in terror, for she was too weak to follow him, and some parts of the stream were deep. She succeeded, however, in attracting the notice of a man in an adjoining field, who was singing blithely as he followed the plough.   This man kindly rescued the child from the water and tried to reason with him :

> " But his young heart was swelling
> Beneath his snowy bosom, and his form
> Straightened up proudly in his tiny wrath,
> As if his light proportions would have swelled,
> Had they but matched his spirit, to the man."

" Ye maun hie hame," said Annie, " and change yer droukit claes " ; but with a determination which surprised her, he quietly told her that until the tag was recovered, or properly searched for, he would not return.   Presently the sound of merry voices coming down the hill announced that the schoolchildren were on their way home, so he climbed up the bank on to the road and told them of his trouble.   They were highly amused, and the bigger boys were soon wading in the Bogie.   A shout and a loud " hurrah ! " announced its recovery, and a long-legged, red-haired boy, with a twinkle of humour in his eye, restored it to the rightful owner, with the caution, " Dinna dry it ower fast, or it'll be a' the harder for its doukin.' "

On the way home, after reflection, he said, " Perhaps it is best you should go, Annie, for you used to try to make me good, and how can I be good without a tag ? "

" Ye are aye gude, my bairn ; ye never do naething wrang, except forgettin' to learn yer lessons, and ye shall nae be whipped for that.   Ye canna help forgettin', whiles."

"Yes, I ought not to forget, because if I cannot say my lessons immediately after breakfast, papa has no time to hear me all day. Have you forgotten about the pilgrims and the black man, Annie?"

Annie, wishing to divert his attention, affected ignorance.

"Well, you know, Annie, the pilgrims had stopped all night with the shepherds on the Delectable Mountains, and when they were leaving, the shepherds gave them a note of directions for the way. They forgot, however, to read the note, and they got into a black man's net before they knew, and had to stop there a long time, till a shining one came to them, with a whip in his hand. He let them out of the net and put them on the right way again; but after he had heard their story, he asked them if the shepherds had not given them a note of direction, and they said, 'Yes.'

"'But did you read it?' and they said, 'No.'

"'Why did you not read it?' and they replied, '*We forgot;*' so he ordered them to lie down on the grass and he whipped them sore. Then he bade them get up and go on their way, and *not to forget again*. And the pilgrims thanked him for his kindness, and went on their way softly."

Annie lived some years after this scene, and many a time she told the story of the boy's inflexible rectitude.

CHAPTER III.

TRANSMITTED IMPULSES.

"Things of high import sound I in thine ears,
  Dear child, though now thou mayst not feel their power.
  But hoard them up, and in thy coming years
  Forget them not."   ANON.

THE life of Alexander Mackay is not a story of self-help in the common acceptation of the phrase. The atmosphere of his early home was high and pure, and his surroundings were very stimulating to literary cultivation. Until he was fourteen years of age he was never sent to school, but enjoyed the valuable instructions of his father, who was conservative in his ideas of education, and believed a good classical and mathematical grounding to be of the greatest assistance, not only in learning English and modern languages, but for science and general literature also. His father was very apt at making instruction interesting, yet he never gave his pupil much to learn by rote, but taught him to apply his reasoning powers to what he read. Indeed, after seven years of age, his

reading **lesson** was the leading article in the newspaper, which was explained to him paragraph by
paragraph. Thus he had a great variety of subjects,
and his mind expanded beyond his immediate
surroundings. Nothing delighted the father more
than to satisfy the boy's intense craving for knowledge, and in their walks abroad nature became an
open book affording many a captivating study.

The hum of the bee in the golden summer air
would suggest a lesson on the important part that
insects play in the wonderful mechanism of nature,
and the unerring wisdom which adapts each created
thing to its own special purpose ; the hoar-frost on
the ground, on a wintry morning, one on aqueous
vapour and its results ; while excursions to the
neighbouring sandstone quarry, armed with geological
hammers, were red-letter days in the boy's memory.
Frequently he accompanied his father to cottage
prayer-meetings, and to " catechisings " in the various
districts of the parish. Weather permitting, they
lingered on the way gathering botanical specimens ;
after a sumptuous tea in the hospitable home of
one of the " elders " they adjourned to the barn, or
gathered round the fire of the low-roofed kitchen,
where, after religious exercises, the doctrines contained in the Shorter Catechism were practically
opened up ; and on the way home his father stimulated his interest in astronomy by teaching him to
distinguish the *fixed stars*, by their twinkling and

CARRYING A BOAT IN SECTIONS.   [p. 69.

pale silvery light, from the mellow, steady ray of the *planets.* Thus the boy was initiated into many of the mysteries of nature, by the close and minute observance of every object which attracted his attention.

There is no doubt, however, that, as in the case of Dr. Moffat, the influence which biassed the mind of Alexander Mackay towards *missionary* enterprise was the gracious example of his godly mother. Piety does not run in the blood, but it frequently runs in the line ; and it was so in this case, even through generations. Margaret Lillie was alike remarkable for her elevated principles as for her prudence, tact, and thrift. Her sympathies were far-reaching and her affections deep, and her memory is still fragrant in Rhynie, although it is now over a quarter of a century since she entered into the joy of her Lord. She was a true helpmeet to her husband in his literary pursuits, and had great facility in the acquisition of languages. Indeed, during the two years subsequent to her marriage she made considerable progress in the study of Hebrew, under her husband's guidance. Her father, Mr. Alexander Lillie, occupied an influential position in Banff.* He was a Disruption elder, and was sent to represent the Presbytery of Fordyce at the first general assembly of the Free Church. Her venerable grandfather,

---

* Banff is a small town on the Moray Firth, and is well described in the "Life of a Scotch Naturalist," by Dr. S. Smiles.

Mr. William Lillie,* resided at New Deer, Aberdeen-shire.   He belonged to the Original Secession Church, and was an eminently godly man, as most of those old Seceders were.

The Lillies are descended from a Huguenot family who fled from France, after the Revocation of the Edict of Nantes, "rather than live a daily lie to God by forswearing the religion of their con-science."   The tradition is that the name was originally De Lille, and that they came from the town of Lille in the country of the French Walloons.

The love of religious liberty, the self-reliance, the valour, piety, earnestness, and other characteristic traits of the French Protestant refugees, and the cruel persecutions† which drove them from their native land—the land which is so inexpressibly dear to the heart of every Frenchman—were often and

* "Died, at New Deer, 25th February, 1840, at an advanced age (eighty-three), Mr. William Lillie, elder, who had been for nearly forty years precentor in the congregation at Whitehill, and for more than sixteen years an elder. Mr. Lillie was a good, praying man, was much attached to the cause at Whitehill, a most regular attender upon ordinances, and understood the Gospel well. . . . The old are dropping off. May a race be brought forward to do more than fill their places—a race more public-spirited and devoted to the extension of Christ's kingdom at home and abroad!"—"Autobiography and Journals of the Rev. Adam Lind, Whitehill, edited by his nephew, the Rev. Adam Lind."

† Two most interesting books on this subject are "The Huguenots in England and Ireland," and "The Huguenots in France," by Dr. Samuel Smiles.

touchingly narrated to the boy by his mother, with the injunction,

> "O ye who boast
> In your free veins the blood of sires like these,
> Lose not their lineaments."

The impress seems to have been graven deeply, for at an early age he knew all about the "Church in the Desert," while the Tour de Constance, the Bastile, and the galley-slave were familiar words to him.

After the departure of old Annie, his mother became the boy's more immediate associate, and thus his *character* training fell chiefly into her hands. She had a great regard for the sanctification of the Lord's Day; at the same time she used every endeavour to make it a specially happy day, and one to be looked forward to all the week. For the Sunday evening lesson, of course, the Bible and the Shorter Catechism were the text-books, and if the boy knew his lesson well, the reward was a missionary story. Entertaining books on missions were scarce in those days, but she always managed to glean something fresh to arouse his interest in what she considered a great and noble work.

Let us take a peep into the manse study on one of these Sunday evenings. The minister has gone to preach at some distance from home. The night is wild, and hail and sleet beat against the shuttered windows. The lesson is evidently over, for the boy

claps his hands and exclaims, " Now for the story.
Mother ! tell me to-night the one beginning,

> "' Hark ! hark !—'tis the sainted Martyn's sigh
> From Ararat's mournful shades.' "

" We talked of Martyn last Sunday, did we not ? "

" Yes, but that was about his life in *India*, and I
remember Mrs. Sigourney's lines you taught me :—

> "' Light on the Hindoo shed !
> On the maddening idol-train ;
> The flame of the suttee is dire and red,
> And the fakir faints with pain,
> And the dying moan on their cheerless bed,
> By the Ganges laved in vain.'

Well, let us begin at the beginning, and tell me
again how *you* were first interested in missions,
mother. It was through your grandfather's minister,
was it not ? "

" Yes, through the Rev. Adam Lind, an eminently
godly man, and well known in the north for his
public spirit and world-wide sympathies. I was at
New Deer on a visit to my grandfather. Sunday
evening came, and I remember it so well—a lovely
June evening. Roses filled the eye with colour and
the air with fragrance. I was only a little girl then,
probably about twelve years of age. It was the
annual missionary sermon, and I felt deeply interested, as I had heard that Mr. Lind was anxious to
go to the foreign field himself, but that his congregation declined to let him. We went early to

get a good seat, where my grandfather could hear. I expected some dry statistics and facts about Canada, Old Calabar, Jamaica, etc., where the missionaries of the Secession Church were vigorously working; but I said to myself, 'I must listen, for Mr. Lind is always so kind and good to me : whenever he sees me he pats my head and strokes my hair. Yes, I *will* listen.'

" Presently the minister entered the pulpit, and he had such a beautiful look on his face: his whole soul seemed to be on fire. The text was, ' If ye love Me, keep My commandments,' with which he coupled our Lord's Ascension command to His disciples—'Go ye therefore, and teach all nations.' It was a most affecting and resistless appeal as to our duty and responsibility with regard to the work of missions. The burning words of his concluding prayer I shall never forget : ' Oh, what an honour to be an ambassador to the heathen, and to be an instrument to gather sinners to the Redeemer ! Lord, raise up many to visit the dark places of the earth ! Oh that we may be honoured to do something in stirring up some to this work of the Lord ! Determine many to occupy a place in Thy vineyard—men prepared by Thyself, full of faith and love, and of the Holy Spirit. The Sun of Righteousness has arisen on many dark lands, and the cry becomes louder and louder, " Come over and help us." Arise, O Lord, and plead Thine own cause.'

"That night I could not sleep. When the dawn came I rose, opened the window, and looked out. A gentle breeze was blowing across the hay-field, and each time it fanned my flushed cheeks it seemed to echo the preacher's words, ' None of us can shirk our responsibilities.' But what could *I* do? I was only a little girl, and so helpless! And yet I felt sure the preacher looked at me as if the message was to me personally. I lay down again, but with the first sound in the house I rose, dressed, got my sun-bonnet, and went out. The carolling of the birds, the tinkling of the sheep-bells, and the merry sound of the mowers whetting their scythes, together with the bracing morning air, revived my spirits and seemed to make me see things differently. Though I could not go to heathen lands myself, yet I might stir up others, and I might help to get money to send out good men. There is Mr. Lind : when quite a young man he came under the liberalising influence of the enthusiasm for foreign missions. He went through the University and Theological Hall with the intention of going as a missionary to the United States of America, but the Lord sent him here. He has been the means, however, of sending a nephew to the work in India, and he has started the Buchan Mission-ary Society, which sends annually from £30 to £45 to missions ; perhaps I too can be of some use. And I went home comforted, and found my grandfather concerned at my absence. I think he must have had his own suspicions, for his grey eyes looked at me keenly. But he merely said, 'Sunday's food will not serve all the week. We need daily bread, worship, and breakfast every morning.'"

"What field do you consider most important, mother?"

"Christ died for all. What we must pray for is the evangelisation of the whole world. All are important, although the eyes of many are now being turned on the land of dusky Ham, and the cry is—

> "'Will not some daring spirit, born to thoughts
> Above his beast-like state, find out the truth,
> That Africans are men?'"

"Would you like me to go as a missionary to Africa, mother?"

"If God prepares you for it, my boy, but not unless. You must first *come to Him*, and if He has need of you, He will call you in a way you will not mistake. You can throw your soul into the missionary enterprise and yet stay at home; but if the message comes, 'Depart, for I will send thee far hence,' take care you do not neglect it. Remember what Jonah got for his pains. But, as I have heard Dr. Duff say, 'The advancement of the missionary cause is not only our duty and responsibility, but it is an *enjoyment* which those who have once tasted would not exchange for all the treasures of the Indian mines, for all the laurels of civic success, for all the glittering splendour of coronets. It is a joy rich as heaven, pure as the Godhead, lasting as eternity!'"

"I do not think I could like *black* people."

"Not pity the poor captives—who

> "'start at every word
> As meant to mock their woes, and shake their chains,
> Thinking defiance which they dare not speak'?"

"Oh, yes, I could pity them, and would like to help them, but to *love* them—I don't know about that."

Perhaps considering whence the mother came it is no matter of surprise that she was a diligent reader of the *Bulwark*, and that she earnestly sought to impress on his youthful mind that the Reformation is a great trust handed down to us by our forefathers. She spent much time in explaining to him the prominent errors and the lying legends of Popery, so that when occasion offered he would have no difficulty in unmasking its face and exposing its craftiness.

In the spring of 1858, as the father was driving to Gartley station, on his way to Edinburgh, he said to Alexander (who was accompanying him to the railway station in order to take home the conveyance), "Well, what book shall I bring you home from Edinburgh?"

"I think, at this stage, father, I ought to have a printing-press."

The father dropped the reins, and in a tone in

which disappointment and disgust were mingled, exclaimed,—

"A printing-press! What do you mean by a printing-press? The thing is to become a good scholar, and if you have anything to say worth writing, any one will print for you. When at the manse of Keig, the other day, I saw one of Mr. Smith's sons * lying on the study floor poring over a great Hebrew Bible; and you talk about wasting your time with a printing-press."

"I do not think it would be wasting time, father. Skill takes no room in the pocket nor in the travelling-bag, and some day I might find it useful."

"My dear boy, you know that the desire of my heart is to see you become a preacher of the glorious Gospel of Jesus Christ."

"Well, but, father, Martin Luther says that 'printing is the latest and greatest gift by which God enables us to advance the things of the Gospel.'"

It was train time, however, and with a hasty "good-bye" the father was soon out of sight. "What could have put a printing-press into the boy's head?" he pondered. "I expect it is the part it played in furthering the Reformation. I know he has been reading D'Aubigné. He devours every book he comes across. Euler's Algebra, which I brought him home last year, has been a fairy-world to him; and yet every now and then this hankering after miscellaneous crafts crops

* Now, Professor W. Robertson Smith.

up.   He does not play, like other boys; every spare hour at his disposal, I find, is spent in the smithy or carpenter's shop, handling tools of all kinds, and on occasion lending a helping hand.   I must endeavour to remove him from his surroundings. Meantime I shall search for a good book to divert his attention."

With this end in view, the father on arriving in Edinburgh made an early visit to Messrs. Blackwood's choice assortment of new books, but not finding exactly what he wanted, he unburdened his mind to his publisher, who laughingly replied, " My dear sir, don't worry yourself : it would be a queer world if we were all parsons.   No doubt he means to strike out a course for himself.   Give him a free rein, and all will come right.   *You* get the printing-press, and we will be most happy to supply the types ; but tell him he must not *publish* your books as well as print them !"

The Messrs. Blackwood were as good as their word, for in due time a large and varied assortment of types, etc., arrived at the manse ; but little did the donors or any one else think then what the destination of their present would be, or how it would, in Luther's words, "advance the things of the Gospel" on the shores of the sunlit Nyanza.

CHAPTER IV.

RAPID CHANGES.

"He who to manhood grows without a grief
Is but half-rooted ; with a will untamed,
And self undisciplined, he seeks his own :
To him no mellowness of being comes."

H. BONAR

HIPPARCHUS, who flourished 160-125 B.C., and who may be justly styled the founder of the exact sciences of astronomy and geography, traces the sources of the Nile to three great lakes in the interior of Africa. From his day, down through the ages till the middle of the seventeenth century, "the triple lakes" adorn the maps of the Dark Continent, although, as Stanley says, cartographers sketched them sometimes "in line," sometimes many degrees north or south of each other, and on either side of the equator as pleased their fancy. Jacobus Meursius, who engraved a map for "Ogilby's Description of Africa," a large volume published at the time of the Restoration, seems to have acquired a good deal of accurate information regarding the far interior from Portuguese and Dutch authorities. One lake, which he names Zafflan, resembles the Victoria

Nyanza in its general configuration ; but he seems to have been confused about the sources of the Nile and the Congo. Ogilby says : " The great river of Zaire or Congo derives its head out of three lakes, the first intituled Zambre, the second Zaire, and the third a great lake from whence the Nyle is supposed to draw his original. . . . Zambre is the principal head that feeds the river Zaire, being set, as it were, in the middle point of Africa, and spreading itself into broad streams into the north, whither, according to common opinion, it sends forth Nylus."

Strange to say, from Ogilby's time to the middle of the present century the exploration of equatorial Africa made no advance, and the best cartographers erased the lakes altogether from their maps.

In the year 1843 Dr. Krapf heard at a port on the East Coast of a vast inland lake ; and about the year 1856 his companions Messrs. Rebmann and Erhardt traced upon a map " that monster slug of an inland sea," as Speke calls it, which stimulated the Royal Geographical Society to send out an expedition of exploration.

Through a curious blending of circumstances, Alexander Mackay was at a very early age deeply interested in this region, where his own lot, in the providence of God, was ultimately to be cast, and the " Nile problem " was a frequent subject of conjecture between father and son. The " Proceedings " of the Royal Geographical Society came regularly to the home ; and as soon as they were published Livingstone's " Missionary Travels and Researches in South Africa," Speke's " Journal of the Discovery of the Source of the Nile," and Captain Grant's " Walk across Africa " appeared likewise on the scene.

The old map of Africa (see p. 2) was discarded by the father ; but the boy cherished his familiar friend and suspended it in his own room, where he spent many a happy hour in tracing on it the results of the most recent explorations. He used to say, " I like to think that the missionaries had a hand in promoting these discoveries, and that Captain Speke has so nicely acknowledged it by suggesting Karague, Uganda, and Unyoro as favourable fields for missionary enterprise."

" But, father," he remarked one day, " there is one thing that greatly puzzles me. I know that until recent times we had to send across the Channel for *engineers* when we required any skilled work done, such as piers, lighthouses, or bridges, and that they had to bring with them their own workmen to execute the task. Have we had to send for our missionaries too ? or how is it that these agents of the C.M.S. are described as Germans ? Could Bishop Heber persuade none of his countrymen to go

> " ' Where Afric's sunny fountains
> Roll down their golden sand ' ?

Of course I know about Livingstone and Moffat, but they are Scotchmen."

" You see, my boy," said the father, " the C.M.S. is

such a large society and has so many stations that I suppose enough men were not to be found in the Church of England willing to become poor despised missionaries. Therefore when the C.M.S. were short of volunteers for the foreign field they applied to the famous Missionary Institution at Basle, in Switzerland. But I believe that Dr. Krapf, who may be termed the founder of C.M.S. Missions in East Africa, had his attention drawn to the Dark Continent by reading the 'Travels of Bruce,' our own countryman."

"Ah! that pleases me well. Most pictures are tame to me unless there is a Ben or a Loch in the background. But why do you say, 'despised missionaries,' father? I understood that the vocation of an ambassador to the heathen is the noblest of all."

"Yes, for those who are baptised with the sacrificing spirit of Christ; and unless a man receive that baptism he had better stay at home."

"Well, I like to hear about missionaries, but I have no inclination that way; and while on the subject, father, I must tell you that I have a growing distaste for the ministry also. I should like to understand thoroughly the construction of machinery and the principles of projections. I believe that your own love of mathematics and of natural philosophy has biassed my mind in this direction. There is a wide field of usefulness for engineers, but a country parish would be no scope for me and my hobbies."

"My son," said the father, sadly, "it is wholly out

of my power, with my large family, to give you the necessary training. It implies a long apprenticeship with a respectable engineering firm in Edinburgh or Glasgow, for which a large premium is required ; and at the end of that time, unless you have capital to begin with on your own account, you will remain but a subordinate all your days. I believe you have constructive power, and that you have the perseverance and constancy of character which would enable you to rise to eminence in that profession, but without capital it would be a great struggle. Better go on as you are doing, and when the time comes compete for a bursary at Aberdeen, like all other ministers' sons in this neighbourhood. If you are successful that will take you through the University, and then all will be plain sailing. The red cloak is a wonderful stimulus. You will forget all about your hammer and saw when you don it."

In the spring of 1860 the boy became delicate, and his lessons seemed to be a burden to him. Naturally of a quiet and reserved disposition, he became more gentle, more meditative, while the healthy humour which had always characterised him ceased to flow spontaneously. He complained of nothing, but his parents became anxious, and as the local physician failed to detect any cause for the debility, his father took him to Edinburgh to consult Dr. Moir, who at once ordered change of air and a long holiday. Accordingly, in the month of August his father gave

him a tour in the Highlands. Spending some weeks
at Strathpeffer, where his wonderful gentleness won
for him many friends, they proceeded to Tain, and
from thence to the banks of Loch Shin, in Suther-
landshire. Here he led a joyous life. A kind friend
put a Shetland pony at his disposal, and he enjoyed
many a ride across the moors. This was the only
time he saw the wild mountainous scenery of the
north, and on his return home he had much to say
about the red-deer, and the sheep-farms, and the
beautiful lake with Ben More in the distance towering
into the sky. The bracing air perfectly restored his
health, but not his love for books. He learned his
appointed lessons conscientiously, but instead of reading in his leisure hours, drawing, map-drawing, and
printing occupied his attention. He was also a very
useful member of the household. It was he who
cleared away the snow which accumulated every
winter in a huge drift in front of the manse, obstruct-
ing the light, and impeding all communication except
by the kitchen-door—and he who in their proper
seasons superintended the sowing and reaping of the
crops. His energetic disposition forbade idleness.
In fact, he always preferred having too much to do
rather than too little. His mother was very fond of
bee culture ; but, strange to say, her bees were very ir-
reverent, for they not only chose the Sabbath on which
to swarm, but they took the opportunity of doing so
during the hours of divine service. Neither had they

any idea of propriety, for, to crown the proceedings, they almost invariably selected for their new quarters an old ivy-covered chimney in the Established Manse, a quarter of a mile distant ! The boy considered this rare fun. One sultry Sunday his mother said to him; "I have a presentiment that the bees will swarm to-day, so I wish you to watch them while I am at church."

" Yes, mother ; I suppose I can take 'Livingstone's Travels ' with me ? "

" No ; because you get so absorbed in that book that I will lose my bees."

" I only wish to look if there is any more said about the native smith teaching Dr. Livingstone to weld the iron."

" You must not read."

The boy went to the garden, but before ten minutes had expired the monotony was so irksome that he felt he must devise some method to make the bees " improve the shining hour " without delay. He tapped the hive and listened. A peculiar sound betokened some commotion within. So far hopeful, he next got a thin stick, and pushing it in at the little aperture, he moved it gently backwards and forwards to entice them out. By-and-by one appeared, and another, and then the queen, followed by a numerous retinue, thronging and pressing on each other until they hung in a dense cluster on his stick and all about the hive door ; while one or two of a more enterprising turn of mind found their way

up his sleeve and to his bare knees (for he wore the
kilt in those days), and took no pains to disguise their
resentment at his inhospitality. Fortunately, the
apiary was situated on the south side of the church,
hard by the window of the Manse pew, through which
the mother heard an extraordinary buz-z-z, accompanied by cries of pain. The congregation were
standing at prayer, so she made her exit unobserved,
wondering why bees are so profane, and mentally
vowing she would rear no more in future, as they
seemed determined to desecrate the Sabbath !

Alexander Mackay had been well instructed in
religious knowledge, had no foolish companions, had
no desire to deviate from the path of truth and
rectitude, but the quickening influence of Divine love
had not as yet entered his heart. His mother felt
that to force religion upon him might be a mistake,
but she continued to pray for him often and earnestly.
As the time approached when it was desirable he
should prosecute his studies in Aberdeen, both
parents felt concerned lest his natural amiability and
abounding humour might lead him into temptation in
a large city. Just then an old friend of his father's,
a Mr. Hector, from Aberdeen, appeared in the neighbourhood. He was very much drawn to the boy, and
told him that he also had a son,* who he hoped and
believed was going forward to the ministry.

* Afterwards known as the Rev. John Hector, Missionary of the
Free Church of Scotland at Calcutta.

It was ultimately arranged that this youth should spend his summer holiday at the Manse, and, if the companionship proved congenial to both, that Alexander should accompany his friend to Aberdeen, and remain under Mr. Hector's roof until the following spring, when his mother hoped to go to town and secure comfortable lodgings for him. The boys conceived a strong attachment for each other, for they had much in common, and in October 1864 Alexander Mackay began to attend the Grammar School in the " granite city."

This was the beginning of many changes in the old home. In company with his friend he returned to the Manse at Christmas, and in the following April his mother fulfilled her promise. She had been delicate all winter, and was strongly advised to postpone her journey until the weather became warmer ; but with her characteristic spirit of self-sacrifice, she never thought of herself when the welfare of others was concerned. The ten days she spent in Aberdeen ever remained a green spot in the boy's memory, and when he saw her off by the train he little dreamed that this was her last earthly journey, and that her course was nearly run. In three weeks' time he was summoned home, as she was seriously ill. He remained a week, and as she appeared to rally he returned again to school, but on the 8th of June she passed gently away.

His childhood was buried in that open grave, but

her dying charge, faithfully delivered by a relative,[*] to "read his Bible and to *search* it, so as to meet her in glory," kindled a light which waxed brighter and brighter until it illumined all his life.

While his father still continued to wish him to become a minister, and he himself desired the profession of an engineer, God was preparing him for both. Writing to a dear friend at Christmas 1866, he says, " I cannot see my way for the future, but I feel certain the Lord will make it plain in His own time. I shrink from the ministry. I feel so unworthy of that office. Besides, it seems to me that there are already too many ministers. Three or four wasting their energies in each little parish in Scotland may satisfy a desire for sermon hearing, but is attended, I fear, with little practical good. I believe God gives us talents to use in His service, and that we are bound to turn them to the best account ; therefore I must go on with engineering. You tell me 'it is impossible, as my father cannot help me.' That I will never make an engineer unless I can surmount a greater obstacle than that, I at once allow ; but He who has given me the desire will in some way grant it. This I feel sure of."

His way was soon made clear. In November 1867 the family removed to Edinburgh, where for six years he applied himself to his studies with laborious and persistent industry. Two of these

* Mrs. James Flett, now residing in the Grange, Edinburgh.

years he spent at the Free Church Training College
for Teachers ; after which the father abandoned his
own views in favour of those to which the talents
and inclinations of his son were so strongly directed,
and no longer urged him to enter the ministry.

Every hour of the next four years was precious to
Alexander Mackay. He studied engineering and its
kindred sciences at the University, and *practical*
engineering at the works of Messrs. Miller &
Herbert ; and during all these four years, in order
that he might not be burdensome to his father, he
taught three hours per day, either in George Watson's
College Schools or in private seminaries, by which he
earned sufficient money for his class fees and personal
necessities.

During the greater part of this time in Edinburgh
he was greatly influenced by the wise pastoral care
and teaching of Dr. Horatius Bonar, who always
watched with tender affection over the young members of his flock, and especially strove to produce in
them habits of reverent and constant fellowship with
God, and daily study of the Holy Scriptures.

CHAPTER V.

LIFE IN BERLIN.

"Then look not back!   Oh! triumph in the strength
Of an exalted purpose! Eagle-like,
Press sunward on.   Thou shalt not be alone.
Have but an eye on God, as surely God
Will have an eye on thee.   Press on! press on!"
B. B. THATCHER.

ON the 1st of November, 1873, Alexander Mackay embarked in the S.S. *North Star* from Leith for Hamburg, his desire being to master the German tongue and fully to qualify himself as an engineer. Amongst the introductions he took with him was one from Dr. Horatius Bonar to a clergyman in Hamburg, who gave him a letter to the Rev. Dr. Baur, Court chaplain and Cathedral preacher in Berlin.

Although it was a time of great commercial depression, consequent on the late Franco-German war, he speedily found congenial employment in a great engineering firm in Berlin.   In his letters home he frequently speaks of the dangerous fascination attending the designing of machinery.   He writes: "Sometimes a new design so absorbs my whole thoughts that I cannot drive it out of my mind.   It ever keeps coming up for improvement and perfection. I would fain give it the first place, as it is my work to a certain extent; but when it would take such complete mastery of me, I find the word in my conscience, 'Love not the world, neither the things of the world: if any man love the world, the love of the Father is not in him.'" His profession led him amongst Rationalists, and he sorely missed communion with the Lord's people. He says: "Carnality and unbelief have got such a hold upon me, that if it were not that, now and again, in reading the Word of God, I get a fresh ray of light, I would fall away altogether." He soon, however, formed the acquaintance of Dr. and Mrs. Baur, who took a great interest in him, and did for him what Aquila and Priscilla did for Apollos.

Dr. Baur writes: " The image of Alexander Mackay, my friend, I might almost say my son, stands forth clearly to my mind, as it was imprinted by a long daily, intimate life together, and by the reports of his later efforts in the work of our Lord. I remember quite distinctly one day he came to see us. I sat conversing with him for a long time in my study. I hardly spoke any English—he little German. I invited him to come back at any time: he would always be welcome. He answered, with his own peculiar, frank, humorous smile, that he did not wish to *visit* us from time to time, but to *live* with us, as, living in a large town with so many infidels, he

longed for a Christian home. I spoke to my wife, and
as we had room we received the young man into our
house, to our great joy. My wife and I always looked
on him as a dear son, and he was a true-hearted
brother to our own son. At that time he had just
entered his twenty-fifth year, but appeared to be
younger. He was scarcely of middle size, and had a
slender but well-knit figure. He had a fine head, with
a noble forehead and an open face. In his blue eyes,
which looked bright and clever, there was a soft, kindly
light, revealing a deep love to God and man. He
took the most lively interest in my work, which consisted not only in the care of a congregation scattered
far and wide in the great city, and in preaching in
the Cathedral, the Parish Church of the Emperor
and his household, but also in the direction of institutions and societies, in addresses at large meetings,
and Bible readings—in short, in Home Mission work
of the most varied kind. He conscientiously fulfilled
his profession of an engineer, but the centre of his
interest lay in the kingdom of God. I remember how
one Sunday morning, at breakfast, he directed the
question to me with deep emotion : 'What shall we
do to send the Berliners to church?' With his
faithfulness in little things, he did bring many a
young man to church. What was a benefit to himself
he longed for others also to enjoy. He himself went
regularly with us to the Cathedral, and did not feel
repelled by our carefully-selected Litany. With a

friend of ours (Rev. G. Palmer Davies) he sometimes went to the American Church, and joined actively in the Biblical discussions." What Alexander Mackay saw of Christian home life in Germany gave him a great love for the country and for the people. Indeed, some of his most choice friends belonged to the " Fatherland." No doubt his residence there did much also to broaden his sympathies, and to show him that unity in diversity and diversity in unity must ever be a fundamental article of the Christian faith. Writing home in the end of 1873, he says : " I very much deplore the bitter tone of the . . . . papers. While the world stands there is room for all ; for God has not cast all in one mould. All trees are not oaks, nor weeping willows either, but that is no reason why each species should look askance at the other. All are of God, and all have their respective uses and peculiar beauty. Let us therefore strive to be useful in the Lord's vineyard, and to attain to some measure of the beauty of holiness. The Master said in the tersest words, ' Seek ye *first* the Kingdom of God, and His rightcousness.' Just as far as we follow that precept can we claim at all to be His disciples. 'Let each man, wherein he was called, therein abide *with God*. There will then be less bitterness between parties and sects, and more of the love that seeketh not its own.'

For some years prior to Alexander Mackay's arrival in Germany, he had neither read much nor thought much of Foreign Missions, so absorbed had he been in his professional studies ; but, strange to say, a few weeks after reaching Berlin, before he had made any Christian acquaintances, and while he was standing aghast at the infidelity of his associates, a simple account of an address given by Dr. Burns Thomson, in Chalmers Memorial Church, Edinburgh, on Mission work in Madagascar, was put into his hands. This appeal, and the remembrance of his sainted mother's injunction, " If the call comes to you take care you do not neglect it," kept ever coming up before him, until at last the claims of the heathen world took such possession of him that he described it as *a new conversion*. He was greatly encouraged by Dr. Baur to follow out his idea, viz., to become an engineer-missionary. Dr. Baur had been intimately acquainted with John Coleridge Patteson, the martyr-bishop of Melanesia, and at the very time he received Alexander Mackay into his home, he was occupied in writing a short biography of the Bishop for his German countrymen.

Dr. Baur, in his character sketch of Mackay,* points out the great resemblance between these two devoted missionaries, although they were so different in their spiritual origin, Pusey and Keble having influenced the one—Bonar and (he ought to have added) Baur the other. Diaries are seldom interest-

* See Introduction to the German Edition of "A. M. Mackay, Pioneer Missionary of the Church Missionary Society to Uganda."

ing, but a few extracts from one Mackay kept in Berlin show his spiritual experiences from time to time :—

"*October* 11*th*, 1874.—Led the Bible-class in American Church this evening. Subject, John vii. 37-9. May much result from our meeting. A Christian a life-giver. Give me Thy spirit without measure, O God, that I may be mighty rivers. What a barren soil is here to irrigate !"

"*Oct.* 12*th.*—This the last evening of the quarter of a century in which I have lived so much in vain. Lord, forgive me, and enable me henceforth to spend and be spent in Thy blessed service."

"*Oct.* 17*th.*—This day enabled by God's grace to preach to ten souls. But oh, with what feebleness ! Do thou, O Spirit of the living God, open their. hearts every one ; yea, and they shall live. Empty me of self, O God, and fill me with Thee. Oh for more communion with God !"

"*Oct.* 19*th.*—These souls, by God's grace, to seek to save. . . . Mighty harvest ! Lord Jesus, do Thou be found of them all. Thou, and Thou alone, canst save. Give me faith in Thee."

"*Oct.* 20*th.*—Lord bless abundantly two or three grains of seed sown. What an idle day ! God enable me to buy back opportunities, because the days are evil."

"*Oct.* 21*st.*—Oh for nearness to God ! God grant me, I pray Thee, a deep spirit of humility—the broken will and the contrite heart. Oh for the single eye! What pride is in my heart! Carnality and unfaithfulness too! How much in me alone the Blood has to cover!"

"*Oct. 22nd.*—Much departure from the living God. Much unbelief and hardness of heart. Lord Jesus, destroy the power of evil within me. Baptise me with the Holy Ghost and with fire."

"*Oct. 23rd.*—God forgive an empty day. Have done nothing for Christ, yet He has taught me to say, with a fuller heart than ever before, with H. Bonar: 'Lord, sift me—the process may be sore'; and with McCheyne, 'If nothing else will do to sever me from my sins, Lord, send me such sore and trying calamities as shall awaken me from earthly slumbers.'

"Lord, Thou art merciful."

Many such entries show how he bemoaned his sinful nature, and reveal his fervent desire to become a true disciple of the Lord Jesus. Especially does he long for greater tenderness in seeking to win souls by proclaiming the good tidings.

"*November 12th.*—Slept in. Notes from home of Bonar's sermon on 'This is My beloved Son—hear ye Him.' This seems to be the lesson God means to teach me by His rod at this time. How prone I am to do anything but learn. Teach me, Lord, this lesson above all others.

"A seed sown, Lord, Thou alone canst bless."

"*Nov. 23rd.*—Slept in again. No time for prayer or reading God's Word in the morning. Yet the

MISSION CARAVAN STARTING FOR THE VICTORIA NYANZA.

[p. 71.

Lord is gracious to me. Thy goodness is leading me to repentance. Oh for more faith, more hope, more love! How dead I am! Give Thy Spirit, Lord Jesus, even unto me."

"*December* 11*th.*—Attaining day by day to a little more childlike faith in Jesus, and therefore joy and peace. Faith is Thy gift, O God. My Father, give Thy son faith, for my Redeemer's sake."

"*Dec.* 12*th.*—Teach me, my Saviour, to speak to lost souls in *love*, and not in bitterness.

"Prayer meeting. Slight sparks of joy. Oh for the joy of being filled with the Spirit! I believe that is what we ought to be. Sadness must be due to unbelief."

Alexander Mackay had first been led to think of Madagascar as a mission-field, but, on inquiry, there seemed no prospect of any opening in that island for his energies. Thus it came to pass that his eyes were cast on the Dark Continent, and, as Dr. Baur says, " he longed to set foot on it as if it were the Promised Land." One bitterly cold night, shortly before Christmas 1875, he finished reading Stanley's " How I found Livingstone," and on laying the book on the table his eye fell on the words, " Henry Wright, Hon. Sec., Church Missionary Society," in an old copy of the Edinburgh *Daily Review*. His curiosity was at once aroused, and on taking up the newspaper he found the above signature to be appended to an appeal for men to go out as pioneer missionaries to

Uganda, in the very heart of the African Continent, in response to King Mtesa's invitation, sent home by Stanley. Mackay, there and then, although it was now after midnight, replied to Mr. Wright's letter, offering his services to the expedition. The Church Missionary Society corresponded with his referees, and early in January of 1876 he had two communications from them, followed by a telegram on the 17th of the month, appointing an interview in London. He paid a flying visit to England and saw the Central African Sub-Committee, and a few days after Mr. Wright informed him that he " had been accepted for the Lord's work in connection with the Church Missionary Society Mission to the Victoria Nyanza." At this time Mackay was busy with a complicated machine which he had designed for his employers, and he could not honourably leave until he saw it in proper working order ; but he accomplished this sooner than he expected, and as the Church Missionary Society were anxious there should be no delay in carrying out their undertaking, he agreed to have his passage taken by the P. and O. boat which would leave Southampton in the end of March. The sudden death, however, on the 16th of February, of his beloved brother, Charles—

" A noble boy,
A brave, free-hearted, careless one,"

altered his plans, and he did not really sail for Zanzibar till the 27th of April. He was glad to get on board the *Peshawur*, being utterly worn out in rushing from place to place selecting the very liberal equipment with which the Church Missionary Society were providing the expedition. Besides machinery and tools of all kinds, presents had to be got for Mtesa and other sultans, as also cumbrous cloth and bead moneys, which are the only currency known in the interior of Africa. In this, however, he had the valuable assistance of Colonel Grant.

An able writer says that "the chances are that if Mackay had been prevented from going to Africa the elaborate trivialities of our modern life would soon have wearied him, and brought him to an earlier grave—his brave and active nature would have beaten itself to death against the bars of European conventionality." No doubt this is true. Writing to a friend, he says, "English Christianity undoubtedly stands in need of being reformed. There is about it much of what our Saviour calls ' serving God and Mammon.' . . . Nowhere in all the world is there so much bitter poverty by the side of high living as there is in England. Our religion has become crystallised in dogmas and Church doctrines, but it has not become the law of our daily life. I often think if I were in England, how I would plead with Christian men and women to leave the fashions of the world, with the terrible expense which compliance with these involves, and consent to spend and be spent in rescuing a lost world. Has Christianity

become such a half-hearted thing that the beginning
and the end of it is a routine of worship, and putting
on a respectable appearance in the eyes of people?
It is saddening to think of the lukewarmness of the
very saints of God. If *they* fail in the hour of need,
where is help to be looked for? May the Lord have
mercy on our hardness of heart, and give us grace
to devote ourselves and everything that is ours to
His service alone."

He went to Africa full of bright ideas and great
schemes, and in one way he saw them all doomed to
disappointment, but in many others he lived to see
far greater progress in the Mission than even in his
brightest hours he expected. Before he entered the
field he did not see the difficulties to be overcome
and the trials to be endured, ere even a small beginning could be made in planting a centre of moral
and intellectual influence in such an isolated place as
Uganda. What he and the other members of the
Mission band would have liked, was to enter the
country with ease and speed; to find a cordial welcome; to become quickly acquainted with the language;
to preach to eager crowds every day; to find all ready
to listen and believe; to find no enemies, but countless converts; to have no trouble or check, but one
continuous flow of blessing from above, and one
unbroken supply of good health and vigour for their
work, and no thinning of their ranks. Instead of
that they reached Uganda at great expense and with

great difficulty, through great dangers, very slowly, and with much loss of life and property. They received a welcome which was outwardly cordial, but attended with great suspicion as to their objects. Learning the language took months and years of patient, earnest toil, much misunderstanding as to their aims being caused by the natives and themselves being unable to comprehend each other's words, and great ridicule being produced by their mistakes. Instead of being able to give unremitting attention to teaching, preaching, and translating the Scriptures, they had to spend much of their time in manual labour—toiling for their daily bread. Instead of eagerness to receive the Gospel, they found indifference or strenuous opposition to such tidings. The priests of the Lubare—the *Baal* of the Baganda— trembled for their idolatry; the followers of the false prophet became more and more fanatic; while the fact that both Rome and the Reformation were represented in the country caused bewilderment to the king and joy to the attendant Arabs.

Yet in times of great trouble, Mackay had faith to see that the triumph of evil was only temporary, and that the true light would yet shine in Uganda. He loved his black friends, and never lost hope for them, and never was there an instance of less looking back after having put the " hand to the plough."

CHAPTER VI.

UGANDA.

"Africa! what mighty grief
Hidden lies in that sad name!
Millions lost in unbelief,
Steeped in blood, and tears, and shame!
Christians, think of millions dying;
Leave them not in darkness lying!"

REV. R. P. ASHE.

UGANDA stretches along the north-western shores of the Victoria Nyanza, and lies directly under the equator. It now forms a part of the vast territories of the Imperial British East African Company. Captain Speke visited the country a dozen years before Stanley, and suggested it as a favourable field for missionary enterprise. Having been for generations ruled by kings of the Abyssinian type, he thought it might even retain a latent germ of Christianity. The ruling caste call themselves Bahuma, and claim to be of foreign extraction.* They retain a tradition that they were once half white and half black, with hair on the white side straight, and on the black side frizzly. The founder

* The bulk of the people are Negroes of a more pronounced type.

of the monarchy is believed to be Kintu, who arrived from the north-east, and established himself on the north-west shore of the lake, where he and his wife were the only inhabitants. The legend says, however, that the country soon became densely populated, as every year his wife had four twins ; the boys were born with beards, and at two years of age the girls became mothers! Kintu brought with him a cow, a goat, a sheep, a fowl, a banana root, and a potato, each of which multiplied at a prodigious rate. There were soon flocks and herds in abundance—the banana root produced a forest, while the stems of the potato covered the ground. Kintu had been the priest of an ancient race, and had a great aversion to blood-shedding. His children, however, discovered the method of making strong liquors, and became drunken, lazy, violent and murderous. Kintu, therefore, quitted the country, taking with him the animals he had introduced, also the original banana and potato roots. His family sought for him far and wide, but in vain, yet to this day his immortality is believed in.

According to Captain Speke, nine generations back, Kimera, a descendant of Kintu, gave the government its definite form. He had soon an army, a navy, a grand palace, smart officers, and, according to barbarous ideas, every magnificence. Since his time the prosperity of the country has ever been on the increase, and the cognisance which he adopted—

viz., a white dog, spear, shield and woman—is still used by the sovereign.

When Mackay arrived in Uganda, Mtesa was on the throne. He was an intelligent monarch, but had an exaggerated idea of his own importance. Speke gives an amusing account of his first interview with his majesty : how again and again in the course of an hour he inquired, "Have you seen me?" and how he handled the articles which the traveller presented to him, " made silly remarks, and pondered over them like a perfect child, until it was quite dark." Stanley talks of his dignified expression of face, and of the " large, lustrous, lambent eyes that lent to it a peculiar beauty." The missionaries allow that he had many kingly qualities, but that he was very capricious and self-indulgent. Mackay frequently denounced his wickedness to his face, and yet the king was always disposed to befriend the mission- aries. Doubtless his ambition to imitate the ways of the white men, his respect for their courage and conscientiousness, and a keen eye for " bintu " (goods) all prompted him to favour them. Mtesa died in the autumn of 1884, and was succeeded by his son, Mwanga, a vain, vacillating youth, who lacked the common-sense and experience of his father.

Mackay believed that the climate of Uganda was far healthier than anywhere on the coast of Zanzibar, and much less enervating, although more so than Unyamwezi, because moister. The lake itself is a

centre of atmospheric disturbance, and the very
broken nature of the surface of the country certainly
encourages rainfall, yet it is very far from being a
regular rainy region. On the whole, he considered
that rain contributed more to comfort and pleasure
than nine months of drought. There is an enormously
greater rainfall in Busongora, on the west side of the
lake, than in Uganda. He says : " The constant south-
east wind, which blows all day across the lake, gets
its vapours condensed on the bold metamorphic cliffs,
which, rising terrace above terrace to a thousand feet
above the Nyanza, I call the galleries of Busongora.
There seems to be a connection between the amount
of rainfall and darkness of skin of the natives. The
moister the climate the darker the complexion of the
black. The inhabitants of Busongora and Karague
are black as coal, while the Banyoro are more of
a chocolate colour, and the tribes from the hills
of Busoga and Gambaragara are, some of them, not
much darker than Arabs. It remains to be proved,
but is I think true, that the darker the skin the
deeper the degradation ; at any rate, the more
agricultural, and therefore peaceful and timid, the
tribe ; while the lighter shades own herds of cattle,
are freer and livelier, and more addicted to war.
The country is a constant succession of hills and
swampy hollows, and the soil is wonderfully fertile.
It is true of Uganda as of the Promised Land that
each man sits under his vine and under his fig-tree,

for the banana—the king of fruit trees--each bunch being as heavy as the renowned cluster of grapes of Eshcol—flourishes everywhere, as also the *ficus*—from the bark of which the national dress is made. There are several species of fig, which yield the fibrous bark for clothing, some having a pale yellow colour of texture, while others shade into darker rays of red and even brown. The trees never attain great size, being probably stunted by frequent stripping—which is begun at an early age, the younger trees yielding a finer and more uniform bark. The stem is peeled from a height of six or eight feet to close on the ground. The soft fibrous pad is then beaten out into a thin fabric by being laid on a long beam and struck with round (cylindrical) wooden mallets, finely grooved, thus giving the cloth a corrugated appearance. After the bark is stripped off, the stem is carefully wrapped in plantain leaves, firmly lashed to the trunk.

"The tree shows no signs of injury from the process, and a new bark soon forms, which is again removed when ready.

"I have never seen fruit on a fig-tree in Uganda. At Kagei I found plenty, but there the art of bark-cloth making is not practised.

"There are several varieties of plantains, one being manufactured into strong liquor.

"Tobacco is planted indiscriminately among these trees."

Maize has hitherto been the principal cereal, and yields from three hundred to five hundredfold. One can sow and reap any day, and in any month, although not to such advantage as when timing these processes by the equinoctial rains. It is strange that while tilling the soil is health in a cold climate, it is next to death in the tropics. The great amount of decaying vegetation suddenly brought to the surface in freshly turned-up soil produces malaria, which gets imbibed at every pore of the body. When the soil is dry there is less poison generated, but then the ground cakes like brick beneath the fierce rays of the sun and is practically unworkable. Unless after heavy rains, one can no more dig or plough in the tropics than Scotch farmers can turn over hard-frozen ground.

Foreigners are looked upon with some contempt by the people, especially by the chiefs. One reason is that they walk about alone, and unattended by a retinue of idle fellows, as the chiefs are whenever they appear in public. Then, again, the missionaries have no wealth like them—wealth of women, cattle and slaves ; but the chief reason of the inferiority of the white man is that he works with his own hands. Work is only fit for slaves in Uganda, and even *they* refuse to dig the soil. Women only perform such humble tasks as cultivating the ground, repairing dilapidated walls, and making parapets of reeds. The men are warriors, robbers and idle loungers. They almost all smoke, as do the women. Their pipes have a small bowl of black clay, with stems of wood, four or six feet long, sometimes longer. These stems are made of green saplings,—pith wood, the pith being forced out by a long piece of wire.

The missionaries have had to contend against the belief in witchcraft, in the Lubare, and charms and spells ; also a particular fear of the spirits or ghosts of dead men, which the Baganda fondly cling to. Polygamy and general licentiousness all over the country have also been a great hindrance to the entrance of the Gospel. The people are, however, remarkably intelligent and apt at learning. Mackay soon saw that his first duty was to learn the language, and as speedily as possible reduce it to writing. As soon as this was accomplished, and he and his brethren were able to translate portions of the Scriptures and print them, a new world opened to the natives. They flocked to the mission premises, and often crowded Mackay's workshop in their eagerness to learn to read the Word of God, and as fast as they learned they taught others.

At the present time there are upwards of two thousand devout worshippers, and nowhere in the annals of missionary history have converts stood better the repeated tests of fiery trials and persecutions, many having suffered martyrdom for the name of Jesus Christ.

CHAPTER VII.

ON THE MARCH.

> "To heal the bruised, speed ;
>   Oh, pour on Africa the balm
>   Of Gilead, and, her agony to calm,
> Whisper of fetters broken, and the spirit freed."
>
> W. B. TAPPAN.

AFTER an uneventful voyage the SS. *Peshawur* reached Aden on May 17th. Here Mackay was met by Lieutenant Shergold Smith, commander of the expedition, and after a day's delay they embarked in the SS. *Cashmere* for Zanzibar. On board were a Parsee and a Goa man, wealthy merchants in Zanzibar. The latter was named De Sonza. He had supplied Livingstone and Stanley with various articles, and could tell to a shilling how much his account had been with these travellers in each of their expeditions. Of course he looked for patronage from the C.M.S. party, but Mackay made no promises, believing it prudent to act up to the character of a "canny Scot." De Sonza described Livingstone as having had one arm, which he allowed to hang in a swinging fashion by his side, and then he continued, "Livingstone a very good man ; oh yes, very good

man.   Livingstone the best man I ever have seen ;
good for rich man, good for poor man, good for every
man."

After a voyage of about seven thousand miles from
Southampton, they sighted Zanzibar on the evening
of the 29th of May. Mackay says: "The moon
shone brightly, and a beautiful starlit sky served to
throw a clear light on the town, which looked not at
all unlike various pictures I had previously seen of it.
In the morning the mails were sent ashore to the
British Consul, and various people came on board to
hear and to tell some new thing. The Sultan's fleet,
of four or five small steamers, or rather steam-tugs,
lies off the fort, and about a mile from shore is
moored the large English two-decker H.M.S. *London*,
stationed here for the suppression of the slave trade.
The ship sends her lieutenants cruising round the
neighbouring islands and

> . . . 'the coast where the slave-ship fills its sails
>   With sighs of agony,
> And her kidnapped babes the mother wails
>   'Neath the lone banana-tree !'

Every week they succeed in capturing slave dhows.
Last week they caught one hundred and fifty slaves.
The gunship's boats are very active, inasmuch as
they receive £5 prize money for every slave they
capture. But all this is only first letting the stable-
door lie open and then catching a few of the stolen

horses. There are, besides, far too few boats and men."

Besides Lieutenant G. Shergold Smith, the C.M.S. party comprised the Rev. C. T. Wilson, Mr. T. O'Neill, architect, three artisans, Mackay and his beloved friend, Dr. John Smith. By June they had all reached Zanzibar, and then the real work had to commence, and "all hands to the wheel"—clergyman, doctor, and all—was the cry for some months.

East Africa is neither like India nor China, hence the missionary's work must be different from what it is in either of these practically civilised lands. "One thing is needful"; and it is to teach that one thing that Christian missionaries enter Africa, but the means that must be employed to accomplish that object most effectively are very different from the common traditional notions of what the work of a missionary to the heathen should be.

Pictures of tropical vegetation in the background, and in front a pious-looking man in clerical attire, with Bible in hand, preaching to an eager crowd of dark-skinned hearers, boys have been accustomed to regard as correct representations of the manner of the introduction of the Gospel abroad. But such are not only a caricature of the truth, but are very misleading and injurious. The natives of East and Central Africa did *not* want the missionaries, and would much rather they had remained away. They naturally thought they meant to take possession of their land

and ultimately drive them out of what they had held from time immemorial; or, as the Portuguese and Arabs did in succession on the coast, reduce them to a condition of servitude. Mackay says : "We know they *need* our aid, but they do anything but *wish* it. Their minds are too depraved to understand anything to be for their good which does not supply their immediate animal wants. Making as our starting-point the supply of these in a legitimate way, so that we may win their confidence, and not merely tell them, but bring them to see that we are their friends, much of the difficulty is over, and we can lead them on from Nature to Nature's God, we can bring them to believe our tale is true, that by nature they are enemies of God, but by grace may be reconciled to Him. Being in the world ourselves, and wishing to bring men not only who are in the world, but of it, into the family of the sons of God, common sense seems to indicate that by making stepping-stones of their dead selves we may lead them from the temporal things they as yet only can understand, to the higher things, the things unseen and eternal."

To narrate the delays, worries and anxieties which these pioneers had to undergo in starting their expedition to the interior would be endless. Like all African travellers, they soon learned that it was useless to attempt doing anything at all without having first laid in an inexhaustible supply of patience. In fact, if one does not take patience with him to Africa, he must buy it dearly there, at any cost, even of life itself. They had taken out with them a light cedar boat, the *Daisy*, which had been built in three sections for transport by land to the greatest of the Great Lakes, and they found some difficulty in getting all her parts out of the Custom House. Then the three-cylinder engine arrived with its reversing lever seriously damaged, while the box containing the main shaft and stern tube had been carried off to Shanghai and was never seen at Zanzibar. To take an engine up country without a shaft for the propeller is as good as going out to shoot with a gun the barrel of which is wanting. Accordingly Mackay had to prepare drawings for a new shaft and couplings with stern-tube, and with Captain Sullivan's (H.M.S. *London*) kind consent, this was well manufactured by the chief engineer, Mr. Green. The Blake's patent pump and many other articles were broken, and every other day Mackay was up at the French Mission getting some blacksmith or carpentry work done. One day he had the sections of the *Daisy's* boiler carried to their station by a lot of pagazi (porters). Black men cannot work at anything without singing, and as they groaned under the heavy loads, ten at each piece, they chanted all the way in broken Suahili, " White man give plenty pence!" Of course Mackay did so, giving each man twopence for a couple of hours' hard work! But each requires only three farthings a day to live on, so they considered they had extra good luck.

At last the whole was packed in convenient loads, and shipped by dhows to Bagamoyo, on the mainland. Here, Mackay says, the day ran somewhat thus :—

"Get up at daylight ; coffee, oranges, and quinine at 6 a.m. ; weighing goods, packing them into bales of 60 lb. each, directing, arranging till 7 a.m.   At 7 sound the drum and take out my 35 soldiers (?) for drill ; 8 o'clock till 10, packing ; then breakfast. Hard work at hosts of things till lunch, then go at it again till dark, with hundreds of Wanyamwezi, Wahumas, Wasagara, etc.   After dark, dinner ; then work again.   As yet it has been hard times with most of us, physically and mentally.

"Starting an expedition like ours taxes all our wisdom and strength.   It is almost impossible to convey to English minds a correct idea of the manner of life in this part of the world—whether the white man's or the native's.   The floor of the tembe where I write this is thickly covered with sleeping niggers and bales of goods.   This may sound strange, but it is stranger still to have it to go through."

The C.M.S. had given instructions that the Wami and Kingani rivers should be explored, with a view to the expedition taking advantage of a water route, if found practicable.   Consequently, Mackay riveted the three sections of the *Daisy* together, and Lieut. Smith and he went up the Wami for seventy miles, but found it unfit for navigation. Mackay and Mr. Holmwood, Vice-Consul, next explored the Kingani for 160 miles with the same result.

The boat had again to be taken to pieces, and as it was found each section would require twenty men to carry it, Mackay unriveted it into smaller pieces, adapted to two men each, and cut away entirely six feet out of the middle.

The greatest trouble of all was in collecting pagazi (porters) enough to carry the goods, etc., up country. In this they derived much benefit from the experiences of the great travellers who had preceded them. Writing at this time, Mackay says : " As to Stanley, it is hard from the home standpoint to form a judgment. Let critics come out even this length (Bagamoyo), and see how they would act in similar circumstances. Of course retaliation would never do for missionaries, but Stanley is preparing the way for us, and has placed ready to our hands a great deal of information that will be especially valuable to our party. But to talk of Africa having been 'opened up' by the passing through it of Speke, Grant, Stanley, and Cameron is to talk of a large pumpkin being opened up by passing through it a fine needle ! "

At length the expedition started on its arduous march. It was intended Mackay should be whipper-in, and lead the rear caravan, with machinery and valuables and everything else which the others had left behind ; but on setting out on the 27th of August, he could only muster two hundred pagazis, fourteen so-called askari (soldiers), who never had had a gun in their hands before; three carpenters, one mason, and three engine boys, while four donkeys and a little dog served to wind up the list of the company!

The loads were chiefly the *Daisy*—which took about fifty men; beads and cloth took more than fifty. The rest carried machinery, books, provisions, tools, agricultural implements, etc. The valuable observing instruments, medicines, gunpowder, and such-like, were intrusted to Zanzibar men, of whom he had about a score. Again, much barter cloth had to be left, so Lieutenant Smith and the Doctor remained in Bagamoyo to secure more porters.

Mackay says: "Suddenly to have stepped into the position of 'father' to such a large family of children, every day crying out ' POSS-HO!' which may be translated, ' Give us our daily bread,' is by no means a joke. Their little disputes and complaints I have to settle. My interpreter is very poor in English, and makes as much misunderstanding as the reverse. Still we get on wonderfully; at times one method of argument succeeding—at times another.

" It occurs to me often as a poser—if two hundred men on march can give such endless trouble, what anxiety must poor Moses have been in on his march with more than two million souls? The Lord God was with him, seems to be the only explanation, and my fears are all calmed by the fact that this caravan is the Lord's, and He will give all necessary grace for guiding it."

Mackay had concentrated his energies in making rapid marches, but it was fearfully hard work, and the over-fatigue brought on fever and the other disease so fatal to white men in Africa, which so reduced his strength that he could not walk, and had to be helped on to his donkey, which he had been previously using as a beast of burden.

He had very little sickness in his camp, however, which was a matter of great thankfulness, as small-pox was raging ahead and the caravans in front suffered greatly. One fellow, Terekesa, with a Nyam-wesi caravan of his own, left several dead in every camp. The road was actually strewn with the skele-tons of bodies which the hyænas had recently picked bare.

Soon after leaving the coast Mackay vaccinated as many of his men as he had lymph for, and the cases took well, but he only got over two or three dozen. When a few fell ill of the dire disease, he took another route, when practicable, to avoid Terekesa, whom his men shuddered to think of. Hence they had a couple of days' marching through a swamp which they otherwise would have avoided. Mackay says: "It would have shocked the ideas of English doctors to see my small-pox boy wading knee-deep, for a couple of days, with his legs covered by the eruption. But here he is to-day, with precious little doctoring, as well as possible." But while such treatment suited the boy, Mackay became so much worse that he had to send back word to Lieutenant Smith, who then hurried on, with only one man, at the rate of thirty miles a day, on foot, to relieve him of the charge of his great caravan. By mischance, however, he took another road and got on ahead. Accidentally Mackay heard of this and dispatched messengers to catch him up, which they did. The Lieutenant then waited until Mackay overtook him, in a couple of days.

Mackay says : " My dear brother brought me new life and home letters, which so far revived me that I was able to let him go next day right on to Mpwapwa, bringing on my caravan myself, as I had done."

This place he reached on the 10th of October. Much he had vexed himself over the short marches of his men during the previous fortnight, as he was anxious to see his brethren again before they proceeded on to the lake; but a merciful Providence regulated it otherwise, and by means of the delays of the porters, delivered him unwittingly from what might have ended in serious calamity to many of them, and perhaps disaster to nearly the whole expedition.

Mpwapwa may be considered an oasis in the great salt desert. Caravans must all pass through it, and must be provisioned there after the hunger on the marches behind, and with a supply for several days in front. They had all been led to believe the place was a land of plenty, but food was *then* not to be had, except by going great distances for it, and even then paying prices much above ordinary.

One day Lieutenant Smith ordered the pagazi to cut grass to thatch the mission house. He did not know that the men were already almost exasperated at having to pay out their own cloth, owing to the dearness of provisions, and were merely waiting the spark to kindle the fuel of impatience and wrath among them into flame. At once they all picked up their guns and their own cloth and bolted, leaving their loads in camp.

Unasked, and entirely of their own accord, the Wagogo—natives of Mpwapwa—seeing the white man's men desert, turned out of their villages in great numbers, and with martial skill and true bravery drove them all back into camp.

Next day the caravan started, but the men set off, most of them, without their loads. They ultimately, however, returned for them, and by the 7th October Lieutenant Smith saw the vanguard of the expedition finally leave Mpwapwa. Mackay had fixed that same day as the latest date of his arrival at that place, but glad he was and thankful to God that it found him still two marches back. Had he arrived then, or sooner, his men, two hundred and twenty in number, might have joined also in the desertion and demoralisation, and who knows what might have been the result?

Writing on the 19th of October, Mackay says: "Early this morning I found another of my men had died of smallpox. He was the second case of death, and being a man of middle age, like the other, I had given up his case as fatal and looked for his death sooner. His messmates had taken him out one hundred and fifty yards from camp and thrown down the corpse among the *maweri* stubble. I ordered them to take their spades and bury him, which they seemed almost determined not to do. The Zanzibar men would not go near him, being Mohammedans. So, weak as I was, I opened the package of spades—shouldered one, and set off to find the body. A flock of ravens soon betrayed the place. In the few hours he had lain dead the hyænas had already eaten off his feet and scalp! The ground I found far too hard where he lay, so tying a rope about his body with my own hands, so as to save the two or three men who followed me from infection, I caused them to drag him one hundred yards to the bed of the nearly dry river, where we made a proper grave, and interred him in spite of the demand of some natives for cloth from me for the privilege I had used. I told them that 'if burying did not suit them they could disinter the body, but they should pay me for removing a dead man from the field!'"

One of the artisans of the expedition had died in Zanzibar, and Mackay was greatly disappointed on reaching Mpwapwa to find the other two invalided.

BRIDGE OVER THE WAMI.

[p. 82.

The one especially, who was a blacksmith and a handy man in other respects, had become a perfect wreck, having allowed himself to succumb to the enervating power of the East African climate. There he was lying in a mud tembe, up the hill, with no disease whatever—but ready to die if he were allowed. Mackay writes: "The secret of it all seems to be, he wants to go home, and if he recovers home he must go.* But there am I, going on to the lake, with our boat in pieces—a hundred pieces—to be rebuilt, in fact to be made another craft, seaworthy ; here are three steam engines to be made use of. Here we have on the road my boiler in rings and plates, etc., all to be riveted (not merely bolted) together, with red-hot rivets. Forgings without end to do, and much such work, and who is now to help me with it all? O'Neill is not up to the use of my sort of tools, while the Doctor and the Lieutenant are not to be expected to be workers in iron and steel.

"Do not think I am talking of imaginary difficulties. The matter is serious to think of, but will be much more serious when we reach the lake ; but we are not there yet, and much may befall us before then, in the five hundred miles' march. But the same God who has guided us till now, will guide us all through till the very last item of our work is done." Mackay waited at Mpwapwa for Dr. Smith, who arrived on the 19th of October, and having given the new-comers

* Both artisans soon returned to England.

an ox to feast on, he let them rest for a day ; and, finally, the two Scotchmen, at the head of a caravan now increased to three hundred and ten souls, made for Chumio, where they quietly spent the Sunday with Lieut. Smith.

Next morning they all set out on the long and trying march over the dreary Marenga Mkali desert, where neither water nor food is to be had. This they accomplished in two days, when they reached Ndebwe, where an old woman, the " Sultany," with a dried-up skin, brought them a present of some matama (meal) and milk, for which she got more than double the value in cloth. Next they arrived at the villages of the great greedy chief of Mvumi, where the first *honga* (tribute) was demanded of them. After four or five days' palaver they had the matter settled by being robbed of thirty-nine valuable cloths, equivalent to £9 in English money. Right glad to shake off their feet the dust of the place where they had been so blackmailed, they marched to the next tribute man, whose place is called Mtamburu. Honga here should be small, but the dirty, greasy old chief demanded of them a *deole*, or fine large silken shawl, " such as became a king," he said, in addition to twenty-four of their most valuable cloths. They had nothing of the kind among their stores, nor would they give him gunpowder, of which he insisted they had many casks. At last, after losing a day, he relieved them of forty-one cloths, one double-barrelled gun, one powder-flask, and a few percussion caps. But the greatest loss of all to Mackay was his health, which the bad water of the place again deprived him of. The Doctor was also laid down, but he soon recovered, while Mackay, in his weak state, relapsed into a worse condition than before, so that he could scarcely endure being carried in a hammock.

His companions were determined he should return in charge of the doctor, but this he would not agree to, believing that a couple of days' rest at a good halting-place would set him up. Forty miles more marching, the greater part of which was through a delightfully green jungle abounding in large herds of elephant, zebra and giraffe, brought them to Nyambwa, the quarters of the greatest chief in Ugogo, whose name is Pembe ra Pera, which signifies the horn of a rhinoceros. This potentate's modest demand was only fifty cloths! Two days' palaver made him content with forty-five, after which he was to present them with an ox (for which of course they would have to pay), so as to make Lieutenant Smith his brother. The latter was sitting in the palace, or rather hen-house, and the matter of the honga being settled he thought he would entertain the king by showing him some of the wonders of white men. Taking a matchbox from his pocket he struck a light, which his majesty thought good to interpret as an evil machination and a design on his life. Rushing from the audience chamber, he sent to say that for such a grave offence as had been committed, they would have to pay thirty more cloths. Next morning he was satisfied with twenty-five, which with what they had previously given, made a total tribute of seventy cloths, or much more than a man's load, and in value about £20 !

The district over which Pembe ra Pera reigns is a great cattle country. Six hundred oxen were driven into his tembe every night, while many more were the property of the people round about.

Here Mackay would have liked to stay, for some days at least, until he could gain strength enough to be carried back. The three days' rest had already restored him a little, and the king agreed willingly that the sick white man should stop with him, but Mackay felt sure that he should have difficulty in getting out of his majesty's hands without the payment of an indemnity. Accordingly he determined to be off at once, and on the 8th of November he was once more on the shoulders of two strong men, and with eight additional to carry his tent, sextant, chronometer, clothes, cooking apparatus, and some cloth to buy food by the way, he bade a sorrowful " good-bye " to his dear brethren, little dreaming that *their* earthly journey was nearly run, and started eastwards.

CHAPTER VIII.

THE COAST AGAIN.

"Do something—do it soon—with all thy might ;
An angel's wing would droop if long at rest,
And God Himself, inactive, were no longer blest."
C. WILCOX.

AGAIN he came on bad water, which, although filtered and boiled, brought him to such a low condition that he quite expected to die at Mvumi Writing home afterwards, he says: " Thinking the end was at hand, and commending my soul to the Redeemer, I called for my writing-case, and having mixed an ink powder, I was commencing to write my last letter on earth. But just then my cook entered the straw hut in which I was lying with a large matama meal poultice, which gave me so much relief, that I fell asleep, and afterwards repeated doses of ipecacuanha and laudanum restored me so far that I was able to be carried to the next village, where I halted two or three days, as the water was good, and eggs and milk in abundance; but best of all was the arrival of the home September letters, which helped so much to set me on my legs that I could ride to Mpwapwa, where, chatting with the brethren stationed there, and a few days' rest and good food, were blessed by God to make me nearly well. But I was intent on reaching the coast as soon as possible. The rains were expected soon, and I had little hope of complete recovery till I should have sea air for a time on board the C.M.S.S. *Highland Lassie.*

"Before sunrise on the 20th of November, I was off from Mpwapwa with my ten men and donkey, but the latter soon refused to proceed, as it either suffered from, or shammed sickness, so I sent it back in an hour, and resolved to march to Bagamoyo on foot. We made what speed we could over the ups and downs of the Usagara Mountains. The highest point I crossed was 5000 feet high, and the descent from there to the valley of the Wami is most arduous. The whole distance is two hundred and twenty miles, and I accomplished the march in eleven days, being the shortest period on record.

"When Stanley came down with Livingstone's Journal, to make himself famous, he took at least twenty-five days, although he made all the speed he could, only he marched in the wet season and I in the dry; but in the dry one suffers many delays from searching for water, and only those who have been in the long deserts up country know what it is to march with an empty water-bottle."

Like other travellers, Mackay found that those tribes are the 'most degraded where the women occupy the position of slaves ; those where the women have assumed something like their proper position are further advanced and less savage. He says : " At first one looks on people in a state of nearly 'nude' with considerable suspicion, but up country one is not a little shocked to find the *nearly* converted into *altogether*. In Ugogo the boys all run about just as they were born, and the full-grown men pride themselves frequently on wearing a similar attire. The women are still too modest to altogether follow their example, but a little piece of skin is all they need for full dress when they come out to see the white man. You would have laughed to see me squirting water in their faces in Ugogo, to drive them out of my tent when I was washing, or occasionally taking a big, oily, yellow-ochery savage by the shoulders, and pushing him off with what little strength I had.

" While writing on board our mission steamer in the Bay of Zanzibar, I am listening to the pleasant sound of one of Mozart's marches, played by the band of a British man-of-war, stationed here for the suppression of the slave-trade. Here it is warm, like German midsummer, and the lightning is playing among the clouds over to the west. The German music carries me back to the land from which it came, and all the happy ties which bind me to the great Fatherland. The British man-of-war makes me think of ' bonnie Scotland ' and the days o' ' auld lang syne ;' of peaceful England, which does her best even out here to put an end to cruelty and oppression between man and man. The Mohammedan gun makes me sigh over the determination of deluded men to worship God in a way that is no worship at all. The little vessel in which I am conveys the impression that the true way of life is at last represented here too, but is yet only one tiny seed in the great soil which Satan has owned so long, but which we hope to reclaim to our Master's possession."

Finding, his health restored, he set to work about Christmas to fit up another caravan for the relief of his brethren on the Nyanza, intending to go to Uganda with it in order to join the party he had accompanied in the autumn as far as western Ugogo. Porters were far more difficult to be had than when the previous caravans started, so he took a tour of three hundred miles northwards and back along the coast to collect men. He passed through more than twenty towns and villages, and liked the people very much, but, sad to say, he found a mass of evidence to prove that the nefarious traffic in slaves was as bad as ever.

He was frequently on board Arab dhows, and he says : "In no case have I seen any examination of a dhow in which I have been, although they were always full of people. The Sultan professes his powerlessness to check the slave traders either by sea or land. The English boats' crews rely on native interpreters, who are bribed by slave traders to decoy boats in wrong directions while the dhows escape another way. Every artifice is used to deceive the English officers. At Kokotini I found seven slave dhows in a creek, while the *London's* boats were passing outside in the open. Daily, dhows sail from the mainland, with multitudes of women and children who are passed off as wives or domestic slaves of Arab and Suahili passengers, while large caravans pass constantly through the coast towns along the shore. The "Walis," or Sultan's agents, do not interfere, although applied to by me. Indeed, it is their interest to encourage the trade, as they receive percentage on caravans."

He walked along the most unhealthy part of the coast, sometimes near the sea, sometimes miles from it, one day over pleasant grassy land, and many days through long swamps of the so-called deadly mangrove trees ; wading for hours at a time up to the waist in mud and water, and occasionally being carried or having to swim over deep rivers, sleeping in the open air, in cow-byres, in hen-houses or anywhere, and living on mahogo or cassava roots, and anything else that could be got.

One day he had left the town of Wanga, and after wading for more than an hour through a swamp as bad as the *Makata*, up to the waist in water, and his feet far down in the mire below, he came to the edge of a swollen river running at nearly eight knots an hour,

It was too deep to wade and too rapid to swim. But cross he must. So he sent one of his boys back to the town for a rope with which he intended lassoing a stump on the opposite bank, thus meaning to cross over by the rope. He then sat down on the muddy bank, and taking a copy of " Nature" out of his pocket he set to work to master Ernst Haeckel's theory of Pangenesis, or the undulatory theory of molecules in organic life. In such a death sort of place, to turn one's brains to investigate the ultimate principle of life seems rather incongruous!

Many of the towns are large and populous, but most of them are neglected by the Christian Churches. How long—how long?

Islam long ago found entrance, and did not fail to find many followers ; but every Mohammedan is a *missionary*, while many Christians not only are indifferent to the claims of missions, but are ashamed to confess Christianity in the presence of heathens.

Early in March 1877 he received instructions from the Church Missionary Society to defer going on to the Nyanza until after the rainy season, but to "consider what were the best steps to take in trying to do something towards commencing the formation of a road from Sadani to Mpwapwa." In compliance, therefore, with these instructions he handed over the charge of the caravan he had equipped to another (Mr. Morton, an Englishman, formerly on the staff of the Universities' Mission at Zanzibar), and after seeing him fairly started on the 9th of March, Mackay commenced collecting men and tools for the work of road-making. An attack of fever laid him aside, however, for about six weeks, but the skill and unremitting attention of Dr. Robb, the Consular doctor, and the kind, hospitable treatment received in the house of Messrs. Smith and Brown, the British India Steam Navigation Co.'s agents, led by God's blessing to his recovery.

H.H. the Sultan of Zanzibar kindly gave him a fine horse to ride on, and by May-day the work of making the first road into the interior of the continent was fairly commenced, and he and his men encamped with plant and stock at Ndumi. Writing from there, he says : " This little village or shamba stands on a most desirable spot, on the top of a hill only five miles from the sea, but, as I have just finished measuring by my boiling-thermometer apparatus, is two hundred and fifty feet high. The place is so beautifully exposed to both the N.E. and S.W. monsoons that I mean to build a rough house here to live in, for a week or so at a time, when I am obliged to be in this neighbour-hood, instead of living at Sadani, which is very un-healthy, lying in a mangrove swamp. I have got a brick mould, and shall make bricks of the red sandstone mud the natives use everywhere in East Africa to make their wattle houses with. Bricks are entirely unknown here, and when they see me burn them in a kiln I fancy many curious eyes will be upon me.

"The prospect is delightful here on all sides. I sit at present like Abraham in his tent door. My servants, my flocks, and my herds are about me. Westward the land rolls away in densely wooded ridges. To the north, between the line of hills and the sea, are stretches of wood and lawn alternately— all fine soil, but none cultivated. After coming into camp to-day I took a stroll with my interpreter Susi—Livingstone's old servant, and one of those who returned to England with his remains. We could not help remarking to each other how lazy the people are, for not a mouthful of food is to be bought, and hundreds of square miles of fertile land lying all around uncultivated. A few Englishmen, with their houses on this high ground, and their property below, would within a year turn the land-scape, far and near, into most productive ground. East is the village of Sadani, on the sea, and beyond one can see the island of Zanzibar, one of the most fruitful in the Indian Ocean. South are the connected plains of the Wami river and Sadani. If Lot were alive I think he would have gone there, in preference to the plain of Sodom. But in the valley of the Wami he would have had some trouble, for at Bomani, where Lieut. Smith and I went last year, live the Wadoi, who are notorious cannibals.

"On the Kingani river too it is not very safe for

quiet people, for the valley is often attacked by the wild warriors—the Mafitsi, who, Dr. Kirk tells me, have laid waste the whole of the splendid country between Lake Nyassa and the sea. This has been a stockaded village, but the rampart has been allowed to fall into decay. The villages farther up are all strongly fortified, for wars never cease among the tribes of Useguha, and though guns are plentiful enough, the people find they sleep securest within a threefold wooden rampart in the heart of a dense thicket.

" The slave trade is still the cause of great alarm. How many slaves pass between this shamba and Sadani every day, no man can tell. A well-beaten track crosses the road from this to the coast, and I shudder every time I cross it to think how many poor victims are nightly driven along that path. I never thought that this should be my work or my whereabouts now, but it is the unexpected that always happens. Somebody must do this work, and why not I? But I do not expect to get very far on with it, for in two or three months I hope to have instructions from the Church Missionary Society to proceed direct to Uganda. Lieut. Smith has sent down orders for me to come up quickly with some artisans, and to take no caravan with me, that I may march fast. He is anxious to have a steamer made. They can build a boat of wood, but they are helpless in iron and steam. I am, therefore, sending a telegram to London for an engine-fitter and black-smith.

"I am well again, thank God, and camp-life has set my spirits up. My horse, my dog, my goat, my oxen and donkeys, with all my household of nearly seventy men and women, are enough to feed, and quite enough to look after at one time. It is now dark, and all as calm as possible, and my men are going to rest. I have given them their food, and they know I shall take a good hard day's work out of them on the morrow. The insects are at it again —midges, flies, and mosquitoes above, and ants and crawling things below. A cup does for an ink-bottle and a mixture of powder and water for ink; but 8 or 9 o'clock is bed-time with me on the march, so good-night!"

Axes, saws, hammers, picks and spades were handled right and left, and day by day the work advanced, sometimes by rapid strides, sometimes at a crawling pace. Through endless forest and jungle they cut their way: the banks of many rivers and nullahs were sloped down to render them fordable; heavy boulders—tons in weight—were laid aside; along the edge of steep hill slopes they scooped out a passage, filling up the chasms with trees and stones, and crossing mire and moss with a solid pavement of layers of logs. In the valley of the Mkondokwa, at one place where, after sloping down the banks of the old river bed, and cutting a broad way for several hundred yards through a most terrible jungle of india-rubber trees, densely intertwined with the creeping wild vine, they suddenly came upon a village perfectly concealed and protected. A mile from this is the strongly stockaded shamba known as Kwa Mputa Mkubwa, which is a general halting-place for caravans, as a quantity of corn is grown by the natives; hence food is cheap, and the Wanyamwezi spend several days on end, rejoicing in chewing sugar-cane, and boiling huge messes of mtama porridge, sweet potatoes and pumpkins. At other parts of the same valley the spurs of the mountain run right down to the river brink, frequently terminating in an abrupt precipice, with deep ruts and chasms, and travellers by this route had to scramble in many places along the precipitous slope where a footing could scarcely be had. Here the thick wood along the base of the spurs had to be cut down, and for miles they had literally to shelve a way with pick and spade along the steep brow of the mountain. Three weeks' hard work they spent on a short piece of road, which they walked over in less than three hours on their way back to the coast.

The last portion of the road is an uninhabited wilderness, about forty-seven miles long. It is subject to raids from highway robbers; hence travelling in small numbers is always more or less unsafe, and seldom attempted. Food is not to be had, but one great alleviation of the trials of the march to caravans is, that there is a plentiful supply of water at convenient intervals.   In this desert is the Gombo Lake, which has no feeder on any side, and having no outlet either, its waters taste brackish.   The lake is infested with crocodiles, which, however, have not yet devoured the shoals of large-headed fish, which Mackay's men caught in numbers.   The east end of the lake terminates in a field of pampas, growing on firm sandy ground.   The whole is a perfect network of hippo and rhinoceros trails.   The reeds joining overhead leave dark passages or tunnels below, and in these the huge pachyderms make their abode.   For a couple of hours, one day, Mackay crawled in a stooping posture through these coal-mine sort of levels, in his endeavour to find a road round the hill.   He saw numerous footprints of buffalo and zebra, but set eyes on none of the animals themselves.

> "At night he heard the lion roar
>   And the hyæna scream,
> And the river-horse, as he crushed the reeds
>   Beside some hidden stream."

Doubtless the leopard was present also, for he found its marks farther down.   Large trees broken across, and others denuded of their bark, told that the elephant also frequents the place.   Had he been inclined for sport, he could easily have bagged any number of guinea-fowl and other large birds.

About eight miles from Mpwapwa a fearful thorny jungle is entered, with numerous young baobab trees,

and these continue without intermission till the cultivated fields are reached. Cutting a way through
these sweetly-smelling thorns was a most arduous
task, all being brown and leafless, and affording no
shade from a scorching sun, under which they had to
work for days on end, with not a drop of water near.

But it is "a long lane that has no turning," and
Mpwapwa was reached at last, on the 8th of August.
Thus, in less than a year's time from the date of the
arrival of the vanguard of the Nyanza Mission party
at Mpwapwa, not only had a station been planted
there, but a fair line of communication made between
it and the coast—a distance of two hundred and
thirty miles.

Boys may think that road-making was strange
work for the Church Missionary Society to set their
missionary to do, but their hope was to have the
way improved and carried on, so as to bring the
remotest regions of the vast interior within easy
reach of the known world, and enable the emissaries
of Christianity and civilisation to enter in, carrying
their mighty forces with them to the salvation and
enlightenment of Negro millions.

A good road means a regular mail service, and
much else which renders the agency of the missionaries more powerful, their comfort greater, and
their success more sure.

CHAPTER IX.

A RAPID JOURNEY.

"At length I spake—
"No! here I must not stay.
I'll rest to-night—to-morrow go my way.
*　　　*　　　*
The tree tops now are glittering in the sun:
Away! 'Tis time my journey was begun."

R. H. DANA.

MACKAY having completed the track to Mpwapwa, the Church Missionary Society, fully alive to the barbarous method of employing human beings as burden-bearers for some six hundred miles into the interior, next instructed him to try the bullock-wagon system, which has been so successful in South Africa.

It was a work of no ordinary difficulty, as, not only had the oxen to be trained, but, what was a still greater undertaking, the men had to be taught to drive them! It was also an unprecedented rainy time for the season of the year, which was a tremendous hindrance, not only to starting, but to progress. The whole country was deluged, and the wagon track a mere mud swamp. The Church

Missionary Society had, however, sent him out a very active and useful assistant—a young English carpenter named Tytherleigh. He was a first-class workman, and was able to render most valuable service in improving the carts, etc. Having also more muscular strength than Mackay, he could better manage the wilder oxen. Unfortunately they could not encamp in his favourite resort, the village of Ndumi, six miles from the coast, as they found, by painful experience, that the oxen died fast there, so they were obliged to pitch their tents for a month in the heart of a bog or marsh in the midst of the unhealthy Sadani plain. One morning, in the space of less than three hours, the rain-gauge showed one inch and a third of rainfall! Mackay draws an amusing picture of his attempts to sleep under a strong canvas tent, with his waterproof coat on and an umbrella up! It was seldom, however, as bad as that; and active exercise, constant employment, plenty of quinine, and intense earnestness in the work on hand, kept him and Tytherleigh in good health and spirits!

At last they started, in December 1877. Six large carts finished and loaded, eighty oxen trained to draw them, sixty men (the half of whom were drivers, leaders, or brakesmen, and the rest porters), five donkeys, a flock of sheep and goats, and six dogs, made up the caravan.

But every day the carts were upset two or three

times, and each mile was got over by the expenditure of a very great deal of manœuvering with and hard driving of long teams of oxen. Twenty spanned into one cart could scarcely move with a load of half a ton.

Writing to a young friend in the end of December, he says: "We have no Christmas or New Year parties here, nor anything else that would suit your ideas of novelty. 'Nothing new' is the order of every day, but get up at 4 a.m., get the cook up and all hands. Tents down and yokes arranged, and then with the first streak of light the oxen spanned in, while we meantime drink a cup of coffee and quinine with a piece of weevily ship's biscuit. When I get my waterproof leggings on, we are off. Marching or sticking in the mud, yelling, beating the oxen, digging the carts out of holes, cutting trees, etc., take all the forenoon till 11 or 12 o'clock, when we halt. Tents up, clothes changed, and breakfast eaten. Then a *boma* (enclosure) made for the cattle at night Various little things occupy the time till dark, when we dine. Then a little reading or writing till 9 o'clock, when we go to bed.

"That looks rather an uninteresting life. But the care and responsibility of the caravan and all connected with the march make one have quite enough to do, and sometimes more than enough. When you see ——, [a half-witted lad], tell him I require a heavy man to act as ballast for my carts, to keep them from turning over, and probably he would be well qualified to fill the situation ; but he must send in testimonials first, which he had better get printed, so that each bullock may have a copy !

"A terrible scorpion crawled over me just now. I should like you to see half the horrors of the kind I see in a day—snakes and ants below till one shudders from top to toe, and terrible biting, stinging, huge flies all above and about, drawing blood at every bite. Last night I was busy sleeping, when just at my ear a terrible growl of a hyæna made me spring to my feet, seize my rifle and fire ; but 'Bobby,' my dog, was before me, and set up such a furious bark that the beast skulked off before I had time to present it with a bullet. I daresay you think it a dastardly kind of life, to lie with a revolver under one's pillow and a rifle at one's side, but it is necessary here, for anything may happen at any moment, and it is best to be ready.

"About a dozen men have deserted from me within the last four months, generally taking cloth, etc., with them, besides their advance. Still I have a lot of tolerably decent fellows, who I do not think will run away. But they are all cowards, and let their master shift for himself while they have a pair of heels.

"Here I must correct your ideas of getting acclimatised. Does a man who has had repeated attacks of bronchitis or lung disease become the stronger and more acclimatised to stand the severe Scotch winter?

It is with fever as with everything else: the more attacks, the more liability to attack, and therefore the less strength of constitution left to weather out the disease when it takes hold.

"A proper meaning might be given to acclimatisation, by saying it means the having learned by painful experience to know how and what to do to avoid as much as possible the chance of being laid down sick.

"I have just arrived at the ford of the Rukigura river, the first great affluent of the Wami. It is at present in flood, and a mighty rushing river it is, neck deep. How I am to cross it I cannot tell. By putting up ropes and pulleys, much in the same way as life-saving apparatus from wrecks is done, I think I shall contrive to get all the men and the goods across, but then eighty oxen, and the carts and several donkeys, will be no such easy matter. However, it either must be done or we must wait till all the water runs past; and who knows when that will be, seeing every day brings thunder and lightning and rain?

"I have adopted a new flag for our mission—a blue ground with a large red cross in the middle. Each cart has a small one, while a large one waves over my tent door every day.

"But my legs have got cramp, sitting on the ground like a tailor, writing this, so I must have done."

One night, soon after this, he was wakened up by a colony of brown ants, which were leading their caravan right through his tent. He was lying on a mattress on the floor, and they crawled over it and him by thousands. He got on the top of a box, and his men set fire to the whole ground, inside and round about the tent. After an hour's struggle they gradually disappeared on his line of march, but he had to sleep on the top of his box till daylight.

The natives did not respect the road which had been made at so much expense and labour. In some places where they had been clearing, they left trees and bushes right across it, while in many parts they chose to think that the white man's operations in levelling the ground were preliminary to their sowing their corn on it.

The heavy rains had made terrible ruts in the declines, and the pole oxen kept tumbling and falling and repeatedly getting into terrible entanglements. On one occasion, when they came to a steep descent, the first cart wheeled right over into a large hidden landslip, and the goods, which were rescued with great difficulty, were found to have sustained much damage. Of course, it was most trying to find things going to smash, but Mackay was never one to " cry over spilled milk " ; he simply got the cart to rights again, reloaded, and jogged along. About this time he had an accident which rendered him lame for a week or two. He had just succeeded in getting the second cart over a stream, when he got entangled in a bush and the wheel caught his right foot ; down he went, and over it went the wheel, and doubled the shock by going over the calf of his left leg. After roaring a good deal and nearly fainting he got a cup of tea made, and applied Friar's balsam and bandages. Two of his men put their loads into the carts, and getting out the light hammock they carried him along. But it was to be a day of delays, for cart after cart upset, and the chief of the village, hearing of his arrival, considerately took him seven victims to be vaccinated, and one little boy to be cured of spine disease!

In the early spring the heat of the sun was terrible, and in many parts of the route the caravan was pestered with *vipange* (a sort of *tsetse* fly), long brown and huge yellow ones—which alighted by thousands all about, drawing blood from the oxen and stinging Mackay and his men fearfully. This was a bitter disappointment. A track had been made with great toil; oxen had been trained to go in yoke; men had been taught to drive them; teak wagons had been brought from Bombay; the Church Missionary Society had spared no expense in giving the undertaking a fair trial; and by the month of February the half of the oxen were dead, and many more ailing—evidently caused by the poisonous sting of the *tsetse.*

To add to their discomfiture, the farther inland they went the more the natives enjoyed witnessing the mishaps which daily befell them. Their suspicions had become aroused that the great teams of oxen coming along the white man's road were but a prelude to Europeans entering the country in vast numbers. In many places they blocked the way with bushes, drove the cattle back again into the rivers as soon as they had been got safely over, and greatly resented their treading down the corn which had been sown on the track. Indeed, the chief of Mevero sent Mackay word by two gentlemen of the International Expedition, who were on their way to the coast, that if he took his teams by his village he would shoot him !

Writing home on the 21st February, 1878, he says : "It is not all plain sailing in East Africa, but we have it very much easier than the first travellers who went inland, and every attempt is accompanied with fewer difficulties than before. I have not been on the march to-day, but have taken a rest in the lonely forest. Damp and swamp have been trying me sorely. I am just recovering from an attack of fever, and feel very weak, but as the carts had to be repaired, I have been at work all day, though ill able for it. It is indeed a day of small things yet with me, but only, I hope, as a prelude to greater things to come. Small beginnings may lead to something higher and better in the future, but the first steps cannot be anything but tedious. The longest night has always had a dawn when done, and here I do believe no far distant time will see a very different order of things from what has been always in the past. Rome was not built in a day. My friend, C. M——, of Prague, used to suggest 'it was built perhaps in a night also!' We are indeed groping in the dark as to how or what we ought to do first, but great bodies grow slowly, and the garden of the devil cannot be reclaimed for God all in a year.

"This will certainly be yet a highway for the King Himself, and all that pass this way will come to know His name.

"I have received terrible news this afternoon. Two letter-carriers of the London Missionary Society came from Kisessa, *en route* for Zanzibar. They had seen on the way servants of Said bin Salim Governor, of Unyanyembe, who told them that there had been fighting at the island of Ukerewe, in the Lake Victoria, and that the two white men (Englishmen) were killed with some fifty of their men, also an Arab named Songoro, with all his men. This is a fearful calamity to our mission, if true; and you can fancy the state of suspense I am in. I am writing the British Consul at Zanzibar to make inquiries and let me know the truth, as I hear the Arabs at Unyanyembe have sent letters to inform the Sultan of the matter. Lieutenant Smith and O'Neill were the only two Englishmen in the neighbourhood of Ukerewe, as far as I have any knowledge. It is not like Lieutenant Smith to take to fighting. In fact, he is the last of us to do so; but he may have had fever, or been obliged to defend himself.

"Africa is not a country where a tale becomes truer

by telling it, and on that account I have some hope. I have written, however, to the Church Missionary Society and also to Messrs. Smith and Mackenzie, our agents at Zanzibar, to telegraph to the Society if they find the news to be correct."

The fertile valley of the Mkindo river was inundated, and they had to drag the carts through miles of what was as bad as the great Makata swamp at any time—mud and mire and decaying vegetation *ad nauseam*, except where it was covered waist-deep with water, or, what was a greater hindrance, bamboos and tiger-grass twenty feet high, and too dense to yield to the wheel of a heavy wagon. Here the *tsetse* was very trying, and the oxen dying two or three a day.

On the evening of the 24th February he had sent on word to Tytherleigh, who was a few miles ahead, to abandon the carts, and drive on the surviving cattle to the Usagara Mountains, when he lay down, being utterly worn-out with anxiety and fatigue. He was next attacked three times by scorpions, and rose before dawn, unrefreshed, and went on his way with his shattered caravan. He had not proceeded many miles before he was overtaken by letter-runners from the coast (who had crossed his own), bringing news that the report of the disaster at the lake was believed at Zanzibar, and warning him of the danger ahead.

He writes: "Our good doctor—my own dear friend of many years—went to his rest nine months ago, and now these brave brethren, Smith and O'Neill, have fallen. There were eight of us sent out—two invalided and four gone Home! Only two remaining. Poor Africa! When will it be Christianised by missionaries at this rate? But God has other hands in reserve, whom He will bring to the front, fast and unexpectedly, and the work will proceed whether we break down or not.

"The Arabs are all, I hear, vowing vengeance on the King of Ukerewe, so I must hurry up to prevent further bloodshed."

Having got the goods safely stored, and leaving Tytherleigh to get the two best carts dragged along empty to Mpwapwa, he swam across the much-flooded Mkindo river, and started on the 25th of March on a rapid journey to the lake. Going over rough ascents and steep descents he reached Kitange, where the people were tangle-haired and red-ochred, with little clothing, as in Ugogo. There he bought a fowl and forty cobs of Indian corn for two yards of cloth.

Marching over jungly ground and through open forests, and sleeping at night by muddy-looking pools of water which would not stand the test of sanitary inspection, he reached Mpwapwa on the 30th. There he found Mr. Thomson, of the London Missionary Society, looking for oxen, but without success. Mackay spent a pleasant Sunday with his three friends, and in the evening Mr. Thomson preached

FIRST MISSION CAMP BEYOND UYUI.

[p. 114.

an edifying sermon on the words, " Let your light shine."

He had intended travelling through Ugogo with only five men, so that he might not be detained by the chiefs on the way for honga, but found it necessary to take six on from Mpwapwa, as he did not well see how to dispense with any of the small loads. But the problem which he could not solve was speedily solved for him.

They had slept at Chumio, some twelve miles west of Mpwapwa, and plunged into the thirty-six-miles-long pori or waterless plain, called Marenga Mkali. Knowing thieves were often about in this wilderness, he ordered his men to march close together (Indian file), he himself being next to the last. Towards evening of the first day, one of the men happened to fall behind a few yards, without his knowledge, when he heard a cry, " I'll be killed!" and turning back he found a gang of Wazaramo robbers had sprung out of the bush, and giving the fellow a blow with a club on the stomach, had seized his load and disappeared. To track them in the bush was found hopeless, so he had quietly to submit to the loss, which was serious, as the contents of the bale were—

> 10lb. of ship biscuit,
> 3lb. of cheese,
> 1 tin of jam,
> 1 tin of meat,

1 bottle of brandy (for medicine),
2 oz. quinine,
8 candles,
18 boxes of matches,
1 Colt revolver (new) and 15 cartridges,
60 rounds of Mama cartridges,
1 pocket filter,
1 large water gourd,
1 parcel addressed Rev. C. T. Wilson, Uganda.

Thus *all* his provisions and all his cartridges were gone ; but the loss of the quinine, of which he took daily several grains, was the greatest trouble of all. Without this medicine he knew it was useless to attempt going far westward. While he was considering whether he should go back the thirty miles to Mpwapwa, or trust to meet an Arab on the way who might, but not probably, have a little of the famous fever specific, a caravan of Wanyamwezi came up and camped close by. The leader was an Arab trader from Unyanyembe, travelling in a most comfortable manner—tent, Persian carpet, cooking utensils, sweets, coffee, any quantity of fine rice, etc. He entertained Mackay most kindly, giving him a good dinner of rice and curried fowl, and presenting him with a most welcome gift—a packet of candles and a box of matches ! Next morning Mackay sent back, under charge of this trader, one of his men with a note to the brethren at Mpwapwa, asking them to send him some quinine without delay.

Resolving to march by easy stages till "Ramazan" returned with the medicine, they went on right through the desert. After the loss of the previous day he took care the men kept close together, and he himself brought up the rear, keeping a very sharp look-out against thieves. They next came to the densely populated district of Ugogo, where the chiefs are very troublesome in extorting honga, and give but a cold welcome to small parties who carry little to be robbed of. Sometimes they allowed him to put up in their dirty tembes, and sometimes they refused him that privilege, when he slept in a small hut in an old Nyamwesi camp. Such huts are not so large as a cole of hay, and it was impossible for him to stretch himself inside. Still he preferred such places to the tembes, which swarm with vermin of all kinds.

It was providential that he had to delay on the road till his man returned, for he thus barely escaped falling among thieves of a more formidable nature than the highwaymen who ran off with his goods in the desert. This was a band of roving Wahehe,* who hovered about his camp at Mtamburu. Mackay says: "Had they chosen to demand everything I had, I was ill able to resist. But my hope was in God, who will deliver me in time of danger. May He grant us a safe journey to Unyanyembe. In case

---

* See " A. M. Mackay, Pioneer Missionary of the Church Missionary Society to Uganda," p. 63.

of being attacked by them in the desert, I have put in my pocket the valuable gold watch the Church Missionary Society are sending to the governor for his kindness to Lieutenant Smith. I should be very sorry to lose their other gift—a fine Arabic Bible—even more than the watch, but it is too large to conceal about my person.

"I was amused at the old chief here performing his divination last night and this morning, with a few long pieces of stick on the ground, which he arranged in threes, and odd ones together, to divine as to the chance of the Wahehe returning, or as a charm against their coming and taking away another ox.

"It rained heavily all last night, and not a dry spot in the tembe, and no light. Succeeded in finding my waterproof coat, and in covering goods with rubber sheet; but it was very wet in hammock, and floor of dung made a perfect mire. One of my men had his arm bitten painfully by a scorpion, and it swelled badly."

In the forest and jungle, after leaving Mtamburu, there was an abundance of flies, which he believed to be the *tsetse*, only with a double instead of a fourfold style of proboscis. They were of the size of the common fly, but with the back part striped yellow like the bee. They bit and drained blood painfully. There were also many long grey-spotted flies, and a yellow sort with long projecting sword, as at Mkinyo, near Mvomoro. Another variety injected a fine needle out of the proboscis, which it kept straight out and sucked blood sorely. He noticed that the needle swelled very much in the middle with blood, just as ink does in a pen.

Reaching Nyambwa, the seat of the fat old chief Pembe ra Pera, who so blackmailed the expedition eighteen months previously, Mackay halted to dine, and succeeded in buying some *mwere* porridge and a calabash of buttermilk for a little tobacco. Thence he went along many miles of mud to Mwanza, where his person, his clothes, and his arms were the constant theme of admiration of crowds of natives. The mosquitoes were very trying, and as he had to share a corner of a tembe with the father and all the family, who lay on ox-hides, on the floor, he had no pleasant reminiscences of his sojourn there.

The first effects of a fortnight without quinine were now beginning to tell on him. By the time he reached Dahumbi, he felt in the unhappy position which is called "in for fever." Shivering and shaking having come on, he took from his pocket the tiny phial of aconite he always carried in case every other medicine was stolen or lost, and was measuring out a dose, when his eyes were gladdened by the sight of "Ramazan" arriving with two men from Mpwapwa and a small bundle, among the contents of which was a bottle of that invaluable specific, sulphate of quinine, from which he derived so much benefit that he was able to proceed on his journey next day. But constant wettings, and having frequently to wade for hours at a stretch through a flooded country, together with badly-cooked porridge of coarsely-ground grain (the only thing to be had), brought on other symptoms, which rendered him so weak that by Good Friday he could not carry his rifle. For a long time he had been on half rations. Coffee, tea, sugar, and salt were all done. Had it not been for a couple of tins of cocoa, which Mr. Last had kindly sent from Mpwapwa, most probably he would have never reached Uyui. Alas! this also came to an end ; but at this juncture he met a large caravan with more than a thousand porters, carrying a quantity of ivory to the coast. The leader was an Ujiji Arab, who knew Livingstone and Stanley and Cameron, and out of his esteem for these white men he gave Mackay a couple of fowls— a most acceptable present.

At last, on the 30th of April, he caught sight of the chief's village in Uyui. It is a large place, stockaded and concealed among trees. Mackay knew it was his destination, from seeing three white donkeys grazing outside the village. He was quickly shown to the Baraza of the "Wali," where sat the venerable Said bin Salim and his family and followers. This kind old man, a few months before Mackay's arrival, had purchased two hundred slaves who had been brought to Unyanyembe for sale, and immediately after doing so set them all free !

This action so irritated some unscrupulous slave-traders that they turned him out of Unyanyembe where he had been governor for sixteen years, and he had to flee, alone and empty-handed, to Uyui. His children managed to join him by stealth ; but such was the hostility of the new governor, that the old man dare not even send for his goods.

While at Uyui, Mackay was often heart-sick at the cruelties of the slave-trade, which were perpetrated under his very eyes, but being alone, he could only protest against such wrongs.

The caravans started for the coast during the night, so that he might not see them, but he could hear the clink of the chains, and the piteous wails of the mothers who had been separated from their children, and fancy he heard the refrain,—

> "And yet He has made dark things
> To be glad and merry as light:
>
> * * *
>
> And the sweetest stars are made to pass
> O'er the face of the darkest night.
> But we who are dark, we are dark !
> Ah, God, we have no stars !
> About our souls in care and cark
> Our blackness shuts like prison-bars :
> The poor souls crouch so far behind
> That never a comfort can they find
> By reaching through the prison-bars."

As Mackay was the guest of the ex-governor, he was of course associated with him by the hostile Arabs, who did all they could to thwart his progress by preventing him from buying a single yard of cloth or an ounce of coffee, or anything else he needed for his further journey to the lake.

They also in Mackay's absence, and without his knowledge, seized the property of the Church Missionary Society, which he had stored in Said bin Salim's house, thereby subjecting him to much privation and consequent sickness, while the C.M.S. work was greatly hindered.

These Arabs, knowing well that the presence of Englishmen would sooner or later stop their traffic in slaves, had been sending down messengers to agitate among the Wagogo, to cause them to prohibit the passage of carts through their country. They also bribed the chief of Uyui to drive both him and the ex-governor away, and pretended that they had orders from the British Consul to that effect.

Mackay then went to Unyanyembe, and showed the new governor his letters of introduction from the Sultan of Zanzibar and Dr. Kirk to Arabs in the interior, but no explanation was of any avail. Kisessa would "have nothing to do with white men"; and Mackay was glad to shake the dust of the place off his feet.

Just at this juncture, however, he was treated with great hospitality by Sheik Thain bin Abdullah, who had once travelled through Ugogo with Stanley; and indeed he invariably received kindness from both Arabs and natives who knew anything of the great traveller.

CHAPTER X.

THE SILVERY SEA.

HENRY WARE.

JUST as Mackay was despatching a party of porters to meet Tytherleigh, and to carry up the remaining goods intended for Uganda, he received the sorrowful tidings that his invaluable companion had been called to his rest.

Writing on June 4th, 1878, he says: "What a disastrous mission ours has been! I am the only layman left of our little band. Indeed, Tytherleigh did not belong to the original party, but came out afterwards. But God's ways are not our ways.

"One thing is certain, this land will ever remain little else than what it is—dark, benighted Africa, until we can find some easy means of travel and

113   8

transit in it. Very few could endure the trials and hardships we went through together in the early months of this year. His loss is a great grief to me.

" After various fights with *Ruga-ruga*, and endeavours to pass by a more direct road to the lake, I am now in the thirty-miles' desert, north of Nguru, under escort of men belonging to the great chief of Usonga, who is a superior man and brother to Mirambo. I hope to be in Kagei in a few days. I am going (D.V.) to the island of Ukerewe, to see the king who murdered Lieutenant Smith and O'Neill.

" I have had a bad sun fever since leaving Uyui, but am now all right."

A few stages north from Uyui the tembes were plastered outside as well as within, and had numerous circular loopholes for defence. Outside most of them pictures of men and lizards were painted, in red and black and white. At one place the door of the chief's tembe had carved on it, in high relief, the figure of a man nearly life-size, and on the whole well executed. These were the only attempts at sculpture or painting Mackay saw in the interior.

Elephants, hippos, giraffes and zebras were numerous in this desert. After a *terekeza*, or evening march, they arrived one night at a deserted village, where they found water, and having made a fire, they cooked some potatoes and nuts, and lay down to sleep. Mosquitoes, however, never ceased to torment them, and about 10 p.m. the alarm was raised of an enemy being near. Mackay had heard repeated loud reports, which he took for the fighting of gnus or other large game in the distance, but he failed in his attempts to make his men believe it was other than the guns of *Ruga-ruga.* Fire in the same direction only increased the alarm. Panic-stricken, the *Wasukuma* were determined to be off at once, leaving pots and gourds and half-cooked food all about. His reluctance to get up was forced into consent by the terror of his men, who, quicker than ever before, had his clothes, etc., packed up, and seizing their guns took to their heels while he slipped on his boots and followed. The young moon was going down, and the sky was very cloudy. Striking north through the jungle, stumbling and tripping all the way, they came after two hours' quick march on a village called Bushola, where they were received in a friendly manner. In a tembe there was a young man weaving cloth of native fibre, and though his loom was very wide and the process primitive and slow, he succeeded in making a strong, thick material.

Next day they arrived at Mondo, where, as in the Scottish Highlands, the cattle live in the same small huts as the natives. The men were all perfectly nude, and the younger women wore only small aprons of beads. At Marya, about four days' march from the lake, the natives had never seen a white man before, and were most inquisitive, though not rude. Mackay was always glad of every opportunity for the natives to become reconciled to Europeans, believing that frequent intercourse, and just, friendly dealing were the first means to remove natural suspicions. On this account he greatly regretted having to march so hurriedly through the country.

By this time his socks were all worn out. Consequently his heels were blistered, rendering walking very painful. But he was nearly at the end of miserable marching over sandy deserts and swampy plains ; and on the evening of June 12th, to his great joy, he caught the first glimpse of the noble lake. There lay the water, calm and silvery grey, and a refreshing breeze from seaward fanned his sunburnt cheeks.

Some notes from his log-book are now interesting :—

"*June 13th*, 1878.—Reached Kagei. Long talk with chief Kaduma. No news from Uganda, but an Arab with many canoes expected soon. Lkonge, king of Ukerewe, is much afraid of white men coming. He has sent repeatedly to Kaduma to ask, ' Is Mackay not yet come ? ' He fears I will go to take vengeance on him, and protests loudly that he had no quarrel with Smith and O'Neill, and that the massacre was caused by the slave-dealer's treachery.

"*June 14th.*—Went out with Kaduma to see the *Daisy* lying dry on the beach covered with grass. Found her in a terribly dilapidated condition. The machinery also in a deplorable state. Most valuable tools thrown amongst nails and dirt, and all destroyed by rust.

" Next I visited the grave of my dearly loved brother Dr. Smith. There stands the pile and tombstone with inscription, and alongside is the grave of Barker. of Stanley's expedition. I must raise a tombstone for our two dear martyrs, Smith and O'Neill, either here or in Ukerewe.

"*June* 15*th.*—To-day the men left who were going to Ukerewe. I gave them a clear message to Lkonge, Kaduma interpreting from Suahili into their language. I told them that the king need not be afraid of me, and that to dispel his fears of my men accompanying me, I begged him to send a canoe of his own for me, when I should go to the island with *his* men, leaving my gun and servants all behind here.

" I have sorted and assorted machinery, nails, screws, etc., etc., till quite done up, and much still remains to do. To-morrow is the Lord's day, and I shall be glad of the rest and peace it brings. May I use it well!

"*June* 16*th.*—Quiet Sunday. Chief Kaduma came as usual early. I endeavoured to teach him that by God's command we white men keep this day as a great day. I read to him from Steere's Suahili Scripture lessons the account of the six days' work of creation and the sanctification of the seventh day. He understood well, but our lesson was frequently interrupted by the cattle, which took to fighting just at the time. The devil seems to hinder even the entrance of a little light in this land of darkness."

All the natives in the neighbourhood of Kagei

strongly advised Mackay not to trust Lkonge, as they felt certain he meant treachery, and would poison him. They told him that after his brethren fell, the king persuaded their followers to put away their weapons and sit down in peace, as he would not harm them. The *Wangwana* believed him and began to cook their food, when he attacked them and killed many. Mackay writes : " I feel it is a questionable step to take, to put my head right into the lion's jaws ; but our object is to Christianise Ukerewe as well as Uganda, and the sooner Lkonge and we are once more reconciled the better. God can close the lion's mouth, and it is in His service alone I go to Ukerewe. My men are afraid to go, and have asked me not to bid them accompany me."

At length, on the 28th of June, he embarked in a large canoe. The cheerful song of the paddlers, the novelty of the scene and the adventurous nature of his mission, were most exhilarating to his spirits. The natives stood on the beach and watched the canoe out of sight :—

> 'And sang their rude song, like the death-spirit's moan :—
> The stranger has gone where the simoom will burn :
> Alas! for the white man will never return !"

They then retired to discuss the matter over their *pombe* (beer), and by sunset the whole village, from chief down to mothers and little children, were perfectly intoxicated.

After a voyage of two days he reached his destination, when, after rest and refreshment, he was summoned to see the king, who was sitting in his *Baraza*—a circular roof supported by a network of posts, and open on all sides. Lkonge was then only about twenty years of age, stoutly built, with plain but not unpleasant features. He was dressed in a grey rifle suit, evidently a present from O'Neill, with a red pocket-handkerchief tied about his head. His legs and arms were loaded with rings of brass and iron wire, while on his neck hung two strings of very large beads, one black and the other white.

As he saw Mackay approach he went out to meet him and cordially shook hands with him, saluting him in Suahili, of which he knew a little. He then took his seat on the throne, a large wooden stool, flat on top and base, with one central leg—cut, of course, out of the solid, for the art of joining trees, except by sewing, is unhappily quite unknown through the length and breadth of Africa.

The *Baraza* was crowded with men sitting on the ground. Each one, on arrival, knelt before the throne, folded his hands, and saluted the king, who seldom made any response. One man presented his Majesty with a small bundle of something which evidently did not give satisfaction, for he threw it at the donor, who picked it up and withdrew, protesting loudly as to the value of the gift.

After much talk, Mackay could see that certain

men were being selected for some purpose, for about
half a dozen went forward on bended knee and kissed
the palms of the king's hands.   Soon after the court
rose.

Next day, while Mackay was sitting under the
shade of a tree, his Majesty appeared on the scene,
attended by his prime minister and chief counsellors.
Mackay rose to meet him, and after the usual greeting
a stool was brought for the king and another for the
stranger, while the natives knelt or sat on the ground
on both sides.

At a signal from Lkonge, the prime minister rose
and related at great length the account of the massacre
of the missionaries.

Mackay then said "he had come in peace, and in
a friendly way, as the king could see from his having
no arms with him, and that he believed the king's
version of the story—viz., that he had no desire to
kill the white men."   At this remark Lkonge was
much pleased, and said they "must kill a goat at once
and make blood brotherhood."   Mackay continued:
"The Queen of England is a great sultan, and her
kingdom is larger than that of any other sovereign
in the world."   Strong expressions of disapproval
were heard among the counsellors, the king laughing
and saying to them, "Does the *Muzungu* mean to say
that his sultan is greater than the King of Ukerewe?"

Mackay said, "King Lkonge need not laugh, for
the kingdom of Queen Victoria is not only bigger

than Ukerewe, but larger than the whole Nyanza, and Uganda, and Usukuma, and all Barra (the Interior), and her people are very, very many, so many that no one could even count them all." He then told the king that "white men who came up country did not come with guns to fight, but to make friends with black men, and teach them to know all the wonderful things that white men knew. They left their great power behind, in England, and would not bring soldiers to Ukerewe to fight, unless Lkonge first declared war with England."

Mackay next asked the king if he wished him to bring two or three white men to live in Ukerewe, and teach his people and his children to read and write and to know the word of God. Lkonge replied, " By all means. I want white men to stay with me, but my people are afraid of them." Mackay pointed out the absurdity of many men being afraid of two or three, and asked, "Are you afraid of me?" The king answered, " No, because you are our friend, nor would we be afraid of two or three such as you, but you must not bring many."

Mackay next asked the king, as a pledge of his good faith, if he would return the book in which his brother Lieut. Smith had been seen writing the day he died, as it was very valuable, and he was most anxious to send it home to the white man's friends in England. But this took the king aback: he pretended that the book was lost, and the guns and other things also, that his people had taken them, one here and another there, and that they could not be found.

Mackay pressed the point, demanding as a proof of the king's friendship the restoration of the articles in question, adding, that a "great king had only to tell his people to deliver them up and they would be brought." Lkonge said he would "look for the articles," and the interview closed.

Day after day passed, and as neither the book nor the guns were produced, Mackay sent the king his red blanket and a dressing-gown, with the message that " he must now leave."

But Lkonge would not let him off until the bond of blood brotherhood was sealed, but no goat was forthcoming.

Mackay suspected the king was delaying bringing the animal until the demand was withdrawn, so he made fun of Lkonge calling himself " a big king," and at the same time being unable to produce a goat in three days!

" Let the king stop looking for a goat. I will not demand the property of my brethren until I come back from Uganda, when I will be sure to bring a goat with me!"

This touched the right chord, and Mackay was immediately summoned to the *Baraza*, where was a great crowd of people, a goat standing in the midst. The king held the fore legs and the white man the hind. A leading man explained the rite as being a solemn seal of friendship between the king's god and Mackay's God. The executioner then passed a knife rapidly down the middle of the living animal, which was severed at once, the whole company lifting up their hands and sticks to heaven with a continuous yell, which is prayer in Ukerewe!

After many a hearty " good-bye," Mackay started for Kagei, which he reached after a nine days' absence, amidst the screams of scores of delighted natives, who danced for joy on the beach at the return of the white man.

Mackay next set to work to repair the *Daisy*, which was a most arduous undertaking. It was frightfully warped by the heat, while the wet grass which it had been filled with, to protect it a little from the rays of the sun, had harboured myriads upon myriads of white ants, which had played frightful havoc. Another difficulty was that there was no wood in the neighbourhood with which he could mend the leaking planks. At last he succeeded in getting from the chief a few heavy logs which were too large for the natives to use as fuel ; but these had to be sawn into boards ; and the heavy work, together with the hot rays beating down on his head, on the shadeless beach, soon brought on a bad attack of fever.

On recovery, he had the most faulty section of the boat uncoupled and carried under a beautiful large fig-tree in the village, where he subjected it to a thorough repair, hosts of naked natives surrounding

him, intently watching every operation. The news
of the white man and his "big canoe" soon spread,
and many chiefs from the neighbouring districts came
to "make brotherhood" with him. He writes: "I
hope thus by degrees to establish friendly relations
with all the tribes around the lake. This must be one
of our main objects, as it may open many a door."

On Sundays he always endeavoured to instruct the
natives, who thronged about him, in spiritual matters,
and found them always ready to listen. But he says:
"Their dark minds can only grasp a little at a time—
all is so new to them; while their knowledge of Suahili
is imperfect, especially of words and ideas for religious matters. Here also, as in all tropical countries,
the men do no work, and an idle life can never be
a Christian one. What Bishop Patteson calls 'the
second step' we must make an essential part of the
first step, else our teaching will be fruitless."

At length, on the 23rd of August, having been
hindered for many days owing to severe storms of
thunder and lightning, the *Daisy* set sail, with a
favourable breeze, for Uganda; but on the fifth day
a terrific storm arose suddenly and with no baro-
metrical warning, and the crew, or rather live cargo,
became panic-stricken, and refused to render any
assistance. The sea broke terribly over the boat,
and as she was fast filling with water, there was no
alternative but to let her drift ashore on the bleak
coast of Busongora.

The little vessel was so shattered that for the third time since her arrival in Africa she had to be shortened and otherwise repaired. The natives of the place were friendly, however, and not only built huts for the protection of the C.M.S. property, but sent some men with their only canoe to Uganda, to ask Mtesa to send on some canoes to carry the remaining goods, which the now diminished boat could not accommodate.

Cupidity and curiosity kept them continually hovering about the camp; their usual expression on seeing the rotary processes of the white man was that "God must be in the air!" They really thought that the knowledge of such wonderful things could only have come from heaven.

Mackay says: "Every day they see more wonders. We grind our corn with a revolving hand-mill; we sharpen our tools on a revolving grindstone; we produce blast by a revolving fan; we turn round articles on a revolving lathe; we clench articles firmly in a vice by a revolving screw; we bore holes by a revolving brace and bit; and we fasten screws into the boat by a revolving screwdriver. By-and-bye we hope to have revolving motion in our steam-engines, in water-wheels, in windmills, in circular saws, and above all in the cart-wheels which we hope to introduce at no distant date.

"I fear the King of Uganda will be so struck with awe at our endless applications of the principle of *revolution*, that he will be tempted to say, as the President of the Mexican Republic did at the Vienna Exhibition, when he was shown an engine which made a thousand revolutions per minute, ' Dat is more revolutions even dan dey make in my contree ! ' "

The work of repairing the boat was sorely hindered by the weather. In the morning, it was intolerably sultry, then rain fell accompanied by violent storms of thunder and lightning. Not unfrequently waterspouts were seen in the distance, and one day a very large floating island, with many great trees on it, glided along the coast.

Eight weeks were spent on this coast, when they got afloat once more, and after a rough voyage and enduring many hardships they sighted Ntebe, the port of Uganda, on the 1st of November, 1878. The natives saw them, manned a canoe, and paddled out to meet them with drums beating merrily.

On the 6th they reached the capital (Rubaga), but the king was too ill for an audience. He, however, sent his salaams and two very large fat goats. Mackay writes :—

" *Friday, 8th November.*—Eventful day. Word was brought that the king was in his *Baraza*, and Wilson and I were to go at once. We set off, bearing our presents, as the excitable couriers could hardly be persuaded to carry the few things.

"Messenger after messenger came running like madmen to hurry us on, but I was determined not to give way to the frantic behaviour of these excited couriers, and kept a steady step. At length we entered on the grand esplanade, running east and west along the top of the hill and terminating in the palace at the west end, where the law of fashion seems to hold good all the world over. The gates were opened, the grand guard presented arms, and we passed along through the double row of guards, into a large hall, densely lined with retainers. At the far end was a door, through which we were ushered into the presence of the king. Here he was, seated on a mat, dressed in a long white robe and long black coat richly embroidered with gold braid. He bowed politely, and stools were brought for us to sit on, while some Turkish-dressed attendants squatted on the ground. An old woman sat behind the king, a little way off, and watched intently. For ten minutes we eyed each other in dead silence, when a little talk began. Our gifts were presented, and the music-box struck up the fine air ' The Heavens are telling,' from Haydn's ' Creation.'

" After some time the king intimated that he was too ill to sit long, and gave us permission to go. We left, the whole court rising and following us down the hill—small boys, as usual, forming a large bulk of the spectators and followers. In the evening the king sent us no less than ten fat cattle as a present, and a man's load of tobacco, with a like quantity of both coffee and honey."

CHAPTER XI.

AT THE COURT OF MTESA.

"God gives to every man
The virtue, temper, understanding, taste,
That lifts him into life, and lets him fall
Just in the niche he was ordained to fill."
WILLIAM COWPER.

IN early Saxon times the smith was ever regarded as a mighty man. "His person was protected by a double penalty. He was treated as an officer of the highest rank, and awarded the first place in precedency. After him ranked the maker of mead, and then the physician. In the royal court of Wales he sat in the great hall with the king and queen, next to the domestic chaplain." *

From his great skill in handicrafts, especially in all kinds of iron-work, Alexander Mackay soon became as much esteemed by King Mtesa and his court as the early smith was by our woad-stained ancestors. Miscellaneous articles were showered upon him to repair, and much wonder expressed at the burnished

* See "Industrial Biography—Iron Workers and Tool Makers," by Dr. Samuel Smiles.

face he put on metal goods. The native smiths could manufacture hoes and hatchets, also steely knife blades, but the art of *tempering* was unknown. To *Burogo* (witchcraft) the natives attributed the process by which he put hardness into steel and took it out again. Neither had they any idea of rotatory motion, and when he rolled some logs up an inclined plane, he was followed by dense crowds calling out, " Makay lubare ! Makay lubare dala !" (Mackay is the great spirit : he is truly the great spirit.)

Mtesa was very intelligent, and could understand anything if properly explained to him. Mackay told him about railways and steamers : how seventy years ago there were no railways, and now the world is girdled with a network of them. He entertained his majesty with accounts of the telegraph and the tele-phone and the phonograph, and greatly impressed him by saying, " My forefathers made the WIND their slave ; then they put WATER in the chain ; next they enslaved STEAM ; but now the terrible LIGHTNING is the white man's slave, and a capital one it is too !"

Another time he gave the king and court a lesson on astronomy, illustrating it with Reynolds' beautiful diagrams. They very quickly understood the first-principles of the Cosmos. Many Arabs were present, and Mackay showed that it would be impossible to fast a whole month, as the Koran ordered, in the polar regions, where some months the sun never sets, and others he never rises, adding, " Mohammed could not have been a true prophet of God, else he would have known this.   I am no prophet, and yet I know much more than he did."

On another occasion he took Huxley's " Physiography " to the palace with him, to show the circulation of the blood, etc.   Such a subject proved intensely interesting.   He dwelt on the perfection of the human body, which no man could make, nor all the men in the world ; and yet the Arabs wished to buy a human being, with an immortal soul, for a bit of soap !   The argument went home, and the king said, " From henceforth no slave shall be sold out of the country." Mackay told him that was " the best decree he had made in all his life."

Being a layman and having had much to do with large bodies of workmen, together with the valuable experience he had acquired as a Normal School teacher, and being besides a shrewd observer and independent thinker, he derived his knowledge of men from real life and not from books.   He cultivated the society of the natives in order to win their love and friendship, joined them at their meals of meat and plantains, which the Arabs scorned to do, respected their prejudices as far as consistent with his conscience, invited many of them to his own house (or rather hut), and entertained them with a magic lantern, which he contrived to make a chimney for out of a couple of Huntley and Palmer's old biscuit tins, one laid horizontally on the top of the other and tacked vertically into a wooden box. These exhibitions greatly delighted the people. Pictures of houses and details they could not understand, as they had never seen any building beyond a grass hut ; but the representations of animals were much appreciated, especially when the exhibitor tried a little phantasmagoric effect.

But all these mechanical employments were subsidiary to the spiritual, and he never lost an opportunity of introducing, in a happy way, the subject of religion, or of dropping a word that would touch the heart.

In his log-book in the early part of 1879 are many entries similar to the following : " House inundated with small boys reading with me, and watching my operations. They say my heart is good. I wish it were, and theirs also."

" Chief who brought the canoes from Busongora spent last night with me. Gave him one of the white blankets off my bed. Had a long conversation with him on the way of salvation. He has been taught something of Islam, but cares little for that, and took a good deal of interest in what I told him last night."

" Every day I am learning to admire this people more and more."

As he became familiar with the language, however, he heard of many crying iniquities,—

"And oft his wakeful hours were filled by grief and bitter sighs,
   O'er cruel deaths, revengeful blows, and slaves' heartrending cries."

He never shrank from exposing such evils to the
king in open court, and privately to the katikiro
(prime minister and judge) and to the chiefs.

He writes: " It is clearly my duty to point out
their error and to show them a better way. But
great tact is necessary for this, and more wisdom than
human. Yet I believe that, with all my unworthiness,
I have had more than once Divine guidance and aid
in such delicate work. Well I know that such sacred
duties could be many times better done than I can
do them. But my Master above can use even the
humblest instrument in His own hand. The power
is in Him alone."

Every Sunday the flag was hoisted on the Palace
hill, and Mackay held a short service and read and
explained the story of the Gospel, dwelling especially
on the blessedness of doers and not of hearers only.
He invited free conversation on the passage read, and
great eagerness was shown by king and chiefs and
numerous youths to know and possess the truth.
Sometimes Mtesa was so much struck with the
explanation of a parable, that he remarked to his
people " *Isa* (Jesus), was there ever any one like Him?"
It seemed as if the prophecy was about to be fulfilled :
" The kings shall shut their mouths at him ; for that
which had not been told them shall they see, and that
which they had not heard shall they consider."

In the meantime two reinforcements to the mission
were *en route* for Uganda. The first arrived by the

MTESA'S PALACE.

[*p.* 127.

Nile, having ascended that river under the auspices of General (then Colonel) Gordon. Unfortunately Egypt had always been an object of great suspicion in the eyes of the Baganda. Captain Speke, who formed Mtesa's acquaintance a dozen years before Stanley, tells how the king objected to his passing through Uganda to Egypt *viâ* the Nile, and how he only gave way on his promising to do his best to open a communication with Europe by its channel! *

The Egyptian station of Mruli was regarded by Mtesa with very jealous feelings, and the Arabs lost no opportunity to fan the flame. Knowing well that with the presence of the white man the hope of their gains was gone, they told him that the " Nile party " were coming as political spies, and were really emissaries from Colonel Gordon, and that the Turks (as they called the Egyptians) would soon come and " eat the country." Mackay saw that the king was becoming very nervous as the time drew near for the arrival of the expected missionaries. The Baganda had the word *Baturki* as often in their mouths as ever the Romans had the word *Carthago* in the last days of the empire. He (Mtesa) never wearied in narrating all his intercourse with white men : how Speke brought Grant, and then sent Baker ; how

* See "Lake Victoria : a Narrative of Exploration in Search of the Source of the Nile, compiled from the Memoirs of Captains Speke and Grant." By George C. Swayne, M.A. (William Blackwood and Sons).

Colonel Long came, and was followed by Stanley; and now when this party comes there will be *five* white men in Uganda. What do they all want? Mackay tried to assure him that " they were merely coming in response to his own invitation, and that neither the Queen nor Colonel Gordon had sent them, that godly men in London had asked them to come to teach him and his people, etc. ;" and then with tact he changed the subject to one he knew would interest him. But in the middle of it Mtesa, in his abrupt way, asked, " Are these fellows not coming to look for lakes, that they may put ships and guns on them? Did not Speke come here by the Queen's orders for that purpose?"

At length, on the 12th of February, 1879, the king received several Arabic letters from the north, containing gossip about the new party and their stuff. The bearer of the letters was also closely questioned about them, and in a tone of relief Mtesa said to Mackay, " Their guns are only muzzle-loading."

" Only soldiers require breech-loading rifles, and our party are not soldiers."

" Will they bring gunpowder?"

" I don't know."

" Will they bring beads?"

" Not likely."

" What will they bring?"

" I cannot tell."

The following entries in his journal are interesting :—

" *Friday, Feb.* 14*th*, 1879.—Early my friends arrived.
. . . In afternoon I was summoned by Mtesa to give
an account of my brethren. Arranged with him that
we should all come up to-morrow, when he should
give us a grand reception.

" *Saturday*, 15*th.*—Having got our presents ready
for the king, we were called about 10 a.m. Great
crowds lined the way with drums and a band. The
king was dressed and sitting in the great court, or
rather in the adjoining room, while the chiefs thronged
the court. . . . Our presents were produced, the king
and chiefs being delighted, calling Massudi (coastman)
to witness how we gave whole bales of what the
Arabs and coastmen sold at the rate of a couple of
yards for a slave or a tusk.*

" *Tuesday*, 18*th.*—As we were breakfasting at the
oval table (which I had made by screwing together
the two bulkheads of the *Daisy*, and mounting on six
ash poles stuck in the ground, at which we can all

---

* "When the half-caste Arabs saw these gifts their resentment
knew no bounds. Every day they agitated at court, and succeeded
in turning the chiefs against us. I had put them to confusion on
every occasion before, when they brought forward their false creed
at court, and the king had got so disgusted with them that he frequently asked me if he should send them away. I told him, however,
not to do so until English traders came. I knew that if no merchants
at all were here, demands would be made on us to supply articles we
could not meet. These fellows have now got the chiefs to believe
that we ought to have given *them* rich presents also. The king is
much influenced by his chiefs, and allowed much evil talk against
us.—A. M. M."

comfortably sit, like King Arthur and his knights,
without any struggle for pre-eminence), and making
arrangements as to the best manner of dividing the
work every day, an order came down for us all to go
up. . . . When we were called in we were told that
two white men had arrived at Ntebe (the port) in a
canoe, but who they were the king knew not."

These turned out to be the vanguard of a party
of French Romish priests, who, although the whole
continent was open to them, preferred to go where
Protestant missionaries were already at work.   It was
a time of very great trial to Mackay and his brethren.
Hitherto Mtesa had been most favourable to Mackay
and his teaching, but the interference of these priests
bewildered him.   " Every nation of white men has
another religion.   How can I know what is right
and what is false ? " he asked.   Mackay appealed
to the infallible *Book*, and the Roman Catholics to
an infallible Church.   The battle of the Reformation
was fought again at the court of this heathen king ;
and, to complicate matters still further, the Arabs,
ever ready to seize an opportunity of showing their
hostility to white men in general, derided the religion
of both.   It is possible that Mackay's training and
the traditions of his family prejudiced his mind
against these priests, but the following extracts from
his journal are one or two illustrations of their
behaviour :—

" *Saturday, Feb. 22nd,* 1879.—Went up to the

palace, having heard that the men of whose arrival we had heard were Frenchmen. We suspected that they were the Romish priests who were reported by Colonel Gordon to be *en route* for Uganda. On reaching the outer courts, I found two men who had come with them, one being a slave of Said bin Salim, and the other the same old Msukuma who accompanied me to Ukerewe last July. From them I obtained the information that the strangers were padres, that they had left three of their number at Kagei, and that all meant to come here to stay. Thus I was prepared for an audience with the king, which commenced immediately afterwards. Mtesa of course asked me about them. They had sent him a letter in Arabic conveying their salaams. I explained to the king what their system was: that they were followers of Jesus (Isa) as we, accepted the Old and New Testaments as we, but worshipped the mother of Jesus more than the Lord Himself, prayed to prophets and saints dead long ago, and taught obedience to the Pope before their own king. I proposed that Mtesa should send a chief along with Pearson and myself to see the Frenchmen, and bring back word to the king explaining who they were, and why come. Mtesa did not accede to this plan, however, but said he would call the Frenchmen some day, and we should then understand all.

" *Sunday*, 23rd.—We understood that a reception was to be given the French padre to-day (his companion *frère* being sick). We went therefore up. Drums were beating, and the general noise so great that I went to the katikiro, and stated how vexed I was at such profanation of the Lord's day. I said that he had agreed, and the king also, to have quietness at least on Sunday; and now, the very first day a European came, all teaching was forgotten. The judge felt guilty, and said that 'it was the king's order to pay honour to their guest.' I showed the want of necessity to hold the reception on Sunday, as there was no hurry. The head-drummer was at once called, and from what we noticed afterwards, I believe he was ordered to make the reception as quiet as possible. We then retired to the church, where we spent an hour teaching natives to read and understand the Creed, when we were informed that the padre had arrived. The king sat in the side room of the large hall, the throne having been uncovered, but he did not come out to sit on it. We waited a suitable opportunity to ask if we were to hold service, but found none. A tall, stout, awkward white man was then introduced, who made the faintest recognition of Mtesa, and sat down sideways on a camp stool, with his back to us. Evidently he was not aware of our presence at all. Soon the king called me forward, when I rose and shook hands with the stranger, and sat (or rather kneeled) down by him to interpret. He said he knew no German or English, but professed his ability to speak in Suahili or in

Arabic. His attempts at being understood, or in understanding either of these latter two languages, failed, however; and I explained to the king that Pearson could talk French, and thus we might be able to converse. But the padre would not reply in his own tongue to Pearson's questions, answering generally in Suahili (very broken). A present for the king was produced of seven or eight common coloured cloths such as go in Unyamwezi, and a French fifteen-shooter (old). I asked where he had come from, to what Society he belonged, for what purpose he came? Did our Society know of their coming, and was he aware of there being five representatives of a Protestant mission here? He replied to most questions rather unwillingly (at least we thought so). He belonged to the 'African Mission Society,' came from Algiers, had heard of Mtesa's willingness to receive white men (he never said Christian missionaries), that their chief was still at Kagei, that should Mtesa be willing they would all come to settle here, but if not they would go elsewhere. He was not aware as to whether or not our Society, or the English Government, knew of their coming, as he was not chief. He knew there were one or two Protestants here.

"I asked plainly if he was not come to teach the Romish faith? He said they came to teach to read and write, and useful arts. I was cross-questioned by the king about the faith of Roman Catholics, and

I stated that they prayed to the Virgin Mary, to saints, etc., and inculcated obedience to the Pope. I said we wrote in the same character, and our arts were the same, and in all respects we were the same as they, only our religions were totally different. I said that they accepted the Fathers, etc., while we received only the Old Testament and the New, as we were distinctly disciples of *Isa Messiah* (Jesus Christ). On this the gentleman said *politely*, in Suahili: 'You are a liar.' This he explained by declaring that I had called him a believer in *Islam*. I explained calmly that he had not sufficiently understood, that I had not said so, but that *we* believed in *Isa*. For his mistake and rudeness he was not, however, polite enough to make any apology. The king asked if in Egypt and Zanzibar there were not both English and French living together? The padre said that we and they were not different, as there were people of his religion in England, and of ours in France. I said, 'Yes, just as there are Arabs living in Uganda, but who will say that the Baganda in consequence are Mussulmans?' This argument was understood.

"Evidently Mtesa and the chiefs, for selfish interests, would prefer to have as many English or French or other Europeans here as possible, as thus they know they will get more presents, and have prestige added to their court.

" After the Baraza broke up the Frenchman asked us if he might not have a few words with us? We therefore asked him down to dinner at five p.m., and he agreed, but evidently with no goodwill.

"I talked earnestly with Kauta and others on the impropriety of having given a state reception on Sunday, to the exclusion of Divine service. They allowed that they had done wrong, and after much talk we left.

"In the evening our guest showed no signs of coming, so Pearson wrote a polite note in French, and we sent two boys with it to show him the way. No reply came, however, and we dined alone. Towards morning, however, one of our boys woke us up, saying, he and the other had been bound by order of the Frenchman, who said 'he did not want our salaams,' and his servants robbed them of their clothing!

"*Monday*, 24*th*.—Pearson and I went early to the katikiro and asked him to send for our boy, who was still in custody. I explained also to him that if the Frenchmen were brought here we should all leave.* This, he said, would not be once thought of; still he seemed inclined to want the Frenchmen here. He said that no one would pay attention to their teaching. This I declared to be impossible, and distinctly gave him to understand that we should not remain here, and we should tell the king so.

* "This was not my own suggestion. All of our party, at the time, were of the same mind. I thought then, and think still, it was a mistake; but mistakes become *experience*, and the best of us can rise to greatness and usefulness and goodness only in that school.— A. M. M."

"We then went up to the king's, but did not see him. We talked with the chiefs, however, as we had done with the katikiro, but they were evidently inclined to have the Frenchmen come, yet they would not hear of our going away. In the evening I was sent for. I spoke of the French padres, and distinctly told the king that we could not remain here if these men were allowed to settle in the place. Mtesa asked where we would go to? I said the continent was large, and we could find plenty of room, as the padres could do without coming here. He said that it would never do to reject Englishmen in favour of Frenchmen. Besides, he said he could not adopt a new religion with every new comer. I showed how impossible it was for padres to settle here without making proselytes, or doing their utmost to do so, even although Mtesa declared that neither he nor his people would listen to their teaching. I left him in good humour, the head chiefs being also gratified by a present I gave each that morning.

"*Friday*, *28th.*—In the afternoon we proposed sending a note to the Frenchmen, which Pearson wrote in French; and as we wished to make sure of their receiving it, one of my brethren and I went off with it, taking a fine goat also as a present. In the letter we said that we had heard they were both sick, and that our doctor would be glad to see them, and give them medicine, condiments, or anything else they might wish. We took with us the two boys whom they had apprehended last Sunday. After passing the hill on which the palace stands, we met a native sub-chief, who told our boys that if we went to the Frenchmen we should be bound hand and foot. We went on, however, but Juma (our Mganda boy) was afraid, and went to stay at the house of the chief who had thus threatened us. We took him on against his will, and crossed the swamp, when natives were seen rushing in various directions, some past us, to a point on the road in front. When we came up to the place, about thirty men armed with clubs, spears, axes, and guns (their chief being the headman whom I have mentioned), stood up and menaced us should we go on. My companion waved some of them aside, and got half through ; but I saw the danger, as he would next moment have been murdered as well as I ; so I cried out to him to desist, and sat down on the bank by the roadside, he accompanying me. The wild attitude of the gang was truly diabolical. As I sat down, one fellow with a large native axe jumped up behind me, and I expected next moment to have my head in two. I looked up calmly in his face, and his chief had by this time succeeded in driving back the furious mob. I asked what was the matter, and wanted the chief to sit down and explain. This he refused to do, as he was too big a man ; but I insisted, and at length he sat down on the ground. He said he had the king's orders not to allow us to go on. I allowed him to say no more, but said, ' Let us go at

once to the king.'   Back we went, the mob being by
this time increased to nearly a hundred men, all armed.
Half went before and the others remained with us
all the way.   When we came to the second court the
chief went in and we were told to sit down outside.
This we refused to do, and stood waiting at the gate
for a few minutes.   One of the pages came out soon,
and asked me if I had brought medicine for Mtesa, or
what I wanted.   I sent him in to say that I wished
to see the king at once, but I should not wait more
than five minutes for an answer.   As no response
was made we left, bringing back the letter and the
goat.   All hangers-on in the grounds looked on in
silence as we turned to go, but we were not further
troubled.

" Who is at the root of all this we cannot say.
Probably Mtesa had ordered that sub-chief to look
after the padres, and he, on his own responsibility,
acted as I have stated.   Anyhow, we feel matters
have come to a crisis—our lives are no longer safe,
our usefulness is at an end, our teaching rejected,
our medicine refused, Romish priests received contrary
to our advice, and no reply written to Lord Salisbury's
friendly letter.*   May God turn good out of evil.   We
now intend sending Mtesa a written letter, stating our

---

* This letter from Lord Salisbury was anent the massacre of British
subjects in Ukerewe, and the fact that the Nile party were the bearers
of it led the king to think that they must have come for political
purposes.

determination to leave the country unless he gives us a written promise of protection, food, and liberty to go about among his subjects. All promises he has now broken, and we must demand his word in writing in future. I feel confident that all will turn out well in the end, and that even were we to leave we should soon be asked back; still at this crisis it is a time of trouble to us, and only the God whom we serve can bring us out of it."

Matters came to such a crisis that the Church Missionary Society party thought they ought to withdraw from Uganda for a time, and go to Makraka, on the north of the Albert Lake, which appeared to be an open field. On the 7th of March, 1879, they heard " it would be well for them to clear out as quickly as possible, as the king's soldiers were only waiting to kill them all." On the 30th, also, an Egyptian soldier (a runaway for years) informed them that " the king was very ill and had slept in his large hall last night, expecting to die; also that there was a conclave between chiefs and coastmen, when it was resolved to murder all the Englishmen should Mtesa die."

On the 8th of April, however, their hearts were strengthened by the arrival of Messrs. Stokes and Copplestone by the Zanzibar route. There were thus seven C.M.S. missionaries in the country. With the exception of Mr. Pearson, however, they all soon left. On the 13th of April Mackay writes: " To my mind, the most likely way to get the king to grant us what we want (food and liberty to teach) is to live on good terms with him and his chiefs and redeem the time by using every opportunity of teaching the truth. Persuasion is better than force, and tact and patience better than urgent demand. I feel sure that the king will now never grant us what we have begged of him unless we show him that we are his friends, and are actuated towards him by motives of real love. Many missionaries in many lands have been worse treated than we, and have held out for many more years than we have done months, and ultimately the Lord has rewarded their patience and perseverance. No real success in missions has ever yet been won without long opposition and frequent violent persecutions for years. It is therefore unreasonable to expect that it should be otherwise here. I mean, therefore, to stay by my post as long as God enables me. If I am peremptorily ordered by the C.M.S. to return, or if the place becomes too hot for me to stay, I may have to leave, but I cannot just now think any other course honourable or upright.

" *Saturday, 19th April.*—Stokes and I went up to court. I asked the king if he was willing I should bring up my Bible on the morrow and read a little to him (the public services had been stopped). He at once replied, ' Yes, bring the book.'

" Before this he had asked many questions on the future state. What sort of bodies, what desires, what clothing? I explained that we should be like the angels, but I found St. Paul's own excellent simile suit best, the new body given by God to the seed-corn sowed. Mtesa quite caught this, and explained it to all present. A little after he asked what we would wear in heaven? I said, we were not told exactly, for our bodies would require no protection from heat or cold. I stated plainly that Christ had left us in the dark about many things in the world beyond, that we might be the more anxious to get there to know all. He asked me if we had any more knowledge than Jesus taught His disciples and they further wrote? I said we had not. I feared the padre sitting behind me would have contradicted this, but he said nothing. Most probably he did not understand.

"*May 5th.*—In the middle of a multitude of questions about the first and second resurrections, Mtesa abruptly asked me if I knew that the Egyptians had planted a new station in his territory, and within three days of Ripon Falls? 'They are gnawing at my country like rats, and ever pushing their fortifications nearer.' I advised him to send two chiefs to Colonel Gordon to make a friendly treaty with him, settling the question of boundary for good.

"'Gordon is an Englishman, and so are you : why, therefore, do you take my country from me?'

"To this I merely replied that we had nothing in common : Gordon is practically an Egyptian, while we are subjects of Mtesa.

"'Did you not promise me *arms*, and now the Egyptians are upon me?'

"Mtesa knowing well that we never made any such promise, and probably not willing to hear a reply to so foolish a question, dismissed the court at once."

In the month of June, however, the king sent an embassy to Queen Victoria in charge of two missionaries who were returning to England *viâ* the Nile. After their departure the king's friendliness returned, the Sunday services were resumed, and Mackay's printing press turned to good account in supplying reading sheets, and portions of Scripture, and pupils increased in number daily.

Next came Mackay's unavailing struggle against a sorceress who professed to be possessed of the *Lubare* of the Nyanza, and to have power to restore the king to health.*　For a time Mtesa and his chiefs prohibited both Christianity and Mohammedanism, and returned to their pagan superstitions.

The following extracts from Mackay's journal at this time will give some idea of his discouragement after all his attempts to teach the knowledge of the true God :—

" *Monday, Dec.* 29*th*, 1879.—Again at dawn, or rather before it, the loud beating of drums and shrill cries of women let us know that the great lubare, Mukasa, was on her way to pay the king a second visit.　I did

---

* See " A. M. Mackay, Pioneer Missionary of the Church Missionary Society to Uganda " (Hodder & Stoughton), p. 145.

not know before that the individual is a *woman*. Mukasa is not her name, but that of the deity or spirit which is supposed to possess her. Mukasa is, moreover, not a spirit of the whole lake, only of some three or four creeks on the coast of Uganda. I have been told that the formidable foes of the Baganda—the Bavuma, are continually paying visits to the island where Mukasa lives, and plundering the god of cattle and slaves.

"To-day, I believe, the audience was of a much more private nature than the previous one. Some say that not even a single chief, nor a woman, was present at the interview between the king and the witch. The king has ordered the chiefs to bring numbers of cattle, slaves, and cowries, and these have been presented to the lubare in no small quantity.

"I was chaffing some natives about their king being obliged to pay tribute (musolo) to an old woman. 'It is not tribute,' they replied, 'it is *bigali*,' or sacrificial offerings to the deity!

" *Wednesday, Dec.* 31*st.*—Early Mufta came, having been sent by the katikiro to call me. Between 8 and 9 a.m. Pearson went with me. After waiting half an hour at his door, he came out, dressed up like a tailor's dummy, thinking himself remarkably smart, but his appearance tended only to excite our risible faculties. Among other vanities he had tied to his neck a plated railway whistle which I gave him many months ago.

"He said that he expected us early, and that he had an engagement just now, but would soon be back. We sat down thereupon in the inner court, but loud beating of drums, as in a procession, excited our curiosity to go out and see. We found the katikiro standing at his outer gate, while hundreds of people, chiefs and slaves, were squatting on the ground outside. All, including the judge, had on a string of green leaves passing over the shoulder like a sash. As we approached, I overheard the katikiro saying (of Pearson and me) to those round him, 'Here come our boys' (balenzi bafwe), at which they all laughed.

"When the procession came up we found it to consist of a whole host of *Maandwas, i.e.* wizards and witches—each with a magic wand which they rattled on the ground in succession before the katikiro, he touching the wands with a finger. Three or four wizards were dressed in leopards' skins, while the witches were clad in a succession of layers of goat-skins—white and black alternately. The head of the whole—a little witch named *Wamala*—was in aprons of goatskins, and had a head cap of many coloured beads. The consequential air with which they shook their wands on the ground was rather amusing. Many women carried on their shoulders, entirely wrapped up in bark cloth, with a garland of the same green leaves as the chiefs, etc., wore, what were virtually idols, being urn-shaped things called *balongo.* These I did not see exposed on this occasion, but others which I saw before were of the urn-shape, with a large bow handle like a pot. They were entirely covered with beads sewed in neat patterns over a mass of bark cloth, having in the heart the umbilical cord of either the present king or one of his ancestors.

"The katikiro went then to the palace courts with the procession; we thought it useless waiting, and came home. I am told that the king refused to be seen by the witches, etc. Wamala, the head one, is stationed near Unyoro, in Mkwenda's country. She is a rival of the other great witch Mukasa, and once lived on the lake, but having quarrelled with the other spirit, she went far inland to rule the dry land, as the other does the water!"

New Year's Day 1880 brought good tidings to Mackay from Colonel Gordon,—viz., that he had withdrawn all his troops from not only Mruli but also from all the stations south of the Somerset Nile. Mackay writes: "I am truly thankful to God that Colonel Gordon has determined on this. Now that Mruli is abandoned, I hope we shall have much less suspicion lying on us as being implicated in bringing 'the Turks' always nearer. The tone of all Colonel Gordon's letters is beautiful and spiritual, and I cannot fail to profit much by the expressed experience of this truly Christian governor.

"When we told Mtesa that Colonel Gordon advised *him* to occupy Mruli he was very pleased, and said 'his heart was good, and that we were good, and that his remarks at court before Christmas, that we were spies, were finished now.' In other words, that he meant to say nothing of the kind again."

A few jottings from Mackay's journal in the early months of 1880 will give a glimpse of missionary life in Central Africa :—

"*Jan. 1st*, 1880.—Sewed up with silver wire the breast of wounded woman. I do not think any ribs are broken, but I fear the lung is injured from the cough she has. Syringed inside of wound in body and re-dressed the hand, cutting away various broken pieces of bone which I did not discover before.*

"*Feb. 7th.*—Had a day's work at tailoring to-day. Clothes I am almost out of, and have considerable difficulty in dressing with any degree of respectability. A coat of checked tweed which one of the Nile party hung up in his hut one night on the way here was partly eaten up, and partly built into the earthen wall by morning, by white ants. This coat he handed

---

* This was a severe case of gunshot, which happened on December 26th, 1879. "A wife of Kaitabarwa's was handling a gun which went off (an Enfield with iron bullet). The bullet passed into the back of the left side, just under the armpit, out under the nipple, then through the back of the left hand, shattering the metacarpal bones connecting the forefinger and the wrist. The bullet passed out under the thumb ; we amputated the forefinger, sewed up the hand, and applied styptics to the wounds in chest. The woman has had a severe shock to her nervous system and has lost much blood. They brought her in a hide and we sent her back on a Kitanda." By March 7th she was almost well, and able to trip about nimbly.

over to me, and I have succeeded in putting patches into the back of it so as not to be very noticeable. I wish I had got some lessons in sewing before leaving England.

"*Sunday, Feb. 8th.*—Continued translation this morning. Read with much edification a nice little book entitled 'The King of Love,' by the author of 'How to Enter into Rest.' There are most beautiful thoughts throughout the book, and much I would seek to live in the realisation of them. 'God is never so far off as even to be near.'

"*Feb. 9th.*—Patched up an old pith helmet inside and out. Cut up and stitched a white umbrella cover, as cover for my helmet. On the whole I have made a decent head-gear.

"*March 18th, 1880.*—It is now announced that another army is under orders to go again to Busoga to subdue rebels there. Sekibobo is commander-in-chief. A whole host of chiefs and subs are now going off with him, and of course as many men as each can muster. All is feudal system here. I wish I knew the real nature of this war, and if I found it to be a war undertaken to capture cattle and slaves, I should not fail, God helping me, to show Mtesa and his court the evil of such terrible work.

"*Sunday, March 21st.*—Kago, one of the most powerful chiefs, and also one of the strongest up-holders of the witchcraft religion of the country, called to-day.

"He told me a series of lies.   He said he was not going to war, while I know he is.   He said that the cattle and slaves which they brought so frequently from the East were only presents from the people! etc., etc.   I reproved him for telling such falsehoods, he being an old man, and a chief, while he should be an example to the people.   Then I spoke solemnly to him about the evil of making these raids for murder and robbery.   I said that, however Uganda might meantime escape from punishment for such evil work, yet Almighty God saw it all and would one day call the king and chiefs to account for it."

On the 2nd April, 1880, Mackay started for Uyui for a supply of cloth and other barter goods, as the mission store of such things was all but exhausted, and he and Mr. Pearson were entirely dependent on the caprice of the king for subsistence.   The Frenchmen kindly lent him cloth to pay his expenses down to Uyui, and would listen to no promise of repayment. Sorely as they tried to injure the work of the C.M.S. missionaries, yet in everything else they were disposed to be friendly.   On the above date Mackay writes: "This day two years ago I started from Mpwapwa for Uyui, and now I am on my way to the same place once more.   May the good Lord, who has preserved me amid no ordinary troubles and dangers since that day, keep me on this journey and bring me safely back to Uganda.

"Ten *Baziba* carried the luggage to Admiral Gabunga's. The king gave me a present of five thousand cowries, as he said, to buy food on the way, and not to rob ! Paid four thousand cowries, however, to carry the ten loads to Gabunga's.

"*April* 16*th.*—Having succeeded in getting a few canoes, we embarked. As the season was early for marching through Usukuma, harvest not commencing till June, we did not hurry the canoe-men, allowing them to take their own time. Some of Gabunga's men who were going to Unyanyembe to sell ivory had joined us, and altogether we had fourteen canoes in our expedition.

"*May* 11*th*, reached Kagei safely. Several men of the Romish mission had arrived there, *en route* for Mtesa's."

Strange to say, among the frères was a countryman of his own, a Mr. Charles Stuart, from Aberdeen ! He had been educated at Blairs, on Deeside. Mackay had several talks with him, but did not expect he would hold out long, as he lay about all day doing nothing, and imagining himself ill from greasy French cooking. Mackay says : " I felt sorely tempted to say to him, ' Och, man, I could hae forgi'en ye a' yer Popery, but what for hae ye forsaken yer parritch ? ' Poor fellow, he had all his clothes stolen from him on the way, nor had he any book to read. I happened to have a Shakespeare, which I had taken to while away weary hours in the canoes, and that I gave him."

The road from Kagei to Uyui is through a most unsettled and unsafe country, with plenty of robbers on the way, and continual demands for tribute at every petty village. Sometimes he had to pay honga three times in a march of seven miles.

But he was mercifully preserved from attacks of natives and from highwaymen in the jungles, although he was only armed with his umbrella. He reached Uyui on the 5th of June, after a march of twenty days. There he remained five weeks, and set out again northwards to Kagei. Though it was the month of July, it was the dead of winter there, and while the sun was sultry through the day, there were piercing east winds every morning, which he found most trying, especially as he and his men, in order to avoid the cupidity of as many greedy chiefs as possible, frequently marched through the night. For instance, on the 4th of August he says : " By 3 a.m. my men wakened me up, saying we should start. Got up and looked at the stars (my only clock), and told them it was yet several hours to daylight, and we might lose our way in the forest, but if the porters were willing to start, I was ready. Struck tent, and packed up in dead silence, and by clear starlight set off. Lost our way at one point, but got on right road again, and the cocks crew as we stole silently past the hut of the extortionate chief. After more than an hour we got into the jungle, where we could breathe freely ; but walking was difficult, as in many

KING MTESA.

[p. 127.

places there were deep holes like wells caused by the tread of elephants."

At the next village he came to, he and his party were detained many days before the matter of the toll was settled. He could get nothing to eat save a few ground nuts, and a glass of milk was scarcely to be had. But he learned to be patient of such delays, and embraced the opportunity to instruct the Baganda lads who were with him, and at the same time he gained much knowledge from *them* regarding the superstitions and language of Uganda. He had made such a rapid journey on the former occasion that much escaped his observation, but he found now that a common act among many of the tribes was the kidnapping of boys, such as goat-herds, etc., who were generally alone, at some distance from the villages, there being always plenty of Arabs and Wangwana about, ready to buy such children. At such times the wails of the poor mothers overnight, and every now and again breaking out through the day, were most piteous. When will this traffic in human flesh cease?

At most villages great crowds of women and children followed him to feast their eyes on the fair face of the white man. Sometimes, to please them, he got out a music-box, with which they were en-raptured ; and, strange to say, the popular tune was " God Save the Queen ! "

Then they must see his arm and his bare foot,

while they stroked his hair and compared it to an antelope's. Until he bared his foot they believed that his boot was part of himself! But perhaps the greatest curiosity he could show them was his lamp, for artificial light is quite unknown.

Owing to the many detentions for honga, he was forty-five days on the way back to Kagei. While there his three Baganda lads were nearly murdered. They were sleeping in a hut behind Mackay's house, when some men they had quarrelled with went and fired a volley into the hut. A terrible scuffle and chase ensued. The three lads ran for their lives, and the murderous party after them. Mackay was half-down with fever, but managed with great exertion to persuade the leader to sit down and talk to him (having previously secreted the objects of his malice). The Beloochees and Arabs next appeared, armed to the teeth, expecting to find that Mackay had been attacked, when they were prepared to aid in murdering him. The chief of the village also arrived, after making sure that the fray was over. With much trouble Mackay got them all to fire off their guns and go home.

The Frenchmen never went to Mackay's aid, although they knew how ill he was, but simply looked over the fence at the fight !

The journal continues :—

" I remained at Kagei two and a half months. I sent on a man to Uganda with a large load of cowries to Mr. Pearson, as also his English letters, which I had brought with me. Many days I spent packing all boxes, etc., in raw hide, sewing the whole with stout twine, to make our goods waterproof on the lake. Much time I had to spend in bed from repeated and severe attacks of remittent fever.

"*Nov. 2nd.*—Having secured five canoes, I embarked for Uganda with my loads and servants, leaving the iron boiler parts and machinery well packed in Kaduma's care. Last of the Frenchmen left for King Roma's in canoes which he sent for them. (Roma owns all the west side of Smith's Creek, and the road from thence to Msalala). Père Levesque alone goes to Uganda, and is commended to my protection.

"*Nov. 3rd.*—Camp on Juma Island. Père Levesque and I cross over channel, and spend a few days at Roma's capital.

"*Nov. 20th.*—At Makongo. Went with Père Levesque to visit Kaitaba, the king of Busongora. Gave him a present, and received a fat bullock in return.

"*Dec. 2nd.*—Arrived at Ntebe, with everything safe. Lake journey has thus occupied thirty days.

"*Dec. 14th.*—After much delay at Ntebe, and on road, and repeated messages to Mtesa, got sufficient men under two chiefs to carry all our goods to capital (a distance of twenty-six miles). Met Mr. Pearson at mission-house, soon after noon."

Dec. 16th.—King held Baraza in great hall and

received the Frenchmen in state, as also the messengers from Roma. The Frenchmen gave presents of gunpowder in kegs and in tins, guns, caps, bullets, military suits, a drum and sundry small articles.

" Mr. Pearson and I agreed that we had better not attend the reception along with the Frenchmen, as we resolved to give no present of anything in the shape of arms or ammunition, and the contrast between our presents and those of the Frenchmen might prove unpleasant.

" The French party now at Roma's had given that king a large present of cloth, guns, a revolver, gunpowder, etc., etc. Every one of these things Roma sent on to Mtesa by some of his own men, these accompanying me. The revolver alone he kept for himself, asking me most imploringly for my revolver, offering me ten boys for it, promising me also a road to Mirambo's, or anything I liked ; and when all these were declined by me, he tried hard to get me to exchange the one he got from the padres for mine. But I was inexorable, saying that I would give such a weapon neither to him, nor to Mtesa, nor to Mirambo. Roma's object in sending the presents to Mtesa was to ask his aid to fight against (*i.e.* spoil and murder) Kigaju, the king of Bukosa, while he asked me to write a letter from him to Mtesa begging the Uganda fleet. I flatly refused to do so, saying that we white men came to bring *peace* into the country and not war Strange to say, Roma took me and not the Frenchmen into his private conference with his head chiefs when he proposed begging Mtesa's aid. Even afterwards, when I was leaving, and the Frenchmen all present, he asked me again to recommend him to Mtesa, but did not ask them. I said before them all that I was a messenger of God, and would willingly ask Mtesa to make an alliance with Roma, but I would bear no message asking aid in war.

"Père Girault, who is head of the mission there, felt offended that he was not consulted by Roma in the matter, especially after *he* had given the guns and powder, which were being sent as the price of the army, and walked off in apparent ill mood.

"*Dec. 18th.*—Mr. Pearson and I went to court. After friendly greetings from the katikiro and chiefs in the outer court, we went into the inmost court (except the king's own). After waiting nearly half an hour, the king called us in. The house was full of naked women, probably nearly a hundred. The king apologised for making no public reception on my behalf, on the ground of his illness.

"Our present to Mtesa consisted of a few doti of coloured cloth, two fine large knives, and a score of flags of diverse colours. We explained that the flags were international, and none of them English. (They were a set of the ordinary "commercial code.")

"We read the king a Suahili translation of part of the Committee's letter, informing him that his men had reached England, had been received by the Queen most graciously, and had been shown every honour, and that Her Majesty had sent them to Zanzibar in one of her own men-of-war.

"Mtesa said that 'the fact of his men being so well received in England raised in his mind the longing to go there himself, but he said the Arabs asserted that he could not reach there.' (This is not true, for the Arabs have always, in court, told him that he would find an open way, and that the English would be so overjoyed at his condescension, that they would send at once *a hundred* large ships to Zanzibar to convey him to London.) I merely said to him, 'A great man can overcome many difficulties.'"

Mackay then showed the king some pictures in the *Graphic* of Queen Victoria receiving his envoys. He was delighted, and seemed never to weary looking at them. The next day Mackay went to court he found his majesty still entertaining himself with them, and he greeted Mackay with the remark : "I am determined to go to England, to consult a doctor about my ailments, and I will leave the queen-mother on the throne, in my absence."

The haughty chiefs, however, opposed this, saying : "Why should a great monarch like Mtesa go to England? Queenie (Queen Victoria) sends only *small* men to Uganda. Speke, and Grant, and Stanley were *only travellers !*"

CHAPTER XII.

HOSTILE ARABS.

> " Now, the pruning, sharp, unsparing :
> Scattered blossom, bleeding shoot ;
> Afterward, the plenteous bearing
> Of the Master's pleasant fruit."
>
> F. R. HAVERGAL.

CHRISTMAS of 1880 and the early months of 1881 were times of sore and grievous trouble to the two brethren (Pearson and Mackay). The Baganda regarded them as having been created to give away articles gratis, and fleeced them of everything. Indeed, the popular impression was that " there was no place in Europe for white men, and they settled in Uganda because it was the most delightful spot in the world ! " All the barter goods which Mackay brought from Uyui were ultimately disposed of, and they were frequently reduced to beggary and to temporary starvation. Mackay had to keep a sharp look out lest the brass cocks and other small fittings of the engines were stolen for ornaments. He had to work hard at the vice and lathe for daily bread, but in consequence of a great drought in the country, in the beginning of the year 1880, the chiefs were unable to pay in kind for work done, complaining that owing to the famine they could not even feed their large retinues of wives, and were obliged to send them to their country farms to subsist as they best could, by digging up the plantain trees, and eating a semi-solid stuff, found at the root of the stem.

The missionaries went on quietly teaching a few lads who came to them, and Mackay, by the aid of his faithful pupil Mukasa (named after the lubare), translated St. Matthew's Gospel into Luganda, regarding which he says: " In studying the sacred words, word for word, I see more beauty than I ever saw before, and I hope the Holy Spirit will bless it much to my own soul, and to that of my assistant. He often admits the beauty of the words of Jesus."

The new year of 1881 dawned in Uganda as everywhere else ; but while we in Europe were enjoying family reunions, the missionaries received a bitter disappointment, by the arrival of two Arabs who confessed to having left their expected gift of home letters at Kagei. Moreover, these men were imbued with a deep and hereditary hostility to the Christian faith, and were especially angry with Mackay on account of the influence which he had gained in the country. For, although the tide ebbed and flowed, he ever remained a favourite with the king, who respected his bold witness for the truth. Mtesa was really favourable to the Christian faith, but he felt that it demanded a nobler life than the Mohammedan code of morals did, therefore he accepted neither.

The contrast between the following scenes at court, at Christmas 1880, and Bishop Tucker's wonderful account of his visit to Uganda (see Chap. XXII.) at the same season in 1890, is very striking, and may be described as A PICTURE IN TWO PANELS.

Under the one may be inscribed—

> "Now, the sowing and the weeping,
> Working hard, and waiting long;"

and under the other—

> "Afterward, the golden reaping,
> Harvest-home and grateful song."

The hope of the "nevertheless, afterward" sustained Mackay through it all, and he writes: "God's will be done. The cause is His, and also the issue of all our plans. May He bless our efforts and bring a speedy end to this sore and exhausting time of trial and persecution. After such a night as we have had, and still are in, we look for a happy morning.

"*Dec. 22nd*, 1880.—Mr. Pearson and I went to court, where we found MM. Levesque and Lourdel. The latter goes every day with some *drug* for the king. It would be a farce to call his mixtures '*medicine*,' for none of their party have any idea of medicine.

"After a little the court opened, and there being

many chiefs present, we were seated in the very back corner, *i.e.*, behind them all.

"Mtesa began asking his chiefs a host of questions about the gods of the country. Some under-chiefs had returned from plundering in Busoga, and the charms which their sorcerers had taken with them were presented to his Majesty. This was probably the occasion of Mtesa's asking his chiefs, ' Which is the greater, the king or the lubare?' Some said the king was the greater, others said the lubare. Talk continued on the matter for a long time, to little or no purpose, as all the chiefs are profound sycophants and echo everything Mtesa says, although one moment he said that their own gods were nothing, and Katonda all in all, and next moment, that the idols and sorcerers had divine power. Finding it difficult to hear distinctly where we sat, I called out to the king that unless I sat nearer I could not understand what he was saying. (His talk was only in Luganda.) I said that formerly I used to have a seat in front, but that now we had got pushed behind every one, nor did I know what wrong we had done to cause us to be thus degraded. He at once ordered me to bring my seat forward, but not one of the jealous chiefs moved an inch to give me room. I therefore stepped out before them all and sat down on the floor between the king and them.

"Mr. Pearson then asked if anything would be done to any one who embraced Christianity? Mtesa replied that there were many old people (women chiefly) in the country, who had power, and these would be sure to kill any one who despised the gods of the country. Mr. Pearson replied that he (Mtesa) was King of Uganda, and that if he gave the order that men embracing Christianity were to be let alone, no one could touch them. Mtesa then said that if any one went to the Bazungu (white men) to read, he surely committed no criminal offence. 'To read,' he said, 'was not robbery, and one could not be condemned for that.' I then explained that merely learning to read was not to embrace Christianity. I said, 'If a man becomes a Christian he will know that the religion of the lubare is false, and hence will not be able to attend court when any of the lubares make a demonstration there. If a man is baptised, either a chief or a common man, will he be punished for refusing to join in the ceremonies of the lubare?' To this no answer was given, but talk was continued on the power of the gods.

"'What is Nende?' asked Mtesa.

"Kyambalango replied, 'Nende is a man ; Nende is a god.'

"The Katikiro said, 'Nende is an image.'

"'Sekibobo!' said Mtesa, 'what is Nende?'

"(Sekibobo is one of the three greatest chiefs.) Sekibobo was sitting a little behind, as he was troubled with catarrh, and etiquette forbade him to sit in his usual place. But before Sekibobo could make up his mind, not as to what Nende *is*, but as to what answer would please the king most, Mr. Pearson, who was sitting behind the chief, called out, 'Nende is a liar; Nende can neither walk, nor speak, nor eat.' Mtesa repeated this for the benefit of all, and from many a sycophant came the echo, 'Nende is a tree, and cannot speak or eat.' Some, however, dissented, saying that Nende is a god; when I proposed that Nende should be brought and set on the floor before us all, that we might see what he is. This created some merriment, while others were shocked at the idea of such sacrilege, and the katikiro replied, 'The woman who has charge of Nende will not allow him to be brought.'

"Again we asked if people could with impunity come to us to be taught the knowledge of God?

"Mtesa replied that before Stanley came he was a Mussulman, then he became a Christian, and when Lieutenant Smith came here he used to teach one part of the day and he (Mtesa) the other. I said, 'Those were happy days, but they are long gone by.' The king laughed and continued, that now he found so many religions in the country, each asserting itself as the true one, that he did not know what to do. He then called M. Lourdel forward, and also Babakeri (an old soldier of Baker's, and a heathen, but a favourite counsellor).

"We put the question very plainly, repeating it again and again, that there should be no mistake.

We said that we did not ask the king to *order* his people to follow Christianity, we only begged that he would give permission (*rukhsa* = liberty) to any one in the kingdom, high or low, to accept any religion he chose; if any one liked to continue a believer in the lubare, he might do so; if any one chose to go to the Frenchmen to be taught, he might do so; if any one chose to become a Mohammedan, he could do so; and if any one chose to come to us to be taught the Book of God, he might do so.

"First the Arabs were asked by the king if he should grant our request. They replied that they had nothing to say, as the older Arabs were not present that day. One old fanatic, however, commenced a harangue on the absolute truth of their creed, as they stuck to the Koran and the patriarchs. I declined to have them consulted in this matter, as, I said, they had come for *trade* and not as teachers, and no one wished to take their Koran from them.

" Next Mtesa asked Babakeri if he should give the liberty we begged. This fellow, after some hesitation, replied, 'Yes, sir, give liberty.' Mtesa, too cunning to listen to good advice which he feared might result in leaving him less absolute than he is at present, tried a new artifice to evade the question. 'Suppose,' said he, ' I divide the country, and give *Singo* (Mkwenda's country) to the English to be taught, and *Kyagwe* (Sekibobo's) to the Frenchmen, that they may teach every one; then will there not be rows between them?' We replied that in Zanzibar both English and French lived and taught in peace, and in Europe also, and that we should make no trouble with the French teachers.

" M. Lourdel did not assent to, or dissent from, our proposition for liberty, nor did he say that his party would cause no dispeace on our behalf, but he said that he and his brethren would treat in the same friendly way all comers, whether believers in their teaching or not.

" The next objection raised by Mtesa was that if the people adopted a different religion from himself and the chiefs, there would be rebellion in the country. We explained that the religion of Jesus Christ taught men to honour the king and every one in authority.

" M. Lourdel assented to this on behalf of their teaching, saying that they taught nothing wrong, but such commandments as ' Thou shalt not steal,' which no one could object to. Mtesa then proposed that the Frenchmen and ourselves should first agree on religious matters, and then he would listen to us both. This was merely a *ruse* to try to get us to enter on discussion, which he enjoys, especially if it occasion ill-feeling between the disputants. We were silent, however, and his *ruse* failed.

" The king, finding our request still strongly pressed by us, in spite of his evasions, proposed to defer his answer until he had first consulted with his chiefs.

The katikiro, in his usual time-serving manner, declared that the king was a follower of Katonda, and all the people were followers of the king, therefore they were followers of God. Seeing that this was given out merely as an off-put to our request, we reasserted that liberty was the source of all intelligence, and that Baganda were *men, not sheep,* merely following blindly any belief; for Mtesa was truly king of the Baganda in this life only, and it would not do to answer God at the great judgment that they had simply followed the king's religion.

"In the course of the discussion, Mtesa said that M. Lourdel had given him to understand that he and his brethren were padres (= teachers of religion) alone, while we, *i.e.* Mr. Pearson and I, were *fundis* (= workmen). Of course we dissented from this, casting no aspersion on the padres, but asserting that we were teachers of religion *just as they were,* and had been sent here for no other purpose; any skilled labour we had done we did merely out of friendship, and not because we were sent here to do such. At one time we could have given Mtesa credit for sincerity in such discussions as that of to-day. Now I fear there is no desire in the man's heart except the gratification of his lusts and desire for riches.

"In the midst of the talk on the gods *versus* the Almighty Creator, he suddenly sent out for a calabash, and having got it, made some obscene observations to his chiefs.

"Before the talk on religion was finished, he listened to the report of the plundering batongole just returned from Busoga. A chief was ordered at once to go to bring the women, cattle, and slaves, which they had left a day's march from the capital. One of the returned batongole, being accused, I fancy, of appropriating too much of the spoil to himself, was ordered without ceremony to be killed. An executioner, of whom there is always a host present at every court, jumped forward with perfect delight in his face, rope in hand, to drag off the delinquent. The fellow bought himself off, however, with the greatest calmness, for some women and cattle. The executioner stepped back disappointed.

"In the discussion, a few moments afterwards, Mtesa said, ' God hears everything I say. He hears when Mackay speaks, He hears when Mapera or the Arabs speak ! ' Oh the savour of death unto death which our teaching seems to have been to him and to the whole court ! Human life and eternal life equally despised, while his conscience has become seared against what he knows, as well as we, to be great sin. Lasciviousness seems to have turned his soul and mind, like his body, into utter subjection to itself. The first chapter of Romans most accurately describes the state of this king, court, and country.

"After mentioning the solemn fact of all having to answer to God in the next world, Mtesa suddenly asked me if he could get a white princess by going to

England! Prudence prompted me to answer, 'I am not an English princess, therefore I cannot give you a reply.'

"The conference ended by Mtesa laying the case thus before the court : ' If we accept the Muzungu's religion, we must then have only one wife each ; while if we accept the religion of the Arabs, we cannot eat every kind of flesh.'

"Thus it is that a trifling restraint on the flesh is balanced against eternal life and peace with God. It was not possible to-day for us to say more on this subject, but we pray the Lord to give us another opportunity of presenting, not the disadvantages, but the enormous advantages of Christianity, before the eyes of this lascivious king and his equally lascivious courtiers.

"On the way home, P. Levesque said to me, that he was quite delighted with the nature of the request for *liberty* which I had so strongly pressed, as being as necessary to them as to us.

"A page was sent in haste after us, with orders to M. Lourdel to come to court *next* morning.

"*Dec. 23rd.*—Expecting to find the subject taken up again to-day, Mr. Pearson and I went early to court. We went in to the inner court, where we found P. Lourdel already sitting. He shook hands, but seemed guilty of something, for he could not look me in the face. We sat down, but were soon told by Koluji that the king asked us (*i.e.* Mr. Pearson and myself) to go farther away, into the next outer court! We went at once, while M. Lourdel remained where he was.

"Soon after, we were joined by Mufta, who told us that M. Lourdel had gone back to the court *last evening*, and had had an audience of the king. Mufta was also there, but outside, and overheard M. Lourdel denouncing us Protestants as 'rebels' from the true Church. That of course meant that they alone should be given liberty to teach in the country, while we, who had asked liberty alike for them and for ourselves, were to be denied it! This, however, exactly accords with what M. Girault said to me at Kagei, when I told him that we Protestants were very tolerant towards *them*, and were willing to acknowledge to Mohammedans and heathens, for our mutual benefit, that they and we were alike believers in Jesus Christ and in the same Book of God. M. Girault replied that 'they would not, however, be tolerant of us, for God was intolerant of error, and it was their *devoir* to teach everywhere that we were teachers of *lies*'!

" By-and-by court opened, and we got in through the crush. The great and only business of the day was the appointment of chiefs to go on *two* great plundering expeditions. Wakoli had been here some time, having brought some ivory, to beg for a large army to aid him against his neighbours in Busoga or beyond it. Another chief from Gambaragara, whose father had died, but who was not chosen for the throne, had been here some time begging Mtesa to send an army to place him in power.

"It is not necessary for Mtesa to have much of an excuse for sending an army to ravage. Two great forces were therefore granted, one for the east and the other for the west. Four great chiefs were appointed to each, with of course their subalterns, and all their retainers. A young lad, now a big Mutongole, called Mukaalya, was appointed captain of the force, against Busoga; while Tole, a renegade coastman, for a long time a settler here, was appointed commander of the force against Gambaragara.

"Our blood could not but boil within us, as we beheld the mad excitement in the whole court, when these fellows were ordered off to murder and plunder. ' Nyaga, nyaga, nyaga, nyo ! ' said the ' *humane king,*' as he gave the captains the orders, *i.e.* ' Rob, pillage, plunder ! ' One's heart sickens at the thought of the carnage—rather cold-blooded butchery—that will result, all, too, on the strength of English guns and gunpowder.

"This is the fifth time in the course of two years that a great army has been sent by Mtesa into Busoga, not to war, but avowedly to devastate and murder, and bring back the spoil—women, children, cattle, and goats. The crime is awful. The most heartrending of Livingstone's narratives of the slave hunts by Arabs and Portuguese on the Nyassa and

Tanganyika shores, dwindle into insignificance compared with the organised and unceasing slave-hunts carried on by this 'enlightened monarch and Christian king.'

" This is the man who yesterday was claiming to be a spiritual guide to his people, and *summus episcopus* in the state. Only yesterday he uttered the sentiment, ' God hears every word I utter while I lie here.'

" Almighty God, look down on the enormous accumulation of crimes of this bloodthirsty, avaricious king and court, and bring to confusion their cruel expeditions against their poor neighbours.

" The Arabs delight in these expeditions, and generally send men to bring a share of the spoil in slaves, these being more cheaply obtained at first than after the return of the army to the capital. To many an officer, whom we met afterwards on our way home, and at our house begging powder (but in vain, for we refuse *in toto*), we solemnly gave the charge to spare shedding blood, for God's eye was over all.

" Munakulya, the only one of the chiefs who has all along continued (after a fashion) an earnest inquirer after truth, and a diligent reader of the Word of God, went this day back, rising up in court and begging the king to appoint him also to join the plundering expedition, that he might get a share in the booty. We feel sorely downcast. Our last hopes seem gone. The lads who had learned the most, and seemed most impressed, have been put out of the way. Others who have been taught more or less (and they are many) are afraid to come to us any more. The few chiefs of whom we had hopes have gone back, while the other chiefs and the king seem only daily to become more hardened and hopelessly sunk in every form of vice and villany.

"But is any case too hard for the Lord?"

"*Christmas Day.*—This time last year the great reaction in favour of the lubare was at its height. To-day, after all that has happened between, matters seem little farther advanced in favour of the reception of Christianity here."

"Many, many hours of discussion, and many occasions of prayer on our sad prospects, have been spent by my brother Pearson and myself during this month. God gives us guidance in our perplexity and deep searching of heart, that we may put away all that has hindered us from having His blessing.

"*Monday, Jan. 3rd*, 1881.—Down with fever. Mr. Pearson went to court, Mufta being there also. The king commenced asking questions on religion, ending in nothing as usual. After this had been going on for some time, Mr. Pearson asked if anything would be done to any of the people who embraced Christianity? Wilfully misunderstanding the question, Mtesa replied, 'Do you mean to make me a Christian by force?'

"Again and again he was told that we used no

force, and no one demanded that he should be a
Christian ; we only wanted his people to have liberty
to come to be taught. 'To be taught what?' he
asked. 'The Book of Jesus Christ,' answered Mufta.
'Do I not know that Book? have I not read it?'
'You know it by head, but not by heart,' answered
the lad again.

"'Well,' said Mtesa, 'if you want liberty, you must
fill my belly; you must give me a daughter of the
Queen to be my wife: unless you do that, you shall
not have liberty to teach—that is my only answer.'

" *Wednesday, Jan. 5th.*—Being considerably better
from the attack of fever, I was able to accompany
Mr. Pearson to court. We expected that the newly-
arrived big Arab would be there, and we were anxious
to hear what news his letters from the coast brought.
He allows having got letters for us at Uyui, but
he left them behind at Kagei! Very considerate!
Probably enough, he would not bring them on that
we might have no information independently of him.

" This Arab generally goes by the name of *Kambi
Mbaya* (bad camp), but his proper name is something
like Rashir bin Shruhl (?).

" Court opened as we went up the hill. The letters
were being opened as we entered. There was one
from Seyed Burgash, but short, and so far as we could
make out, only compliments. We saw none from the
Consul. The Arab presented a musical box (of which
Mtesa has already several), and a revolver. Then he

asked for canoes to bring his goods from Usukuma. Gabunga (Grand Admiral) was called forward, and a Mutongole appointed to get fifty canoes quickly.

" I have heard the Wangwana say that this man has brought four hundred guns—a present from Seyed Burgash, who asks Mtesa to fight Mirambo—while he brings one hundred more guns on his own account not to sell, he says, but he will not refuse ivory if the king gives him any !

"Then he stated that Seyed Burgash had sent a force of two thousand soldiers to Unyanyembe, determining to open the road from the coast to there, while he (Burgash) asked Mtesa to open the part from Unyanyembe to Uganda—abolishing honga and Ruga Ruga. Further, he said that it was necessary to fight Mirambo, 'who was only a Mpagazi,' but had usurped power in Unyamwezi.

" Then Mtesa of his own accord asked Mufta what it was that we had demanded the other day. Mufta replied that we asked liberty to teach in the country ; to which Mtesa answered that he would give no answer until his men returned from England. We said nothing ; but the way in which the new Arab gave himself out to be some great one, tempted us to say to Mtesa that the expense, which we and our friends had paid, to take his envoys to England and bring them back, was a greater present to him than the sum of all the presents he had ever received from all the Arabs together, yet for all that he despised us and

treated us worse than his commonest subjects.   To
this he replied that he believed England to be very
far away, and he knew that the expense had been
great.

"'Seyed Burgash,' I said, 'after he saw England,
gave a concession of land to both English and Frenchmen to settle and teach.'

"*Mtesa.* 'Yes, and when I come back from England,
do you think that I shall refuse to give you a concession of land?'

" *We.* 'But we have already taken your envoys
there, and now they are near.   Please send quickly
to Usukuma and fetch them; for collecting canoes
enough, usually six months are required, and we
cannot wait so long for supplies.   When Mr. Pearson
was working for you, he nearly died of hunger.   It is
not the custom of white men to beg, and we will not
ask you always for plantains and goats, but you own
the whole country, and it can cost you nothing to
give us a fair patch of ground with plantain trees
on it.'

" *Omnes.* 'Oh! you want to get a chieftainship!'

" *We.* 'No, we want no authority in the land, we
only want a place where we can grow our own food.
We mean to buy and not to beg, and we are prepared
to buy a piece of land if you refuse to give it us
gratis.'

" *Mtesa.* 'This country is like a woman; it is our
mother; we cannot cut off an arm of our mother and

give it to you. And do the Frenchmen want to buy land also?'

" *P. Lourdel.* 'No, *we* do not want to buy land.'

" *We.* 'Even if we buy the land, it remains here; we cannot take it with us when we go.'

" *Mtesa.* 'When will you go?'

" *We.* 'We are prepared to go to-morrow if you order us, or to stay if you like, only we do nothing by force; we came here by your permission, and will go when you like: only if we stay we must be allowed to teach any people that like to be taught.'

" *Arab (Kambi Mbaya).* 'What can they teach?' (with a sneer).

" *We.* 'We wish to teach the great truths of eternity and God.'

" *Mtesa.* 'When my men come will they not bring a letter from the Queen, asking *by force* that I give you land?'

" *We.* 'No, our Queen will ask nothing of you by force.'

" *Mtesa.* 'She wants only friendship?'

" *We.* 'Yes.'

" *Arab (Kambi Mbaya).* 'Ask them, whom they have got in Zanzibar to listen to their teaching? The white men in Zanzibar have got no land, nor do they build; they only rent houses at a high price.'

" *We.* 'That is not so;' (to the Arab) 'Do you forget about the English mission at Mnazi-Moja and at Bweni, and the French Mission at Bagamoyo? They have got land from Burgash, and cultivate it and build on it.'

"*Arab (Kambi Mbaya).* 'I don't know anything about that.'

"[N.B.—This man has just come from Zanzibar, and knows everything about the missions there.]

"*Mtesa.* 'Are there both French and English teachers in Egypt?'

"*All Arabs.* 'No, there are none."

"*We and P. Lourdel.* 'There are many teachers, both French and English, in many parts of Egypt.'

"*Arabs.* 'These men lie.'

"*Mtesa.* 'You are vexed and angry, then, about food. Why, if any one is hungry, he need only tell me, and I will give him food at once. Why did Mr. Pearson not tell me that he was in want?'"

"[N.B.—Mr. Pearson did tell Mtesa repeatedly that he was in want, while he only begged the king to pay him some of the many thousand shells which he (Mtesa) was owing him for cloth, etc., which he had sold to him; to this day, however, Mtesa has paid only a fraction of what he owes us. Of course the remainder, never.']

"*We.* 'No, we are not angry about being left to starve, but we are vexed to find that you are playing with us and with religion. One day you have said that our religion is the only true one, another day you adopt the religion of Mohammed, and a third day you follow the lubare.'

" *Mtesa.* 'The Frenchmen have one religion and you have another; they cannot be both true: first agree to have one religion in Europe, and then come and I shall let you teach my people.'

" *Mufta.* 'The English and the French have only one religion; their religion is *one*, but their *mode* is different.'

"[N.B.—We have ever striven to make the heathen and Mussulmans understand that the Frenchmen and we are both alike followers of Jesus Christ, and differ only in small points (something like the sects among the Mussulmans themselves). But the Roman Catholics will not assent to this, foolishly (for themselves) asserting always that *they* only are proper Christians. P. Lourdel did not contradict to-day, however.]

" *Mtesa.* 'When I was well and able to go about, I was able to see what condition every one lived in. Now I am sick, I cannot get about. These white men, what do they want? The Arabs were here in my father's time, and are virtually now adopted children of mine: but these white men are strangers of but yesterday.'

" *Arabs.* 'We are sons of the country; but what do the white men want here except to make dispeace?'

" *Mtesa.* 'I have a regiment of drilled soldiers, and my father had none. Has not Seyed Burgash new institutions which his father had not?'

" *Arabs.* 'Yes. You and Seyed Burgash are just the same. You are the only two kings in Africa!'

" *Mtesa.* ' The Arabs want ivory and slaves, and they bring me cloth, and guns, and powder ; but the white men will not take ivory or slaves,—they say that they want only to teach the people. What do they mean ?'

" *Arab (Kambi Mbaya).* ' We hunt only for a few tusks, which we sell to get our daily bread, but these white men want to eat up the country !'

" *We.* (to the Arab). ' What country are we eating up ? (*i.e.*, conquering). Who has eaten up Zanzibar, and the coast, and Unyanyembe ? and who is just now bringing an army into the interior to fight ? Are these white men or Arabs ?'

" *Arab (Kambi Mbaya).* ' The Arabs want only to make peace in the country, and you therefore cry out against them, because you want the country for yourselves.'

" *We.* ' It is not well so to abuse white men, for you must remember that although the Arabs bring here guns and powder, yet every gun and every keg of powder comes from the country of the white men, and all are brought in their ships. It is only by permission of the white men that these things can ever come at all. They could stop sending them if they like.'

" *Arab (Kambi Mbaya).* ' Try to stop our trading in slaves on this lake, as you try at the coast. I defy you ! I shall march past Mpwapwa with all my chains full, and my hundred guns loaded, and who

THE RIPON FALLS, VICTORIA NYANZA.

[p. 147.

will hinder me ? I shall go right to Zanzibar with gangs of slaves and defy the English Consul to touch me. I come from Seyed Burgash, and care nothing for the Consul—I am not afraid of him.'

" [N.B.—This speech was made with great vehemence and great bitterness. It appears that Kambi Mbaya had been reported by the Mpwapwa missionaries to the court for having passed them with slaves. On reaching Zanzibar he was apprehended by Burgash, but released at once (he says) on asserting that he used the chains only for thieves and deserters.]

" *We.* 'We have not come here to say anything against you. It is not our business to apprehend slavers. When you Arabs bring guns and other goods to sell, we never interfere with your trade. We only ask that you will not make unprovoked attacks on us, who are only talking with the king on religion and on private matters of our own.'

"*Ahmed Lemki* (Arab). 'I can tell what these white men are doing at Nyassa to eat up the country.'

"*Mtesa.* 'Tell us.' [This Arab seems to have been apprehended with a crew of slaves on the coast by one of our cruisers.]

"*Ahmed.* 'At the coast they place a boat with steam and cannon at each side of every port, and watch for every dhow that passes and seize it. Formerly we could buy any amount of slaves at Nyassa for two doti (= 8 yds. calico) each. Now these English have conquered *the King of Nyassa* and taken his country, and put a steamer on the lake, and we have no more trade.'

" *We.* 'There is no King of Nyassa. The country there is like Unyamwezi, full of petty savage chiefs, but the English have conquered none of them.'

" [It pleased Mtesa to hear that there was no big king near Nyassa, to compare with himself.]

" *Mtesa.* 'What did the white men come here for?'

" *Arab (Kambi Mbaya).* 'Yes; just ask them if they were ever asked to come here, and if they had any recommendation from the coast.'

" *All Chiefs.* 'Nobody asked them to come here.'

" *We.* 'The king himself sent to Ukerewe more than once begging Lieut. Smith to come to him, and again he sent to Mruli and brought Mr. Pearson and others.'

General hubbub and discussion.

" *We.* 'We ask Mtesa if Stanley told the truth or a lie, when he wrote saying that he (Mtesa) wanted Englishmen to come to teach Christianity?'

" *Mtesa.* 'I asked Stanley to send me white men to make cannon and guns and powder. I collected brass and charcoal for Mackay to make me a cannon to fire salutes (!) with, but he refuses.'

" *Mackay.* 'When we talked about the cannon I had only come to the country, and did not then know that you sent these expeditions to ravage countries.'

" At the word *ku-nyaga* (= plunder and murder), Mtesa feared we should rebuke his wanton robbery and devastation of Busoga, etc., so he immediately dismissed the court.

"[Mtesa wilfully misconstrues always what I had said to him two years ago about making a small brass two-pounder. He had been pestering me for many days about making such things, while I had always been begging for pupils to teach work in wood and iron. I then told him that if he gave me ten lads to teach, I should give them knowledge enough in working metals to enable *them* to cast a small gun *after they had been with me three years*. The lads were promised, but never came, while soon after Mtesa was sending to Busongora and other parts to exact coils of brass wire from his tributaries. I have ever since refused to say anything on the matter, as he did not fulfil his part of the engagement. It must also be remembered that small cannon (of which Mtesa has over half a dozen) are of no use whatever to him, except for firing an occasional salute. Baganda have no idea of artillery practice, nor could they afford the gunpowder necessary for it.]

"Mr. Pearson and I, unwilling to have any more such humiliations in court similar to this day's, sent a note to Mtesa asking permission to go to Kagei in the canoes which he sends for his envoys. We put it on the ground that many months must elapse before these can be brought here, and our supplies must fail long before then.

"After much prayer and deliberation we have come

to the conclusion this is, on the whole, the best step to take, as once at Usukuma we could send on his envoys and presents from England, and safely state the only terms on which we could return again to the country.

" May our God grant us a peaceable answer !

'Showing that they still remember something of what they have been taught at court, I may not omit the following remarks, which were made in the course of to-day's Baraza :

"*Katikiro.* 'They want to teach the common people. Are *our* people *their* children?'

"*Mtesa.* 'They say that all men are their brethren.'

"*Chiefs.* 'Yes ; our people have bodies like them, and heads like them, faces and bellies like them."

"*Mtesa.* 'They say we shall all be burnt in the fire after we die !'

"*Katikiro and Chiefs* (jeering and laughing). 'Oh, we shall be burnt in the fire, but the white men will be let go, eh !'

" Much laughter and idle talk followed these remarks, there being no opportunity in which we could well say a word. Why they should have chosen the doctrine of future punishment to make merriment of, I do not know, as in all my teaching I never preached much, if anything at all, about retribution for sin in the next world. I always spent most of the time in trying to impress on them that God is love, unlike their lubare (= spirit), which they are ever in fear of, and making offerings to, in order to conciliate.

"*Thursday, Jan. 6th.*—At midday, the usual hour, seized again with this wearisome intermittent fever—cold shivers, pains all over, ultimately settling in the head, and sickness. Got into bed, but a hundred blankets could do nothing to give heat, even if I had them. A fire lighted at the side of my bed, on the floor, makes no warmth in the first stage of the attack. After half an hour, a burning fever, and one tosses about as if in severe pain, yet only a feeling of wretchedness remains. Then a few cups of hot tea bring on perspiration, and a dozen hours of broken dreams and fantastic visions leave one next morning weak and sick and fit for nothing at all. Emetics and purges and doses of quinine seem to do good, although the remedies are worse than the disease, and leave permanent effects for evil afterwards,—weakened organs and a deranged nervous system. One has during recovery always the discomfort of thinking too that a similar attack may occur next day or the day after. I have just had three attacks in a week.

"*Friday, Jan. 7th.*—Mufta came early, saying that he had read our letter to the king last night. Mtesa replied that he would not let us go until his men came back, adding that he did not detain us as hostages on their behalf, for when he sent some men to the coast some time ago some of them died on the way, but that was no one's fault. His saying that probably implies that he does detain us on that ground, for we have no idea of where Stokes is with the Baganda.

In fact, we cannot tell if they arrived safely even at Zanzibar. Kambi Mbaya told us that after he left Uyui he heard that Stokes was in Ugogo, but when questioned by Mtesa, he said that he had no news of Stokes whatever.

"The Frenchmen sent us a note in the evening saying that Ahmed (the little Arab who has a hatred of the English because they deprived him of his slaves), and other Arabs, this day in court were pouring down calumnies on my head. Were it not that our dependence is alone on the omnipotent arm of our God, we should stand every day in great danger from these wicked Arabs and from the equally wicked king of this country.

"*Saturday, Jan. 8th.*—Mr. Pearson went up to court alone, but was refused admittance even at the outside gate. This is something entirely new. We have often been denied entrance at the inner doors, but the outer courts were never closed before. He asked for Mufta and was told that he was not there, while we found that he was there. Pearson then went to call on the Frenchmen, to get from them some account of what evil things had been said by the Arabs against us yesterday in court.

"Their tale narrates the most diabolical series of falsehoods that evil men could have concocted. The newly-arrived Arab called *Kambi Mbaya*, whom I never saw until the other day, when he opened fire on the English in Baraza (nor have I seen him since), and *Ismail Belooch*, who comes to us almost every day professing the most sincere friendship—these two men yesterday in open court laid to my charge a series of terrible crimes. They had evidently made up beforehand the part which they meant to act in concert with the king, for Kambi Mbaya had an interview with Mtesa the day before, while Ismail we know has been 'making friends' with Kambi Mbaya. M. Lourdel and Mufta were both present at the Baraza, and their reports agree with each other. Mtesa is said to have commenced the subject, saying, ' Makay mulatu ' (' Mackay is mad '). All chiefs thereupon repeated, ' Makay mulatu,' the Wangwana asserting the same also. Then Ismail and Kambi Mbaya declared that I was a felon of the blackest type ; that I had fled from England because I had murdered two men there ; that I had got on board a steamer with two revolvers in my hands, and threatened to murder the captain instantaneously if he didn't convey me at once to Zanzibar ; that in Zanzibar I committed more murders and had to flee from there again ; that in Unyanyembe I had gone about with the two revolvers trying to shoot Kisessa, the governor ; that here my presence was certainly dangerous to the king, for I was insane and only went about to kill people ; that I was terribly afraid of the story of my crimes reaching Mtesa's ears, and that on that day I had given Kambi Mbaya a present and implored him on my knees not to make my evil-doings public !

" They had no crime to allege against me as having committed in this country, except that one day when a number of the Arabs called on me I asked them ' why they all came into the house armed with their dirks ? '

" No doubt all this story suits the king's purpose admirably. M. Lourdel says that he (Mtesa) is unwilling to quarrel with the English generally, yet he must assent to the Arabs' hatred of us, while he does not want our religious teaching ; hence he has devised the scheme of throwing all possible charges upon one individual, hoping by not accusing the other to keep on good terms with him, and thus have Stokes brought. on with a new supply of valuables to fall a prey to his own clutches. As the Frenchmen say, ' *he has the heart of a tiger.*'

" Meanwhile we have sent another letter to Mtesa asking that both Mr. Pearson and I be allowed to leave, I for England and Mr. Pearson for Usukuma, with the view of finding where the men who went to England are, and of hurrying them on with the king's present.

" Of course, if God enables us to reach safely the south end of the lake, Mr. Pearson will not come back here, nor permit another missionary to fall into the trap, until from an independent position there proper conditions be obtained, on which alone our mission can again be planted here.

" God is over all, and He is our God and our sole

defence. In fever, when one's nerves are weak, many doubts arise in the mind, and through morbidly dwelling on the number of our bloodthirsty enemies, faith almost fails. Yet the fever subsides, and courage rises with better health, and one cannot but feel a deep inward peaceful consciousness that, though we are absolutely shut off from every human help, yet we have protection more secure than any Consul can afford, even the omnipotent arm of Jehovah. 'The wicked plotteth against the just, and gnasheth upon him with his teeth. The Lord shall laugh at him ; for He seeth that his day is coming.'

"This evening, after bearing such false witness yesterday against me, Ismail called with most cool impudence on Mr. Pearson. The latter would not see him, however, but called out from inside the house that he refused to see him because of the lies he had told yesterday in court against me. Ismail asked confusedly, 'What lies ? when ? who told lies'? Mr. Pearson made no answer. The Belooch went on, 'Oh! the Frenchmen must have been telling lies to you. *They* have told falsehoods, and not I.'

"This is not the first occasion on which Ismail has openly played the double part of friend and poisonous snake. None of us have ever given him any occasion to abuse us, yet he has invariably given evil counsel against us whenever he had opportunity, all the while professing sincere friendship to us. He is a fanatical Mussulman, although entirely ignorant of his creed.

He is a fair specimen of the Wangwana who are our daily enemies here.

" Every fresh arrival of Arabs creates a fresh outbreak against us. The whole of their malice I *do not hesitate for a moment* to attribute to our public testimony as Christians and as Englishmen against *slavery*. Some of them use the pretext of their religion for blaspheming the Nazarenes, while others raise rumours of English aggression, and others again merely fabricate charges against us individually.

" All this will go on so long as the supply of slaves is here unlimited, and the demand is apparently as great as ever in Arabia and Persia.

" The efforts of our cruisers on the coast are successful only in driving the traffic by a land instead of the easier sea route. The slave dealers are only harassed, not crushed, and, like wounded animals, rendered only more vicious than before.

" Driven from the Nyassa region as being now unprofitable, and too far south for the risks of the land route to the northern ports (Brava, Lamoo, etc.), they are coming to Uganda in increased numbers every year ; for here protection is sure, living is cheap, and human flesh cheaper still. Where in all Africa are raids for cattle and slaves carried on on such a gigantic scale as by the King of Uganda ? I may safely say that he keeps a fresh force of ten thousand men, without a month's intermission all the year round, engaged in the openly avowed act of devastating the neighbouring tribes, merely for the sake of slaves and cattle. Mtesa is the greatest slave-hunter in the world, and he carries on his murderous raids on the strength of guns and powder, brought up country, by Arabs it is true, but supplied to the Arabs by Banyans and Hindus, subjects of the British Government ; while the Banyans and Hindus in Zanzibar purchase the powder and the guns, destined to be used in first buying slaves, and then in murdering the parents in order the more easily to catch their children for slaves. They purchase these articles from Europeans in Zanzibar,—many of them Scotchmen and Christians too !

" The powder and the guns bought by slave-hunting Mtesa from slave-buying Arabs, who get them from British subjects, who again get them from the British themselves, are mainly carried to Zanzibar from Europe in steamers belonging to the ' British India Company,' the directors of which are philanthropists and Christian gentlemen, giving largely in aid of missions, and themselves actively engaged in opening up the Nyassa region to legitimate trade.

" Thus, while with one hand these energetic, praiseworthy men are taking the best possible steps for the abolition of slavery on the Nyassa, they are with the other hand carrying on the terrible traffic in women and children on the Victoria Nyanza, and every year causing death to thousands of more distant savages, who cannot procure the deadly weapons supplied only by the British merchant, for Banyans and Hindus are British merchants.

"For the above terrible charges laid against me, some proposed in court that I should be put to death. Even the charge of carrying my revolver is false, for I almost invariably march unarmed, only my umbrella in my hand. Mtesa, however, said that the best thing to do was to send me home, as being a raiser of much noise and row in court. He knows very well that this charge too is unfounded. Even one of the Romish missionaries complimented me on the quiet manner in which I talked with Mtesa, while Arabs and others spoke with vehemence.

"We now can understand to the full the meaning of that blessing which we are promised when men shall *revile* us, and persecute us, and shall *say all manner of evil* against us falsely for His sake. We are His, and it matters not what man can do to us."

Mtesa had no intention of allowing Mackay to leave the country. In fact, the latter had found great difficulty in getting permission even to go as far as Uyui. Mtesa really disliked the Arabs, and knew very well the above charges were pure inventions ; but he wanted guns and gunpowder, therefore it was his policy to appear friendly towards these traders.

CHAPTER XIII.

THE PLAGUE.

> "And it was so—from day to day
> The spirit of the plague went on,
> And those at morning blithe and gay,
> Were dying at the set of sun."
>
> J. G. WHITTIER.

IN the spring of 1881, *Kaumpuri* (the plague), which is terribly dreaded by all, from king to slave, broke out suddenly in the country. It was probably due to the drought and consequent famine of the previous year, when many died, and many more had to struggle for life by eating roots of plantains and other trees. Mackay believed that the filthy state of the huts in which the Baganda live had not a little to do with it. *Kaumpuri* is also the name of the *lubare*, or deity supposed to be the cause of the evil. Several sorcerers belong to this deity, and are believed to be possessed of the evil spirit, and of its power to visit any particular house and garden, when the natives at once flee. On this occasion it broke out in the royal palace among the king's wives, several of whom died in a few hours. Hence there was a stampede of the king and chiefs from Rubaga to the hill of Nabulagala. One sorcerer set to work to check the disease. He made a pipe some five or six feet long, in which he put some noxious weeds, and walked round the courts of Rubaga, smoking the formidable charm ! Mackay remarks that the treatment might disinfect the place, or at any rate himself.

Meantime Mackay and Pearson endured many hardships and privations. For many days at a time they had nothing but plantains to eat, and to buy these they had parted with all the clothes they could spare. The following entries in his journal at this time give a glimpse of the much-talked-of " luxuries of missionaries."

" *March* 13*th*, 1881.—The hours of daylight are very precious, as we have only one candle left, and we do not know when we may get more. Fat and butter are not to be had. Hence every hour of light must be filled up with useful work, for after dark we must just sit in the dark, as we have had to do for some time, and for many days at intervals before. I miss a nightlight, especially for reading or writing a little. I have always grudged the hours of day for these purposes, but now I must do without the evening hours of reading for improvement. How I thank my dear father for my well-stored mind, which enables me to enjoy many an hour's meditation."

Then comes a red-letter day, which missionaries in distant lands can well understand.

' *March* 14*th*.—I had been busy all forenoon trans-lating, and had set to work continuing printing our first book of texts, etc. I had my composing-stick in hand, and was in the middle of the line ' God so loved the world that He gave '—when I heard a shout outside. It was our boys welcoming the man whom we had sent to Usukuma two months ago. On goes my slouch-hat and white canvas coat, and out I run to hear the news, and open my eyes for letters from home.

"Question and question tumble one on the top of the other, with fragments of answers and salaams from this and that white, black, and yellow friend in the lands south of the Nyanza. Pearson opens the small bundle which had left the hands of Stokes that morning on the lake, where he and Rev. Mr. O'Flaherty had arrived the previous day. God be praised for their preservation from every danger by land and lake, and for this bundle of letters from England!

" Pearson is letter ' sorter.' ' Mackay, Mackay, Mackay, *Pearson*, Mackay, Mackay.' Three of mine to every one of his, and I chuckle with glee and think of the contents. My total is nearly forty letters, and Pearson has fifteen. Not satisfied, but craving more, I call out, ' Where are my papers? I know my folks always send me lots of papers!' We only hope that the papers will come by Stokes himself, and we proceed to read what we have. My last from home was dated June 5th, 1880 ; now I have a pile running on to September 23rd (six months ago). Other letters from England and Germany and the interior of Africa fill up the rest of my budget.

"The moon is full and the sky clear and calm, and by this light I continue to read long after the sun is down. Our remaining candle we light, and read and remark on events till a late hour.

"Many good men are dead, but saddest of all to us is the news that our dear and *true* friend Rev. Prebendary Wright is now no more. Salisbury Square seems strange to us already.

"We have nothing to go upon here as to when to expect letters. After we get a packet, we expect nothing for three months, and then we begin to think that before another three months are over we may hear again. When we send a mail off, we have much more trouble than merely stamping and posting. First, we have to consider which of our men we can spare, then some of these are sure to refuse ; so we try others, till we make up a complement of four. Then each has to get calico in advance, to wear, and calico to buy food with on the way, as also cowrie shells. Next, each has to get a gun and powder and caps, and invariably each has some request of his own—petty debts which we must pay for him, etc. Meantime we have arranged with the leader of some canoes that mean to start for the embarkation of our men. His demands have to be satisfied, else the letter-carriers will be refused passage when they reach the lake. Frequently, after paying for their passage, they have had to return to us, as they were refused permission to go on board! When their backs are turned, I am glad, for generally we have been writing till very late the night before, and in the morning the packet has to be made up and sealed, and then sewed in strong calico, with a band so as to be slung round the neck of the carrier. What would we not give for just a good Scotch herring-boat on this lake! But the time is, I hope, near, when I shall be able to set about building a steam launch for ourselves."

A new era dawned on the Mission on the 18th of March, with the arrival of the Rev. P. O'Flaherty. Mr. Stokes accompanied him, but started again for the coast on April 1st, and a few days afterwards Mr. Pearson also left the country. Mr. O'Flaherty brought with him the three Baganda envoys who had been sent as ambassadors to Queen Victoria, but it is questionable whether their visit to England in any way promoted the interests of the Mission, for they all returned to their old ways and their old superstitions, and one of them (Namkade) conceived a great dislike to white men, and continued ever after to be an open enemy to the missionaries. On one occasion he bribed the katikiro with presents he had received in England, to take back from the missionaries a piece of ground the king had presented them with.

The king was very fond of controversy, and

greatly enjoyed the discussions at court between Mr. O'Flaherty and the Mussulmans. Indeed, he frequently, out of a spirit of pure mischief, asked questions which he very well knew would lead to bitter feeling and angry words. Each time the Arabs breathed out venom and opposed Mr. O'Flaherty to the utmost of their power.

Still many pupils—chiefs and slaves—were allowed to go to the Mission Station, which was the desire of Mackay's heart, as even although after a few months they might be suddenly ordered off to some other part of the country, the good news was disseminated. The Baganda are very eager pupils, and are besides very clever at learning to read and write. As a rule it only took Mackay a couple of months to teach the younger lads to read fluently, although they did not even know the alphabet at the beginning of that time.

Regarding his teaching, he says : " I feel sure that in this respect alone the Christian influence of the Mission is very great in the country ; it is unquestionably felt, otherwise there would be less fear at court of our perverting the minds of the youth of the land."

The work of God began to take root again, as it did during the first happy months of Mackay's residence in the country, and his heart was greatly encouraged, notwithstanding the open hostility of the Arabs, and the trials caused by the French Romish priests, who, although on good terms with the Protestant missionaries, never ceased to play their old game of proselytising.

Secular work also prospered, and Mackay describes himself humorously as "engineer, builder, printer, physician, surgeon, and general artificer to Mtesa, Kabaka* of Uganda, over-lord of Unyoro, etc."

By the month of June the plague greatly increased, and in most cases proved fatal. Many applied to Mackay for medicine, but the disease being new to him he declined to prescribe for it. He, however, did his utmost to get the king first to *understand*, and then to enforce some sanitary measures, so as to check and ultimately stamp out the pestilence. The king himself had long been ailing, and the "Queen Dowager" (of whom Captain Speke says much, in his "Journal of the Discovery of the Source of the Nile") came to visit him. She was one of Suma's wives, and generally looked upon as Mtesa's mother ; but his real mother was sold by Suma to an Arab, and by him carried out of the country—where?

As Uganda has its kabaka or king, so there must always be a mother to the king, occupying her own capital, holding her own court, and having her own chiefs, each holding an office corresponding to Mtesa's officers of state, *e.g.* katikiro (premier), Mkwenda, Sekibobo, etc. The old heathen had been a great

* The word kabaka is higher than king, being synonymous with Kaiser.

hindrance to the entrance of Christianity into the country. When *Mukasa*, the incarnation of the lubare (or the devil), went to court in great state, at Christmas, 1879 and Mtesa, at Mackay's earnest instigation, refused to see the national deity, it was old Namasole, the Queen Dowager, and her court of females, who succeeded in persuading the king to abjure Christianity. After that, however, she did not interfere with the missionaries.

She seldom visited the king, and on this occasion her object was to prescribe for his complicated maladies—the cure being that he remove from the country all the donkeys!

Now, Mackay had procured a donkey for Mr. O'Flaherty to ride on to court every day, and had forged a bit and a pair of stirrups, and manufactured a saddle. The mission station, at this time, was situated three miles distant from the royal quarters, and as Mr. O'Flaherty was getting old, he felt the walk there and back too much, in the great heat. Mtesa at once remembered the mission donkey and objected to her Majesty's proposal, but of course he had to yield. Accordingly, some pages were sent to Mackay to say, that " the king wished the loan of the donkey for Père Lourdel, as he was sending the latter to see a distant chief who was very ill!" Mackay believed the tale and let the ass go. It is needless to say, it was never again seen. Mr. O'Flaherty, however, was able to walk to court pretty frequently, and on one of these occasions Mackay gave him a list of six measures, begging him to submit them to the king's consideration, for the relief and suppression of the plague.

" 1. All persons attacked to sponge repeatedly every day all over with tepid or cold water, as they find most soothing. Also to drink plenty of water, hot preferable to cold.

" 2. Each patient to have a new, small, airy hut built at once, with a bed off the ground.

" 3. Every house where any one has been sick or died of the plague to be burnt to the ground, at once, as also all their mbugus (bark-cloths), etc.

" 4. Every house in the land, whether of chief or peasant, to be clean swept out once a week (say on Friday), and new grass strewed on the floor." [The custom in this country is to have old hay rotting on the floor as long as the house lasts, occasionally sprinkling new grass on the top of the old filthy stuff!]

" 5. In poor men's houses, and women's quarters, where goats are generally kept in the house, to sweep clean out every day. Also nuisance not to be allowed in the houses, as is universal at night.

" 6. All dead persons, from any cause, poor as well as rich, to be *buried* and not thrown into the swamps, as is universally done with all the poor and victims of the executioner.

" These suggestions Mr. O'Flaherty took much

pains in explaining in open court, and the king called the attention of the chiefs most strongly to them. What will be the result remains to be seen, although if the fellows are alive to their own interests they will attend to the king's advice to see these suggestions carried out. I shall be very glad if they take our advice, and life is thus saved. They may listen next to our lessons for the cure of the greater plague of sin and eternal death. The Lord grant it!

" I have heard that all the dead are ordered to be buried, instead of being thrown in the swamps. Those killed by the executioners will, I fear, continue to be chopped in pieces and thrown into the jungle as formerly. The fact that the potters (who get their clay in the swamps) have been especial victims of the pestilence, shows, I think, that the swamps have much to do with fostering the terrible scourge.

"One result of Mr. O'Flaherty's instructions is very manifest. On all the roads bands of women have been set to work to hoe and scrape and sweep all the highways, burning much of the rubbish, but of course not all. Certain petty officers were appointed to see the work carried out, and they have already done wonderfully well. Their method has been to compel the owner of each garden to clean the road in front of his fence. All poor slaves passing by are, of course, forced to lend a hand, whatever they are carrying being detained until they have done a good piece of work. I was much amused the other evening at seeing two women hoeing on the road near our place, when there came past a lad with a stick in his hand and a bunch of plantains on his head. The women ordered him to help them to carry off the weeds. He declined, when suddenly one of them—a strong young woman—rushed at him to catch him. The fellow ran, and the woman after him. Down tumbled the poor lad, and the stout woman tumbled over him. She seized his stick, and guarding the bunch of plantains compelled him to take her hoe and work for her. So the man had to yield to the Amazon and fall to work, amid the merry jeers of the females. I complimented her on her feat, and walked away.

"But the outside of the cup and platter are easily cleaned, and I have seen no attempt made as yet to purify the filthy houses. Doubtless the very style of building universally adopted in Uganda must prove unhealthy, even although the inside were scrupulously clean—which it never is. The houses have no walls; all is roof, like a beehive, with the grass coming down to the ground, and therefore the lower part, being buried to carry off the rain, always rotting. When I show them how to make bricks they will begin to learn how to build more healthy houses. Some say that the king has ordered all old huts to be pulled down. That alone will help to diminish disease."

The year 1881 was a time of great rain, forming a striking contrast to the drought of the previous

year. After the mission was reinforced Mackay
began to build a house for their accommodation. He
writes : " Rain and thunderstorms very frequent, and
are really terrific at times. Close on the equator and
near the lake, we are in the centre of atmospheric
disturbance. The rustle of the wind among the great
green fronds of the plantain trees sounds wild, like a
cataract. Squalls rise at any moment from a dead
calm, but they never last long, although they are
violent. The roof of my hut is nearly blown off, and
leaks badly in many places. Under the hut, however,
the ground brings forth abundantly, and one may as
easily *see* the crops growing, as the Irishman *heard*
his cabbages growing larger. I mean to make the
house fire-proof, as far as the materials will allow,
and also sufficiently comfortable for an Englishman
to live in. The plan I have fixed upon is novel. To
use sun-dried brick would arouse suspicion, as the
Arabs have told the king that we build *military forts*
with bricks. I am therefore erecting a great framed
structure of wild palm (which is the only wood proof
against white ants and other insects), and a thatched
roof, which, with a wide verandah all round, will keep
off rain from the wattle-and-daub walls. The house
proper will have a flat roof of trees and clay, and
between that and the sloping thatch there will be a
large space, which we may use as an upper storey."
Mtesa was much interested in the progress of the
house, and supplied poles, grass, etc. ; he also issued

an order for all the workers in wood and iron in the country to go to Mackay for instruction in handicraft, the old men sending a lad as an apprentice, and the younger ones working themselves. As the apprentices lived far away, the missionaries asked the king for a piece of ground on which they might build temporary huts. He at once increased the mission land to about twenty acres, part of which contained many hundreds of plantain trees.

Meantime, while Mr. O'Flaherty represented the cause at court, Mackay was more than occupied in teaching reading and writing, and other school work, teaching artisan work, building, designing, planning, providing food for all, and giving medicine to numerous patients. He says: " I only wish I could spend the whole day learning and teaching with books. . . . Every man should be encouraged to acquire a thorough knowledge of the language. Others can come and at once take their place at manual labour, but it must always be the men who have become most familiar with the language who can teach and preach. . . . Among the savages we have got to be savage, or at least semi-savage. Their little loves and hates we have to take an interest in, perhaps much on the same principle on which passengers on board ship show great interest in the play of a porpoise or any other trifle. Still it is necessary that we make ourselves *at home* among the people and learn to like them and their country. Thus alone can we elicit their sympathy, and get them to regard us as their friends, and thus only too can we become acquainted with the *finesse* of their language, so as to be able to express ourselves without exciting their risible faculties. It is an easy thing for a European to learn a smattering of these black men's tongues, just as negroes learn pigeon-English, but it is a very difficult matter to talk 'like a nigger,' and until we can do this we fail in being able to teach them, as we ought, the knowledge of God and His Redemption.

"The Church of England is not the best for giving elbow-room to a layman, therefore I am determined, if God spares me to return home, to go up for ordination by the Church of England. I am even studying for that at present, my object of course being to come back to Uganda immediately after taking priest's orders, for the mission here is not at an end. I have all along seen that a great and effectual door is open to our work here, although there are many adversaries." * Some jottings from his log-book are interesting at this time :—

---

* Later on, as the work developed, he gave up all idea of taking orders, believing that it was best in the interests of the mission that he should continue to be a layman. He found he had more influence as such. His manual labours brought him into immediate and constant personal relations with a large number of boys and men, whom he taught not only to handle tools, but also to read and understand the Scriptures, and to whom his life was a constant source of instruction. The unconscious influence of a good man is often more influential than his verbal teaching, and certainly the *living* epistle is the most valuable of all commentaries upon the printed one.

THE CAPITAL OF UGANDA.   [p. 172.

"*Oct. 20th*, 1881.—To-day my pupils finished reading St. Matthew's Gospel. I think they have understood it all to a certain extent, and at all events they express their joy at what they have read, and their belief in the sacred Word. I hope now to take up the Acts of the Apostles with them, as I have several copies, and there is great value in bringing before these heathen inquirers the story of how the heathen world of old first heard the story of salvation.

"*Oct. 23rd.*—Soon after noon we had a very severe thunderstorm. The quantity of hail which fell was remarkable—great pellets, larger than pigeons' eggs. For a short time the ground presented a white appearance, and this under the equator! A ridge some six inches deep lay along each side of the house, where it fell from the slope of the roof. Our boys gathered bucketfuls, and I initiated them into the pleasure of snowballing. Much remained unmelted until the next day, showing that the temperature of the hail must have been very low. But what a blasted appearance all the country has assumed since! Every plantain leaf is turned to shreds, and many trees felled. All the standing crop of Indian corn terribly damaged. Pumpkins, tobacco, and cassava all leafless, and the ground strewn with foliage, like autumn in England. The natives predict much hunger in consequence. Upwards of two inches were shown by the rain gauge, but the real amount must be much more, for the lumps of hail rebounded as they fell, like ivory balls.

"*Nov. 6th.*—The country is recovering from the terrible havoc produced by the hail. So rapidly does vegetation rise, that Stanley described Uganda well, as being 'a land that knows no Sabbath.'

"Door and window frames of smoothly planed hardwood I have been fitting into the new house, to the great astonishment of all visitors. The walls too we are building up to plumb and squaring, and soon all posts and wattles will be concealed. This is the first house of the kind in the land, and people never tire of coming to see it.

"Once more Mtesa has been talking on the subject of marrying the Queen's daughter! 'I would put away all my women,' said he, 'and give you a road through the Masai country by which to bring your ships (!), if only you bring me an English princess. These Bazungu are strange men ; I would give them wives here if they like, but they have one, only one each in Europe ; their heart seems bound up in that one : I cannot understand it.'

"*Nov. 21st.*—The king's cows are in the habit of wandering about with no herd. They fatten best in that way. One has been speared by some fellow who wished for a piece of beef. The cow was afterwards slaughtered for the king's own use, but over forty men were arrested and punished severely, while four or five were burnt alive as a warning to the public!

"*Nov. 23rd.*—A young elephant was captured recently, and of course presented to the king, who sent it down by a chief to me, saying that he wished to hand it over to my charge, that I might teach it to obey and carry loads, etc., like Indian elephants. We were unwilling, however, for such a charge in addition to all our other work, which is already too much for our time and strength. Neither could we afford to keep the hungry animal. We therefore sent back word that if they first built a suitable house to put the elephant in, and supplied two men to attend it, with food *regularly*, for the men and elephant, we should not object to look after the animal. This we knew they would be slow to do.

"*Dec.* 10th.—Yesterday in court complaints were made that we are building a castle of stone, and bribing many Baganda, under pretence of teaching reading, to join us as soldiers to fight in the new fort. ' They are teaching our children to rebel,' said some counsellors; others, 'They teach evil things;' others, ' We shall arrest all lads who go to the Bazungu to read.' ' No,' said Mtesa ; ' send first some one to spy, under pretence of learning to read, and then we can find out how many go to read and what they are taught.' A great chief (Kyambalango), who is an old pupil of mine, ventured to defend us, saying that he ' had seen our house, and that it was no fort : that Mtesa had given Mackay, long ago, permission to build as he liked,—let him therefore go on.' "

Writing home at this time Mackay says : " Père Girault has returned from King Koma's (see p. 159).

He speaks very contemptuously of the place. He did not do so a year ago, when he went there to establish a station just on hearing that I meant to reconnoitre there. I look on his troubles there as a judgment from Heaven on his false dealing with me on the matter last year when we were together. I cannot but regard the presence of the Romanists in Uganda as a warning to us to be less lax in our standard for admission into the visible Church than we might have otherwise been, and at the same time an incitement to us to be more faithful and more active in the great work of evangelising. If the Protestants of the world have let three centuries pass before stretching out their hands to direct the lost negro to the way of salvation, they cannot expect to begin, at this late date, under the same favourable auspices as they might have begun upon much earlier. It is also a crying shame to Christianity that Mohammedans have been here before us. There can be no possible excuse for our allowing Islam to first degrade all Africa before we take the first little step to elevate it."

Mackay toiled in the sweat of his brow and applied himself to all sorts of manual labour; indeed, there was nothing he was unwilling to do, so as to remove prejudice, and promote the spiritual good of the Baganda, and assist the cause of the mission. He often writes : " Oh that I could win their love, and that they would put away their childish suspicions and learn that I am their friend !" It was always a source of regret to him that so much of his time was occupied in building and other industrial work. He would have liked better to have spent it all in studying the language, teaching, translating and conversing with the natives; but his intense earnestness of soul would never *alone* have given him the great influence for good which he acquired in the country. His physical and mental power and his readiness of re-source in emergencies (for which his training as an engineer had peculiarly fitted him), had all to be brought into play in this pioneer stage of the mission, and attracted around him vast numbers of Baganda, to " see the wonderful things the white man did."

He was always welcomed at the palace whenever he chose to go. One day he took up a glazier's diamond with him, and showed the king how to cut glass. He also produced a yoke, and showed how oxen are harnessed. Mtesa said: " There must re-main nothing more for white men to know—they know everything !"   " We only know yet the be-ginning of things. Every year we make advances in knowledge," Mackay answered.

" Can Baganda ever become clever like the Bazungu ? " asked Mtesa.

" Yes, and even *more* clever." The king laughed and said, " he did not believe it." The chiefs all laughed too. " Is it not the case," said Mackay, " that the scholar generally becomes wiser than his teacher ? The skill of the Bazungu to-day is much greater than their skill a year ago, while to-morrow they will improve on the wisdom of to-day. The pupil stands on the shoulders of him that taught him. He sees all that his master sees, and a great deal farther too."

This they all understood, and seemed delighted with the idea. The court rose soon after, when Kyambalango and other chiefs took him by the hand, in the Uganda fashion.

Writing at this time, he says: " It is very hard to get the natives to do anything. They are willing enough to stand and see their slaves work, but I insist upon them digging themselves, along with me, else no food. Of course I shall give a little calico to steady workers. Here it is where a practical Christianity is so essential. Any amount of mere preaching would never set these lazy fellows to work ; and if only the slaves work, what better are matters than before ? I have made work so prominent a part of my teaching that I am called *Mzungu-wa Kazi* (white man of work). I tell them that God made man with only one stomach, but with two hands, implying they should work twice as much as they eat. But most of them are all stomach and no hands ! That *I* work with my hands is a great marvel, and should be a salutary lesson."

Concerning Christmas 1881 he writes :—

" CHRISTMAS DAY.—All our Wangwana turned up early, expecting something, as they believed it was a ' great day ' with us. We gave them four yards of strong calico each, as well as a hundred cowries per man, to add some luxuries to their beef and bananas. Having got them all sitting round the room on mats I had spread for the purpose, I gave them then a lesson on the meaning of the day to the whole world, and exhorted them earnestly to leave off their life of mere animalism, and reflect that there is a world beyond this, in which we must stand before the Great Judge. These men are nominal Mussulmans, but neither professors nor practisers of the creed, for they know nothing at all of it save to swear by ' Allah.' What would I not give to see some, were it only one or two of them, coming back again at times to ask something more about the coming down of God Himself as Man, which I spoke to them of this morning !

"Having bought a large earthenware pot for the occasion, with lots of bananas and native beer, I got our boys on to cook with all their might. Bundle after bundle of firewood disappeared in the flames, and ever on I gave out more, while meanwhile I tried my hand on a semi-dumpling, semi-plum-pudding. We had asked all our pupils to come, and by midday we had a crowd waiting. All being ready, we spread mats on the *floor*, with a spread of exquisitely green fronds of the banana ; then, in came the basketfuls of mashed merè, and junks of meat. Plenty of salt being our only relish, we said grace in Luganda, and all fell to with a will."

CHAPTER XIV.

GOING TO MARKET.

WRITING on 1st January, 1882, Mackay says :
" Once more we are spared to open a new
year. May it be more of God than the last, and
whatever it brings with it, may the kingdom of our
Lord Jesus be more advanced, and His blessed name
much more fully known and believed in, in this
heathen land. The work is great and the time is
short, but the strength is not of man, but of God.

"*Jan. 8th.*—Had a pleasant afternoon with my
young men, studying two of the Psalms. Oh, how
welcome is Sunday when it comes round, bringing a
few hours' leisure to obtain some spiritual refreshment
in this land of carnality!"

Much secular work continued to be prosecuted
during this year. Mackay finished his wonderful
house, and the fame of it spread far and wide, so
that high and low, rich and poor, went to see it.

Windows! and hinged doors with locks! a double
storey, and a stair with a balustrade! Such things
had never been dreamed of. Then, more strange still,
" the white man had made an oven in which he baked
bread." The consternation of the native potters
knew no bounds when Mackay got two clay pots and
cut a square door in the side of each, and a hole for
a chimney in the crown of the larger one. He allowed
them to bake the curious-looking sherds in their own
way, after which he contrived to make a very practical oven, by building the two one over the other,
with fire below, and the smoke passing up between.
He also made a brick-kiln, and having at last succeeded in getting his steam machinery from Kagei,
where it had been lying rusting for years, chiefly
owing to the intrigues of hostile Arabs, who were
especially jealous lest he should build a better boat
than their own, he erected a steam saw-mill. But
the wonder of wonders was *the cart*, which he painted
brightly in red and blue.

One day, when Mr. O'Flaherty was at court, and
there was some talk on wealth, and what the wealth
of a country consisted in, he told the king that he
ought to cultivate his land, and work his iron, and
make a market where people could buy and sell daily,
adding, " This seems to be the last country in the
world that God made, for everywhere else people
buy and sell, and have markets, and become rich
thereby, but here there is nothing of the kind."

Immediately it was decreed that, there and then, an enclosure was to be built in the palace grounds where people could buy and sell; but so ridiculous were their ideas of barter, that the court not only decreed that anyone selling anything anywhere else would be chopped in pieces, but they agreed at this sitting what was to be the price, in cowries, of every article!

Mackay having broken in a couple of bullocks to pull the cart, set off one day to the market, three miles distant, to buy a load of plantains. When he got there, it was raining heavily and no one about, so he unyoked, and went to see a young elephant which had just been caught. Meantime the·king, to whom every trifle is reported, heard that Mackay had come to market and had left disappointed, so he ordered his wives to go at once and sell plantains, and to take a good look at the cart so as to be able to tell him all about it!

After an amusing description of the native curiosity as to how he fastened the oxen in, most believing that he tied them on by the tail, he continues: "Off we went, and the crowd after us, down the steep hill, when I clapped on the brake, and thus kept the cart from overpowering the oxen. At the foot I jumped in amid the delighted yells of all. At every step the crowd grew, and yelled, and screamed with delight, and at every yell the oxen increased their pace; but all ran along, before, beside, and behind, until I had a roaring retinue a thousand strong, a procession quite as great as if the kabaka himself had headed it. Panting and breathless they followed to the swamp, or more than a mile. Here we had to outspan and cross with care, but with no mishap. Yoked again, and drove home, when a new crowd collected, and it was difficult with their noise to prevent the oxen from being injured by going so fast."

A few days after this adventure, Manoga, a chief, the king's tailor and factotum, called on Mackay and remained to dinner. He said that " they had been talking in court about the journey in the cart, and that the king had been told that the vehicle was a most formidable affair, that it was uncontrollable and killed people ! "

Mackay put the chief in the cart and drove him along the walk in front of the Mission-house, with his own hands. He was delighted, and expressed his wonder that people should say such things about the cart, seeing that it could be made to go slow or fast, at will.

One wonders at such childishness, but he had ever such idle suspicions to contend with. Whether he drew water from the depths of the earth, and made it flow through a pump, or whether he showed them how to catch the sun's rays in a lens, until they danced and screamed with delight, sooner or later the majority were sure to attribute the marvellous powers of the white man to witchcraft. Still, as such secular work awoke the interest of the natives, and helped to educate them, he did not allow himself to be discouraged, but continued to prosecute all kinds of works for the public weal. He made them bridges and viaducts, which excited as much astonishment as Stephenson's railway over Chat Moss did the English public. He spared no pains to prove to them that he had their interest at heart; and time removed suspicion and enabled them to see that he who did so much for their temporal needs must be in earnest when he pressed home Divine truths also.

Writing to a German friend, he says: "As to the opinion that a missionary's life is richer in faith and nearer to God than the lives of other Christians, I believe that this ought to be so, but in actual life everything seems to join in preventing this from being the case. Though we may do much, our teaching is feeble, the example of our daily lives feebler still. God be praised, who in spite of our unworthiness and feebleness can and does bless His own word!"

When his friends pressed him to return to England to recruit, he replied: "I cannot forsake my work till God gives me some indication that the time for that is come. With our present feeble force, and work of many kinds growing in our hands, I have no right to leave while I have strength left me."

Spiritual fruit began to be gathered in the spring of 1882, and on the anniversary of the arrival of Mr.

O'Flaherty, five young men, whom the missionaries believed had received the truth, were baptised. In his journal is the following entry :

" 18*th March*, 1882.—The week is over, and I feel glad, not only that it is so, but also for the events which have transpired.

" Several days' hard work I had in cleaning out the house and rearranging the rooms, so as to receive our guests to-day. For not only would our house be full at the dinner, but we expected some of the Frenchmen also, while a suitable place had to be prepared for a sort of chapel in which the candidates should be baptised.

"Five lads were to-day enrolled in the visible Church of Christ; through baptism, by Mr. O'Flaherty.

" 1. *Sembera Kumundo*, who received the Christian name of *Mackay*.

" 2. *Mukasa* (same name as the lubare), who received the name of *Edwardo*, after Mr. Edward Hutchinson.

" 3. *Mukasa*, who received the name of *Filipo*, as Mr. O'Flaherty is generally called here.

"4. *Buza Baliao*. He has received the name of our beloved late friend, *Henry Wright* (spelt *Henri Raiti*).

" 5. *Mutakirambule*. He has received the name of *Yakobo*.

" Our earnest prayer is that these lads, all of them grown up to manhood, may be baptised not only by water, but by the Holy Ghost and with fire. Lord Jesus, make them all-in-all Thine own, and may they be indeed the seed of Thy Church in this land. We have long looked for this day. Now that we have seen it with our eyes, may we give our Lord no rest until He will give these young Christians His grace and Spirit.

"There are many other lads reading here regularly, and who are candidates for baptism. Many of our best pupils have gone to the country also.

"The Baptismal Service we translated into Luganda during the week. The service was over early. All forenoon I had plenty to do in getting dinner ready for about thirty lads. M. Père Levinhac made himself very pleasant. I had baked a loaf and made a raisin pudding or dumpling. We slaughtered a cow yesterday, and made a good brew of banana beer. Two days ago I went to the market with the cart, and brought back eighteen large bunches of plantains. I had four large potfuls boiled, besides two pots of beef. So all had enough and to spare, for there remained over, and all seemed delighted with their treat. Our female servants and guests were not forgotten either, and came in for a share of the beef, bananas, and beer."

CHAPTER XV.

MACKAY AS UNDERTAKER.

W. ALLSTON.

COLONEL GRANT, in alluding to the surprising confidence in which the Baganda held Mackay, refers to the funeral arrangements of Namasole, the Queen Dowager of the country, with which he was entrusted, and the extraordinary fame he won thereby.* In writing his father, 27th March, 1882, Mackay says: " The King's mother has just passed away, and not only she, but an old man, an elder brother of the king, has died to-day also. The drums are now being beaten at the palace, to frighten away the ' King of Terrors,' and escort the departed spirits into the unseen world. The ghosts of kings and great men alone are here thought to live after death. They are said to enter certain sorcerers and sorceresses,

* See *Blackwood's Magazine*, May 1890.

225

who henceforth become privileged persons. This belief is something like the Hindu dogma of transmigration of souls. The old queen died of typhoid fever, as Père Lourdel, who saw her, informs us. He was asked by Mtesa to give her medicine, but she would not take the Muzungu's (white man's) medicine, nor even allow any one near her wearing calico or anything foreign. So her diviners brought their charms, and the native druggers drenched her with their physic. She collapsed next day and died."

Continuing his letter on the 7th May, he says: 'Since I penned the above all hope of sending off letters was knocked on the head. The Royal mourning lasted a month, during which time no work was allowed to be done in the land. No boat could start, nor any one carry a load, until the queen was buried. But while all had respite from work I was toiling hard night and day, for thirty days, for all were waiting for me. The morning after Namasole died, Mr. O'Flaherty and I went to court to pay our respects to the king. All the chiefs were clad in rags, and crying, or rather *roaring*, with their hands clasped above their heads. Mtesa determined to make a funeral to surpass in splendour any burial that had ever taken place in the country. Such is the desire of every king to outstrip his predecessors. Fifty thousand bark cloths were ordered to be levied in the land, besides some thousands of yards of English calico. Mtesa asked me 'how we buried royalty in

Europe?' I replied that we made three coffins, the inner of wood, the next of lead, and the outer of wood covered with cloth. I knew the custom of the Baganda in burying their kings, viz., to wrap the body—after mummifying it—in several thousand bark cloths, and bury the great pile in a huge grave, building a house over all and appointing certain witches to guard the grave for generations.

"'Would you be able to make the three coffins?' Mtesa asked me. I replied, 'Yes, if you find the material.' He said he had no lead, but he had a lot of copper trays and drums which he would supply, if I could manufacture a coffin out of them.

"Frequently we had been twitted by the king and court for failing to work for him; accordingly I agreed to be undertaker, thinking it a small affair. But then the dimensions! Everything was to be made *as large as possible!!!* Immediately all the copper in the king's stores was turned out, and sent down to our Mission. Fine large bronze trays of Egyptian workmanship (presents probably from General Gordon), copper drums, copper cans, and copper pots and plates—all were produced, and out of the materials I was to make a coffin for the queen. All the artificers were ordered to my assistance." The rest of the description is chiefly taken from his journal:—

"Next morning I went off to Rusaka, some three miles distant, to measure the body. Much objection was made by the royal ladies there at my going in to measure the corpse. But my friend Kyambalango was there, as master of ceremonies, and he explained that I was commissioned by the king. But I was somewhat taken aback on being told by some of the other chiefs that I should have measured not the corpse, but the dimensions of the grave, and make the coffins to fit the latter! I told them that there was not copper enough in the land to make a box larger than necessary; that if there was, I would willingly make a coffin as large as a mountain, but as it was, I could make the inner coffins to suit the body, and the outer one as large as a house if they liked.

"Meantime Gabunga, the 'Grand Admiral' and lord of the lake, had gone to the forest for wood. I got all the native smiths together, and converting the building, which we were fitting up for a school, into a smithy, all hands were set to work beating out the copper into flat plates. Tools, of course, *we* had to supply for punching, shearing, and riveting, but before a couple of days were over, the native smiths thought good to steal a drill. How many copper nails they stole no one knows, only these disappeared far faster than the work required.

"Gabunga first brought broad planks, adzed by canoe builders, but so irregular and crooked that they were fit for little or nothing. A huge tree had been chopped down to make two boards! I asked him to fetch some solid logs. These he declared impossible to transport; however, he tried, and next evening he returned with some two hundred men dragging a large slice of a tree, by the natural creepers they had tied round it. I laughed at the shapeless thing, and declared I could carry it alone! At once I took the body of the cart off its wheels, and lashed the log under the axle with leather ropes. Then with one hand I pulled along the road a log which had taken a regiment to drag, to the consternation and joy of all. They yelled and clapped their hands and jumped about with delight at such a wonder, each one rushing up to me and taking me by the hand, in ecstasy at such a prodigy. 'Mackay is truly the lubare' (= the devil, but their god).

"So they must have the cart to fetch trees with, in spite of my protestations that they did not know how to manage it, and would be sure to break it or come by an accident to themselves. Before they were out of the plantation they landed it several times in the ditch! Still they were determined, so I sent a couple of Wangwana with them, and was agreeably surprised to find them come back next day with a fair-sized log under the axle, and the cart actually safe and sound. But they did not want to take the cart again.

"In ten days' time we had finished the two inner coffins, the first being of wood, cushioned all inside with cotton wool, and covered all over, inside and out, with snow-white calico secured with a thousand copper tacks. Ornamental work I made by cutting patterns out of black and white pocket-handkerchiefs, and tacking them on. The copper box measured seven feet long by three feet wide and three feet high, shaped like a coffin. But the king's copper was enough for little more than the lid and ends, so we had to supply for the sides four sheets of copper plate, which the king paid for at once in ivory, as we did not think well to give these away out of the Mission stores gratis. We gave our workmanship and skill and time gratis, besides the tools, and all the iron nails (no small quantity). We received copper wire as an equivalent for the copper tacks. Even the copper coffin we neatly lined all over inside with white calico tacked on to laths which were first riveted to the copper plate.

"It is needless to describe the worry and trouble we had, working late and early, and sometimes all night. At every hour of the day pages were sent down to inspect the progress and ask when we would be done. The native workmen, especially the head men among them, would do almost nothing, and generally spoiled what they did. They preferred sitting down all day smoking, and watching how I did. I was able to get some assistance, however, from several of the younger fellows.

"When we had the two boxes carried up to the court and shown to the king, he expressed unbounded satisfaction, and asked us what we wanted for our work. We replied that we wanted nothing at all.

But he gave us ten head of cattle on the spot, in addition to several cows and a hundred bunches of plantains, besides many gallons of beer, which he sent while the work was in progress.

" But even in the execution of a small work like this, which all allowed to be far beyond their own powers to accomplish, there must needs be an exhibition of jealousy and ill-feeling on the part of some—chiefs and Arabs.

" They told the king that we made the coffins small, much too small for Namasole, because we wanted the timber to finish our own house with ; that we had already secreted in our house a lot of boards ; that perhaps we might show good workmanship, but we could not work fast.

" The Arabs also asserted that it would take us some three months to make the large outer box. Then Namkade (one of the envoys who went to England) was called in, and was asked how the English built? How long did it take them to build a house ? were they like us, who had been a whole year over one house, which was not finished yet ?

" Namkade (no friend of ours) replied that the Bazungu were very slow in building ; in fact, that they built a piece of a house, and then lived in that while they worked at building the remainder ! [Probably the envoy had seen repairs going on at some large mansion while the people were living in it, or perhaps his ideas could not be separated from a

Baganda hut, which can be commenced and finished in one day, being entirely of reeds and grass, and which, when needing repair, is simply pulled down or burnt in five minutes and a new one knocked up in its place.]

"Mtesa alone stood our friend. He refused to believe that we had appropriated any boards, while he said to our accusers that what was done well could not be done in a day. 'Can a woman cook plantains well if you hurry her?' asked the friendly king.

"We had commenced to cut wood for the large outer box, which was to measure twelve feet long by seven feet wide and eight feet high. I was sharpening the pit-saws and setting them, when an order came that all the native artisans were to go and make a box after their own fashion at or near Rusaka (where the queen died). We knew that this order did not come from the king, but from the katikiro and chiefs. Of course the smiths and carpenters left at once. Mr. O'Flaherty went to court, and was told by Mtesa that *we* were to make the box. Still the native artisans did not return, while a few Mutongoles came with gangs of men, and carried off all the planks they could from here, leaving only the huge logs which Mr. O'Flaherty had cut himself in the forest. So we put on our own Wangwana to the saws, I having previously marked off each log into boards. But who could use the saws? Such work at first! Zigzags of every style; each board varying in thickness at every inch. But we held on, and by-and-bye they got more into the way of it.

" We gave them large supplies of beef and beer every day, and in a week's time we had about a hundred boards cut and squared to fit, and nailed together with strong ribs like the sides of a schooner. When together, it looked like a small house rather than a coffin !

" In another couple of days we should have been done of the job, but suddenly our braves decamped, all except two, leaving us in the lurch. We sent word to the court, and had the native artisans fetched at once. These had to be initiated into using the long saws, but they soon learned, and in a few days' time we had enough of boards for the lid. Then we covered the whole outside with native bark cloth, and lined the inside with pure snow-white calico. Each side was a piece by itself, made so for transport. A thousand men arrived to carry the segments, and most fortunately it did not rain. We put them together before the king, who challenged all to say if such workmanship could be done in the country by Baganda, or if anything of the kind had ever been seen in the land?

" Next day we had the king's orders to go to the burial. He wanted us to go the same day, but we were too tired, having for a full month been constantly at saw and hammer from dawn to midnight, and often later.

" The grave was a huge pit, some twenty feet by fifteen feet at the mouth, by about thirty feet deep. It was dug in the centre of the late queen's sleeping-house—a monstrous hut, some one hundred and fifty feet in diameter, as usual all roof and no walls, and a perfect forest of poles inside, the centre ones being good enough for frigate masts.

" Rusaka stands on a hill of dry sandstone, clay, and gravel. It is well the stratum is so firm, other-wise serious accidents might have happened from the sides of the grave slipping.

" Nearly all the excavated gravel had been carried away, while the monster pit was neatly lined all round with bark cloth. Into this several thousand new bark cloths were thrown and carefully spread on the bottom, filling up the hole a long way. Then the segments of the huge box were lowered in with much trouble. I descended and nailed the corners together.

" After that I was summoned to the ceremony of putting the corpse into the first coffin. Thousands of women were there, yelling with all their might, and a few with tears in their eyes. Only the ladies of royal family and the highest chiefs were near the corpse, which by this time had been reduced to a mummy by constantly squeezing out the fluids with rags of bark cloth. It was wrapped in a new mbugu, and laid on the ground. The chiefs half filled the nicely padded coffin with bufta (bleached calico), then several bundles of petty charms belonging to the queen were laid in. After that, the corpse, and then the coffin was filled up with more bufta. Kimbugwe, Kauta, and the other chiefs in charge, carried the coffin to the court, where the grave-house was, when much more yelling took place. I screwed the lid down, but such was the attachment of some of the royal ladies to the deceased that I had to get them peremptorily ordered away, with their crying and tears and hugging of the coffin, before I could get near to perform my duties as undertaker.

"Then came the copper coffin, into which the other was lowered by means of a huge sheet. The lid of that had to be riveted down, and that process was new to the chiefs standing by. 'He cuts iron like thread,' they said, as the pincers snapped the nails. 'Mackay is a proper smith !' they all shouted.

"With no mechanical contrivances, it was astonishing how they got the copper coffin, with its ponderous contents, lowered into the deep grave without letting it fall end foremost into the great box below. The task was effected, however, by means of the great multitude of men.

"Thousands of yards of unbleached calico (shirting) were then filled in round and over the copper coffin, until the big box was half full. The remainder was filled up with bark cloths, as also all the space round the outside of the box. The lid was lowered, and I descended once more to nail it down. Several thousand more mbugus were then laid on till within three feet of the surface, when earth was thrown in to the level of the floor.

"We returned at dusk, but the burying was not completed till nearly midnight. Next morning every man, woman, and child in the land had their heads shaved, and put off their mourning dress of tattered mbugus and belts of plantain leaves. The country had been waiting till we were done with our carpentry.

"Mr. O'Flaherty and I made an estimate of the value of cloth buried that day in the grave of Queen Namasole, and we reckon the amount to be about fifteen thousand pounds sterling! The Arabs made an independent calculation, counting the calico and mbugus in equivalent of ivory, and their reckoning agrees pretty nearly with our own. Such-like is the barbaric splendour of the court of Uganda. Who would have thought, in the civilised world, of burying fifteen thousand pounds' worth of cloth in the grave of even a queen?

"Being so inaccessible, one would not have believed that there was so much cloth in the country, ten or twelve yards of the dressed calico being sufficient to buy a slave here, or twenty yards of the coarse stuff at threepence or fourpence per yard in England.

"What an attempt at achieving a short-lived immortality! The woman died a pagan, but her burial was one fit for a Christian. The text is a good one from which to preach many a sermon here. Such

THE CAPTURE OF AN AFRICAN SLAVE BOY.   [p. 194.

1. The Boy.   2. His Home.   3. The Slave Dealer's Attack on the Village.

prodigality in trying to procure a short-lived immortality, with no care at all for the immortal soul."

Among the native artisans whom the king sent to help Mackay in this formidable undertaking, was Walukaga, or Nua, the head blacksmith. A great friendship sprang up between them, and Walukaga visited Mackay afterwards and listened eagerly to all he was told of the Gospel, and cried out, " How is it, when we were making Namasole's coffin, you told me none of these good things ? "

Mr. Ashe describes this man as " a splendid Christian, and one of the most intelligent Africans he ever knew." In the time of the deep trouble of the mission in connection with the fate of Bishop Hannington, the Church Council frequently met in Walukaga's enclosure ; and on one of these occasions Mr. Ashe baptised the young Admiral Gabunga.

CHAPTER XVI.

"THE ELEANOR."

> "I looked, and thought the quiet of the scene
>   An emblem of the PEACE that yet shall be,
> When o'er earth's continents, and isles between,
>   The noise of war shall cease from sea to sea,
> And married nations dwell in harmony;
>   When millions, crouching in the dust to one,
> No more shall beg their lives on bended knee,
>   Nor the black stake be dressed, nor in the sun
> The o'er-laboured captive toil, and wish his life were done."
>
> W. C. BRYANT.

THE Roman Catholic missionaries withdrew altogether from Uganda in the end of 1882, as they considered the field hopeless. The reason they gave the king was that of *ill health!* but they told Mackay, that "it would not do to state to the king the real reason"! Most probably they were disappointed at not being able to baptise the population *en masse.* Mackay says: "Were it their purpose to put the Scriptures into the hands of their pupils, they would not call instruction entirely lost when these are sent off to different parts of the country, or to war, as then they would carry a lamp with them. But their system is to teach only a catechism of their own peculiar dogmas, and to make their pupils repeat the *Pater Noster* and *Ave Maria*, with invocations to saints. They have purchased since coming here about fifty little boys, whom they have been training carefully. As they will take them with them, they perhaps consider that their duty to the country is discharged when these lads return as *Apostles*.

" The time must indeed come round when this or that member of our mission must return to Europe for the sake of his health, or because he is discouraged ; but may the time never come when the Protestant mission here will be given up. If we can only swim with the tide, and leave off when things prove adverse, we should be no men at all. Converts we are bound to have, even in the most apparently hopeless times. Our orders are to go into *all* the world, there being no limitations as to the *likely places* merely, or those where success is most rapid. Now, at any rate, we will have a fair field and no favour. This has its disadvantages too, but I need not refer to them. I only hope that our hands will soon be strengthened, and the work of our mission carried on with re-doubled vigour in all its branches. Our secret of power is God's own Spirit."

Early in the year 1883 a letter arrived at the mission station from Urima, on Smith's Sound (south end of the lake), saying, " *We* have arrived ; " leaving Mackay to guess who the *we* were. In the end of January he heard that their goods had been for-warded by an Arab dhow, and were lying at the port (Ntebe). Some jottings from his log are now interesting :—

"*Jan.* 24*th.*—Got a young chief from the king to get porters to fetch our loads. Set off at cockcrow with the donkey and four men for Ntebe, to take charge of our loads. Wishing to shake off the fever, I marched much of the way on foot. . . . Found the boxes considerably damaged by wet, but it was too late in the day to do much in the way of opening and drying the bales. Our Arab—Said bin Hamed—is a young man, with a careworn face. He gave me rice and gravy, and cleared out half a tent for myself and men to sleep in. The chief of Ntebe, who is a friend of ours, sent me a sheep and several loads of plantains, besides beer and sugar-cane. I wish I had accepted his offer of a native hut in the adjoining village, for about midnight there came on a terrific thunderstorm and rain, which lasted for hours. I was lying on the donkey saddles, on the ground, in the thin calico tent, and the place being the open beach there was no shelter whatever. In a few minutes my blankets were dripping and the floor flooded. So I got on the top of a bale and sat there, half asleep till morning. . . . Next night I got a hut, but sleep was impossible, for fleas and mosquitos, as the hut was half a cow-byre, half a—well, not a human habitation at any rate. The following morning I examined the bales and spread out the calico to dry. . . . Every tin of petroleum had leaked terribly. All seemed to have *exploded* by the terrible sun of Unyamwezi. This is a great loss to us, as night-light is hard to procure here.

"*Jan. 27th.*—I got porters collected, but just as they were about to start rain came on, and they all fled.

"*Jan. 29th.*—Reached Kijikibezi (nine miles from the mission station), and put up in an open shed with all the goods. For security against theft I arranged bales and boxes so that my servants and I could sleep on the top of them ; but I scarcely shut an eye for the cold, as there had been rain again, and the wind blew chill through the shed, which is all the hotel that exists in this part of the country. I had many long conversations with the natives at each halting-place on social and religious subjects. The plague has been playing terrible havoc among the poor people, and I advised them to clean their huts and thus save their lives. All their charms I showed them were of no use, for there is but one God, who was punishing them for worshipping the devil. In every place they crowded round to listen and hear the wisdom of the white foreigner, who was so different from the Arabs.

" I had been more than a week away, and was glad to get home. I found Mr. O'Flaherty ill. He seems not to be able to sleep, from anxiety and worry, when alone. I had intended starting at once with a few canoes to fetch our new brethren, but I see now that if I leave O'Flaherty by himself for any length of time, I might see him no more for ever. So the canoes must go with some of our servants.

"Much work has now to be done in drying our goods. Our sun helmets are perfectly rotten, as also many articles of clothing to which we had been eagerly looking forward, as we were sorely in want of protection from the strong sun of Uganda. More than a dozen bottles of medicine broken and the contents lost. Still, all in all, we are very fortunate, considering the many risks and the long, long journey. We feel deeply thankful to our Heavenly Father for all His gracious provision for our wants.

"*Feb. 26th.*—Many visitors to-day. One man had been a sorcerer. His master is a sub-chief, who recently took eagerly to learning, and to teaching his women also, but he had suddenly to leave for a distant place, by the king's orders. To-day he sent us the present of a fat bullock by the hands of the old sorcerer. The latter had laid' aside his charms on hearing O'Flaherty teach his master some things about the true God. There was present also an old man, a "medicine man" (*i.e.*, half doctor, half wizard), who said he had heard the fame of our house down at the lake, and came himself to see. The man who brought the bullock wanted medicine for a disease hard to cure. The old "medicine man" volunteered to give him some, but the other refused, saying he did not want lubare's (*i.e.*, devil s) medicine, but the

Muzungu's, as the Muzungu (white foreigner) is a man of God.

"The old 'medicine man' had a string of charms, which I began to show him the uselessness of. 'Oh, but they *do* cure!' said he. 'When you are hungry,' I asked, 'will they cure your hunger? or when you are thirsty, will you quench thirst by putting them on your head?' The former sorcerer added, 'I had once a lot of charms like that, but I threw my idols into the swamp, for I know now that there is but one God, *Katonda*, whom the Bazungu know.' The 'medicine man' seemed to have his faith shaken in his string of charms, and said that he would come another day to see us, and bring his friends at the lake too, to see the wonderful house. I hope he will come back, and that God may open his eyes to enable him not only to throw his idols into the swamp, as the other did, but to see in Jesus Christ the God of Truth and of Love also."

In the month of May, the Rev. R. P. Ashe arrived in Uganda, and Mackay soon recognised in him the same warmth of heart to the Lord Jesus, and the same burning zeal for missions, which had characterised his attached friend Dr. John Smith, who had fallen asleep on the southern shore of the beautiful Nyanza just six years previously. Perhaps no two men were so differently constituted in mind and temperament as Mackay and Ashe, and yet they laboured together harmoniously; each rejoiced in the honour God bestowed on the other, each acted conscientiously for the welfare of the mission, and the spirit of envy never separated their hearts. Consequently the Lord greatly blessed their united labours.

In writing to his friends, Mackay more than once expressed his regret that in the C. M. S. publications and elsewhere, words of commendation had been used regarding him *alone*, in connection with the terrible difficulties that followed closely on each other after the martyrdom of Bishop Hannington. He says: " An undue amount of credit has been given me. It is far from my desire that this should be so. Ashe and I bore our trials together, and praise or blame must rest equally on both."

For some time previous to Mr. Ashe's arrival, Mackay had had repeated severe attacks of malarial fever, from which for two years he had been exempt. His friends urged him to return to England, but he replied: " I do not feel that my work here is yet finished, but it cannot be long before I must leave, for health cannot endure very long in this region. Seven years have told sadly on me. Five is the nominal for India, even with a yearly change to the hills of the Deccan, or Himalaya. In India there is every comfort to be had, while here there is comparatively little as yet, and our work as pioneers has been unprecedentedly heavy. I know mine has been so, and it has told on me. Dr. Smith reckoned that the first single year of the life we had to lead in East Africa should count for three years of residence. I had nearly three of such years; still I should be sorry to leave this place yet. If I am spared by the goodness of God to continue my work with a fair measure of health, I hope to think of turning my steps homeward in a year's time now. But were my health better, I mean were it possible at.all to remain longer, I would infinitely prefer it, to think of going home for many a year to come. A fellow with a long beard, a face brown like an Arab, a careworn look, and head turned grey, is all you must look for when you overhaul a Southampton boat for me."

In the month of June Mackay left his two clerical brethren in Uganda, and proceeded to the south of the lake to build the *Eleanor*, which had been taken out in planks by the last party of missionaries who had gone up country.

Coasting along the Nyanza, in a frail canoe, he reached a sheltered haven in one of the Sesse Islands, where he found a large boat, packed full of slaves in stocks, and much ivory. The poor victims, having endeavoured in the darkness of the night to break loose, were re-secured by their owners, which caused much bitter wailing. Mackay's heart burned within him, but he could only pray, in the words of Pierpont—

> "With Thy pure dews and rains,
> Wash out, O God, the stains
> From Afric's shore;

> And, while her palm-trees bud,
> Let not her children's blood
> With the Nyanza's flood
>   Be mingled more.
>
> " Wilt Thou not, Lord, at last,
> From Thine own image cast
>   Away all cords
> But that of love, which brings
> Man, from his wanderings,
> Back to the King of kings,
>   The Lord of lords ! "

It was a tedious voyage : great squalls arose very frequently, so that they could not land for food, and for a whole week they had nothing at all to eat, at the end of which time a little milk and matama gruel was very welcome. Mackay also suffered much from fever, but at last they reached Kagei, where they found the whole village in mourning, as a young man had died. The natives killed a bullock, dug a grave in the court at night, and set the corpse in a sitting posture in the centre of the hole. They then covered him over with the fresh hide of the bullock and filled in the grave with earth, placing a stone directly on the head, which was half out of the grave !

On arrival, Mackay was met by the Rev. E. C. Gordon, from England. First of all, a site had to be found in which they could build the *Eleanor*, which had been left lying at Msalala, and in quest of this they walked many miles. But the pangs of hunger suggested some refreshment, so they kindled a fire in an old *boma*, by the edge of the creek, and made some matama porridge, which they had to eat with their fingers—a newspaper serving duty as plate! The creek, for some thirty miles, they discovered to be not only fringed, but densely matted with spear-grass and papyrus, rendering the passage of a boat impossible. At length they came to a suitable opening in the reeds, probably made by hippopotami, at Urima, on the east side of Smith's Sound; but the question remained, would the chief allow them to settle long enough in his dominions to build a boat? While they sent to see, they encamped for the night. The neighbourhood was full of *tsetse* jungle, and the papyrus harboured myriads upon myriads of mosquitoes. Hyenas growled about, and towards morning a lion roared for hours, so that they could not get any sleep. Leaving Mackay to settle with the chief, Gordon returned to Kagei to fetch Wise (an artisan, who had accompanied him from England), and tools and other necessaries.

The King of Urima had never come in contact with foreigners, as his country lay far from any caravan route; accordingly he sent his compliments to Mackay, " but he cannot allow him to settle in his country, though he would like to remain friends with him. Mackay may carry his boat to the port, and build it there, but a present will be required for this concession. The king is afraid of the Muzungu [white man], afraid to see him, and afraid of his staying in the village [ten miles off]; he must go farther away."

Accordingly Mackay went and put up in a village near a high hill to the south-west, where the natives were pleasant and gathered in incessant streams to view and interview the strange Muzungu. Another chief in the neighbourhood, Makolo, wished to make blood brotherhood with Mackay, which was performed in a different way from that of the island of Ukerewe. The ceremony took place in the chief's hut, in presence of the head men. A cut was made in the right knee of each, then a drop of blood from Mackay's knee was put on a leaf, mixed with a little fat, and the same done to Makolo. Then each rubbed his blood into the knee of the other. Yelling and firing of guns followed, and the ceremony ended by each declaring friendship with the other till death, calling God and all present to witness. Road to the port was Mackay's gain, and presents of cloth Makolo's.

It not being etiquette to leave at once after the ceremony, Mackay remained till next afternoon, when the old chief gave him a sheep as a parting gift, and he returned to the port. Finding the mosquitoes almost unbearable, he pitched his tent far up the hill, hoping thereby to get rid of them, but after sundown the buzzing of millions commenced in the swamp below. They rose and filled the tent, and even smoke had no effect in frightening them away. After dawn they disappeared outside, but his tent and clothes still swarmed with them, while his helmet was like a beehive.

On the 22nd of September Mackay and Wise (who was by trade a tinsmith, but in every way a handy man) commenced to put the boat together. The awning, which Mr. Ashe had placed over it on his way to Uganda, had been stolen ; consequently the panels and planks were seriously damaged, and the keel twisted and bent by the hot sun. The task altogether proved to be a most arduous one ; neither bolts nor straps had been supplied, not a nail nor a screw to be seen ; but, what was worse than all, there was no timber in the whole neighbourhood which they could use as a substitute for the broken and missing planks.

> "Nothing but drought and dearth, but bush and brake,
>   Which way soe'er I look, I see."

But Mackay was never wanting in resource : he made an anvil by sticking a hammer in the ground, and forged the bolts and straps for the keel joints. A log was procured from a distance, which they got sawn into boards ; a quantity of ground nuts were bought, from which Mr. Gordon manufactured oil for paint ;

> "And around the bows and along the side
>   The heavy hammers and mallets plied,"

and by degrees the little vessel looked more "ship-shape," although many weeks' very hard labour had to be spent before she could be rendered seaworthy or comfortable.

The very day they began to build, the King of Urima sent a message to say, "You must finish your boat and be gone within a month, otherwise you must leave it, and come back next year to finish it, as the rains are near, and your presence in the country may prevent favourable weather for hoeing and reaping the crops!"   In vain the white men pleaded to be allowed two months instead of one;   all their efforts were futile in endeavouring to get the king's courier to understand that God alone gives or withholds rain, and that white men have no power over it.

One day a huge fat hippopotamus was spied by the natives, and hauled ashore amid great rejoicing. They killed the animal by fixing an iron barb into a paddle handle, which they drove into the hippopotamus, and then withdrew the paddle.   The poor animal only drove the iron deeper into his flesh in his efforts to rub away the irritation.   The missionaries got a piece of the flesh roasted for dinner, which made a little variety from the everlasting plantains.

A few jottings from Mackay's log-book are now interesting :—

"*Oct. 29th*, 1883.—Gordon started early to meet caravan.   Wise followed in evening with all his tools, etc.   I do hope that now they will be able to take possession of Msalala in Christ's name.

"I am once more alone, with all the work of boat to do, and every twisted plank calling out,

"'Build me straight, O worthy master.'

"*Nov.* 11*th.*—A week of very hard work, patching broken frames and broken planks. Have had to use up my deal boxes for timber.

" All last week great ado in village. Wizards holding orgies. Much beer-drinking and drum-beating. Children all baptised with ashes and kegs of beer, and initiated into the mysteries of the kingdom of the devil. Such rites are supposed to abolish death and disease !

" *Nov.* 12*th.*—Notwithstanding all orgies, the mother of the chief died this morning.

" Rain has fallen almost every day. Thus diviners are silenced at my stopping rain until my work is done. Tried to explain to the natives that these priests are liars, and that God alone holds the reins of death and rain. These Urima people, degraded though they are, flock about me and watch my operations. Not a few of them listen attentively to New Testament stories I tell them, while I am at work, and to-day I was gratified when one old man came back, saying :—

> "'This snake-skin, that once I so sacredly wore,
> I will toss with disdain to the storm-beaten shore:
> Its charms I no longer obey or invoke ;
> Its spirit hath left me, its spell is now broke.'

" In the evening much drunkenness in village, and much singing. A party arrived here singing in wonderful chorus, led by a poor leper, without fingers or toes.

" Sembera, my Baganda lad, is busy learning to write. On Sundays I always give him a long New Testament lesson, and on all other days, when rain keeps me in camp, an hour or two.

" Every evening, after work, I am too fatigued to teach, my right arm aching, and my knees quite stiff with creeping and crawling and cramping at this boat. The mosquitoes too are a terrible trial, but I thank my Heavenly Father for freedom from fevers and accidents all this time.

" *Dec. 3rd.*—Launched the *Eleanor ;* and christened her in addition—' *The Mirembe* ' (PEACE)."

Much had still to be done ere he could venture out on the stormy lake, in what was after all but a poor, comfortless thing compared with a Scotch herring boat, being perfectly open, and having neither cabin nor deck, nor any protection for the crew from the pitiless rains. But on the 20th December he anchored in Murchison Bay. He says : " All night long the natives beat drums and yelled, and lit great bonfires all along the shore. Got very broken sleep, while I was much in need of rest, having got little sleep for many nights, my crew being entirely ignorant of the use of sails.

" I thank God, however, who has prospered so far my mission to the other side of the lake, and I look for His heavenly guidance and blessing on the labours of the days to come."

CHAPTER XVII.

THE KING IS DEAD.

MACKAY made several other journeys to the south side of the Nyanza, in the year 1884. On one occasion he had been unable to get any plantains on board, at the port of Ntebe ; so he and his men endeavoured to land on the large island of Sesse in order to buy some, but the natives met them with mad brandishing of spears and shields, and they just managed to keep beyond the range of the stones which were pelted at the little vessel. He says : " We held up cowries and said we only wanted to buy food, as we were very hungry, but they only shouted that we were not to land, and continued throwing stones and dancing wildly. More natives came down the hill and joined in threatening us, saying ' they would kill us.' They were now many, and lighted fires on the beach, and beat their drums, preparing to watch all night. I refused to allow any of my crew to reply to their insulting language, and quietly cast anchor for the night. So they yelled away in vain. In the morning I asked them to bring food in a canoe to sell to us, if they were afraid of us landing, but they did not.

" Centuries of misrule and robbery by the Baganda have made the poor people naturally anxious to keep away all strangers. Only a week ago, Mugula, with fifty canoes, went ashore on this same island, and was met with stones. He shot half a dozen of the natives and robbed their gardens. But the *Mirembe* is not a fighting boat. God give us tact and prudence to act patiently, even in provocation and hunger. He will give us our daily bread.

" Most probably had we landed they would all have run away, but that would bring us no nearer buying food, so I turned the boat's head eastward and set sail. They then gathered courage and slung stones, some falling inside the boat. We simply held farther out and departed in peace. A thick fog then came on, and we had great difficulty in finding our way out of this labyrinth of islands. Thunder was then heard to the east through the fog. I dropped the end of lightning-conductor into the sea. Soon a severe squall arose and merciless rain. No inch of canvas could stand, so we just let her drive in trough of sea. After many hours of tossing we approached Alice Island, when the wind fell. I woke up crew, rowed into harbour, and found two or three fishermen, who seemed very frightened at us, but I assured them we had no desire to hurt them. By-and-by, they became friendly, giving me a dried fish, and I presenting them with a string of cowries. Afterwards they brought me a pot of honey."

While at Kagei on this voyage, he writes : "God's holy name be praised! He has saved me from two great perils this day. Said bin Saif and some other Arabs, who came to meet me yesterday, told me that there was a good sandy anchorage round the point east of Kagei village. This morning Said sent his dhow captain to show me the place. We rowed round, and the Arabs met me on the beach. Left boat in charge of men and went ashore to Said's house. Had breakfast, and got mail which had arrived a month ago. Just as I was opening my letters I noticed the sky lowering. Made haste to boat, but crew all gone ashore, save two men and two boys. Pushed off and pulled, but gale rose before I got many boat-lengths. Drifting into rocks which were hidden before, but now visible in the waves. Threw out both anchors. Rode out gale for an hour in dangerous proximity to rocks on both sides and stern. God alone saved us. Had sea risen much more, boat had been dashed to pieces by rock under bow only five feet below. The Arabs came and watched. When the gale lessened we sailed back to anchorage. Later on I waded ashore. On returning I meant to bathe. The natives drove cattle down to drink close by; and just as I was about to enter the water a crocodile dragged off a large cow. I have learned, I hope for ever, not to bathe or wade in this lake.

"Thus boat saved, and my own life and my men's lives in one day.   God be praised!"

King Mtesa had been ailing for several years, and latterly had been getting more and more feeble.   As a natural consequence, he was far less powerful in the land than in the early days of the mission, when he was able to get about.

He continued friendly to the C. M. S. missionaries, but to their great sorrow showed no sign of a change of heart.

The katikiro (prime minister and judge) was also very friendly, as also several of the other chiefs; but some would have liked to banish every foreigner out of the kingdom.

Writing home, Mackay says: "Our future is in God's hands alone, but I think we are justified in using every lawful means to help to secure protection for our mission in case of emergency.

"I do not know that I have ever hinted to you of the extreme peril we should probably be in were our king suddenly gathered to his fathers.

"Heretofore, in the history of the country, such a time has always been one of plunder and much blood-shed.   Mtesa's reign of late has been one of internal peace, but Baganda still remain the same greedy, plundering, murderous knaves. Only the strong arm of the law keeps them down.

"It is agreed by all of us foreigners, Arabs, and English, that were it not for the protection given us by the court, not a single foreigner could be a day in the country without being plundered, if not also killed.

"But God will provide for us, as He alone can in any such serious circumstances. We are by no means anxious, for our defence is omnipotent, and He hears prayer. He has preserved us in great peril before now, and will preserve us again."

The condition of the king was kept a great secret, and he was dead some days before the report was announced, on October 9th, 1884.

Mackay was away at the lake at the time, giving the boat a thorough repair. He had it hauled up on the beach under a large tent, and was quite unaware of the trouble which the news had caused his brethren at the mission.

Four of his men, whom he had sent back to the capital, were robbed of their clothing on the way, and had to run for their lives.

Next day, a messenger arrived to tell him of the sad event, and that already the people had commenced to rob each other, and that the mission boat would be plundered.

Very unfortunately, he had now few men with him, but after many hours' hard work the boat was launched, anchored near shore, and all necessaries put on board. He quite expected the mission-house would be destroyed and that the brethren would have to seek refuge on the lake. He watched all night, but received no news of them.

Next day a band of a hundred armed men arrived from the katikiro to escort him to the palace, as he wished the king's coffins made at once.

What follows is in his own words: " Reached Kitebi after dark. The escort feared to take me farther in case of a fight, as many might take my arrival at the capital, at night, with a force, as an attempt at the throne. Slept in a very dirty house, but the people were very kind, and did everything to make me comfortable.

" *Oct.* 12*th.*—Reached palace early. Main court and space outside filled with freshly-made huts.

" The corpse was laid in state in the Kadulubare's house (the largest within the grounds), while a grave was being dug in the centre of the building. Thousands of women were wailing and men roaring. The katikiro and chiefs told me that Mtesa had expressed a desire to be buried without delay or pomp. They wished therefore to do as he wanted, and set the new king at once on the throne, so as to pacify the country. The first act of the new king is to bury his father. He is not king till then.

" They wished three coffins made immediately, but at last consented to let two suffice."

Mackay went to the mission-house for his tools,

and for the zinc lining of old cases, which had been sent there from England, with stores. He then returned to the palace, and, with a lot of native artificers, set to work at once. By dawn next morning, the huge chests were completed, to the satisfaction of all, and the king placed therein and buried.

A prince was then selected. The katikiro and some others wished to elect a little boy, but they soon found that his appointment would be disputed by rebellion. They therefore chose Mwanga, a lad of about seventeen years of age, and his father's image.

The missionaries felt thankful that this young man, whom they knew well, as he had frequently visited their house, had been elected king, and they were still more thankful when the news reached them that the princess chosen to be *Lubuga,*[*] or maiden queen, was one of their Christians, baptised as Rebecca.

Some of the chiefs proposed robbing both the Arabs and the missionaries, but the katikiro restrained them. Mackay says: "Our Heavenly Father has watched over us during this time of danger, while we have been helpless. His holy name be praised!"

Mr. Ashe tells how on one occasion, after he had given Mwanga some instruction, he asked "how he would treat his old friends the missionaries, if he

* The Kabaka, or King of Uganda, must always have a queen-mother (Namasole) and a queen-sister (Lubuga). If the king's own mother be dead, then an aunt is chosen to support the title. The Lubuga is chosen from the princesses. See "Two Kings of Uganda," p. 87.

became king ? " The reply was, "I shall like you very much, and show you every favour ; " but he was no sooner raised to the throne than he forgot his promise.

The very first time the three missionaries went to pay him their respects, in order to show his sense of his new importance he declined to see them.

As the king was only in temporary quarters, and daily occupied in receiving the chiefs and subs, who went with their serfs to swear allegiance to him, Mackay thought it best, before attempting another interview, to return to the lake and finish repairs and refitting of the boat.

One day he had a scare, as the Bavuma, hearing of the death of Mtesa, went and robbed the country at the mouth of the bay. Fearing that they might go farther up, and sight the boat, which was rather conspicuous, being white, with a black point of forest in the background, he got his men to cut green branches, and closed up the landing-place.

After ten days he returned to the capital, and on the way met Mr. Ashe, who informed him that in his absence he was accused by some of having gone off without seeing the king, while the Arabs said he was robbing plantains, and fortifying himself afloat. This rumour was widespread, and Mwanga had given orders to have his movements checked.

Some extracts from his log are now interesting :—

" *Nov. 5th.*—We all three went to see the katikiro, by appointment, taking a present of four good jorah.

We thanked him for his good government of the country at the past critical time.

"*Nov. 6th.*—Ashe and I went to court, taking king present of three jorah of fine cloth, and an umbrella. Found him in audience, but very haughty. He wore a magnificent leopard skin. By his side was the magic horn (a white tusk of ivory), in his hand was a small mirror, while a larger one was placed in front of him. He soon left, but ordered us to remain to see him privately.

"At the second reception we found him lying on the floor on some rich carpets which the Arabs had given him. He tried to upbraid me for having gone to the lake without leave. Next he tried to bully me into taking a messenger of his own choosing with me to Msalala, to fetch our brethren. I had to positively decline taking this man and prevailed, getting another, who is a Christian, appointed in his place.

"*Nov. 7th.*—Started for lake. Launched boat. Several of our Christian friends came with me to see me off, and spent night at lake.

"*Nov. 10th.*—Strange to say, as many as nine Christian lads on board with me. This is a rare treat, and God grant us a prosperous journey.

"Boys talked till late on politics and religion. I was astonished at Sembera giving them an hour's exhortation on Christianity, especially on the idolatry of the Romish Church, and the need for diligence in seeking after real truth."

CHAPTER XVIII.

THE REIGN OF TERROR.

"It happened that upon the shores of Afric's upland lake,
  Whence the famed waters of the Nile their journey northward take,
  Where Nature spreads her bounteous gifts beneath a tropic sky,
  Three bright young lads were seized and bound, and led away to die!

  * * * * * *

"Not long since they had pledged themselves to serve their heavenly
    Friend,
  And manfully to fight beneath His banner to the end;
  That fight how fierce they little knew! nor guessed the rich reward
  That waits the faithful soldiers of a world-rejected Lord.

  * * * * * *

"The faithful three of old came forth out of the fiery glow,
  To witness for their heav'nly Friend and serve Him here below;
  To these upon Nyanza's shore another lot was given—
  Christ took them from the burning flame to be with Him in Heaven!"

S. G. Stock.

KING MWANGA was not long before he showed himself in his true colours; and the katikiro, seeing his sovereign's mood, became also hostile to the missionaries, although he pretended friendship with them. His enmity reached a crisis on one occasion, when Mackay was about to start in the *Eleanor* with letters for Europe.

The king had given him permission to take the

mail to the south of the Nyanza, but told him he had better get leave from the chief judge also. This worthy not only granted Mackay's request in a most gracious manner, but actually gave him a couple of goats as food for the voyage, while at the same time he had made arrangements to entrap him on his way to the port.

Mackay started for the port on January 30th, 1885, Mr. Ashe and two boys accompanying him. After walking for three hours, and just as they were entering a tangled forest, they were suddenly confronted by a Mohammedan chief—Mujasi—with a band of armed men, who drove them back and insulted and ill-used them, giving no reason for their proceedings. Mackay and Ashe never carried arms, and had only their walking-sticks in their hands. These were rudely taken from them, while the hands of their boys were tied. They, however, showed no resistance, but, tired and dazed as they were, quietly marched back under guard to the capital. When they neared the mission-house they were told to go home, but their boys were carried off and they saw them no more. The missionaries, fearing the worst for their boys, went at once to the katikiro to know the reason. They expected justice from the man who had appeared so friendly on the previous day, but they were sadly disappointed. The judge was enraged, and would scarcely give them a hearing, but ordered their false accuser, Mujasi, to tie them both up and bundle them out of the country next day. They were then driven out of court with great violence ; but the judge, not wishing matters to go too far, ordered that they should be molested no further.

They went home with sad hearts and ordered all their pupils to fly, but had great trouble in persuading them to do so ; but it was well they did, for soldiers were soon sent down to search the premises for pupils, as Mujasi was determined to burn them all. At night, the missionaries, after prayer and consultation, sent up six bales of fine cloth to the katikiro, six to the king, and one to the wicked Mujasi, begging the release of their boys ; but although the presents were accepted, the news reached them that the two dear boys and another young man (all of them baptised Christians) were burnt to death. Some said that in the fire they sang, in the Luganda language, " Daily, daily sing the praises." Mackay writes : " Our hearts are breaking. All our Christians dispersed. We are lonely and deserted, sad and sick.

" *Feb. 8th.*—Ashe and I busy printing all the week. If driven off, we hope to leave some truth in print. We hope also to establish Christian centres with an ' elder ' in each. Now is the time. May God thus make His work to grow, while the converts need not come much to our place. Who knows when persecution may break out again? Any visitor may be accused of serving us, and be burnt."

Meantime the king had sent for Mackay, and

AN AFRICAN VILLAGE.

[*p.* 207.

pretended that the mission lads had been burnt without his knowledge. Mackay feared not to utter his reproof, even though death should be the penalty. He told him plainly that he "had committed a great sin against God in murdering innocent boys."

Strange to say, the danger of this time increased the desire of many to become professing Christians. Lads flocked to the mission house in the darkness of the night, and many were baptised. Many also who were in great danger, being "wanted," were bold enough to go in the daytime, being determined to face the consequences. The missionaries strongly advised them to get away into the country for some months, and failing that, to commence to hold worship in their own houses, but to keep away from the mission house.

By the end of February more clouds loomed on the horizon. Reports were circulated on every hand that the chiefs were threatening rebellion, probably because the new king was entirely in the hands of the katikiro.

One day the chiefs and katikiro went to celebrate a feast over Mtesa's grave on the occasion of the tapestry and hangings of the tomb being finished ; but Mwanga was afraid to go, lest another prince might be placed on the throne in his absence. He felt very uncertain of his position, as but two days previously the katikiro had robbed him of two hundred cows, which were being sent him as a present from Busoga!

Mackay writes : " Mwanga has paid out gunpowder

to officials and servants in the palace grounds ; evidently he fears an alarm. God grant there may be no rebellion ! If chiefs win, there will be no quarter for us. The situation is most serious. Commend ourselves to our God in prayer, and wait for the morrow. Our boat swamped at such a moment seems mysterious. God is leading us, and He will preserve His own."

The greatest difficulty which the missionaries, and indeed all foreigners, had to contend with in the country, was perhaps the want of liberty to go about. The Church Missionary Society men were not allowed to live near the lake, neither dared they go to look after the boat when they heard she was wrecked, without a *mubaka* (messenger) to accompany them. On this occasion Mackay made many attempts to see the katikiro, but in vain ; he then sent him a handsome present, requesting a mubaka at once, as he wished to go to the port, as, if the *Eleanor* went to the bottom in twenty feet of water, no one could save her.

But the answer was, " Mackay must come himself ; " and when he did go, he was referred to the king, who in his turn sent him back to the judge, and so on ; ending in nothing but a promise of a mubaka on the morrow, which morrow of ·course never came.

This was a time of great anxiety to Mackay and Ashe, while the apprehension of danger prostrated

Mr. O'Flaherty with a severe and tedious fever; but God "stayeth His rough wind in the day of His east wind"; and the news reached them that the great chief Mukwenda had been seized and put in stocks, and his all plundered in town and country, also that seventeen other chiefs had been deposed and several friends of the mission put in good positions. Mackay says: "The king has saved himself and us by this sharp stroke. God be thanked."

Mackay now tried to get an audience of the king, who asked him if he did not intend to cross the lake? Mackay said, "No, I am not going away; I only wish to rescue the boat."

Ultimately a mubaka was ordered, and the king appointed Gabunga, Lord High Admiral, to supply canoes to aid in the rescue.

Mackay started immediately, with men carrying ropes, grapnels, buckets, axes, etc., but on nearing the lake they were stopped by armed men, who beat their drums and said they had orders not to let Mackay reach the port. There was no help but to hasten back and again plead with the king for further authority. This was obtained, but, with all the speed he could make, it was the next morning before he arrived at the lake, and found, to his dismay, the *Eleanor* almost invisible and the surf breaking over her. No sign of any of the canoes ordered, so he took four small fishing ones, and joining two and two together, went out to examine the boat. She was lying on her starboard side, with masts in water, and the waves were breaking over her port side. After countless difficulties, too tedious to enumerate, she was at last hauled near shore and baled out, then hauled up the beach and found to be undamaged.

The missionaries now began to appoint regular services in different little communities of Christians, so that they might get into the way of self-instruction and extension, and thus the work of the Lord would go on whatever happened.

Mackay's skill in handicraft again got him and his brethren into favour with the authorities, and for a time there was peace. The following extracts from his journal show the change of mind at court :—

" *May 4th.*—The katikiro shook me warmly by the hand as I was entering Baraza, and said ' I was now a great favourite, and he would give me his daughter.' I merely asked him how many days his favouritism would last? King very gracious. Said that now he hoped former good relations were again restored. Talk about the Mahdi and about European skill and excellence. I told him that it seemed unreasonable that he and his people should value so highly our goods and workmanship, while he would have none of our other world of mind and soul, and was only suspicious of our presence. King said I was right, and the katikiro also said that we ' white· men were evidently men of truth, for our cloth measured exactly as stated, a box of powder held the proper number of tins, with no sand mixed to adulterate it, and guns fired without exploding and killing the purchasers, while Arab traders in salt mixed ashes to adulterate it and make it look more!'

" The katikiro praised my work on his gun, saying that it looked exactly like new. The king replied that *he* had done well in giving his chiefs men of such value!

" *May 9th.*—Several times seen the king again. He repeatedly renewed his assurances of friendship. Set up a shelf for his clock, which pleased him much. Talked to him on the evil of having people killed on the highway, as they were not the thieves he meant to catch. He said he would order it to be stopped, and that it would not be done again. Talked to him on the folly of beating people, and tried to show him that liberty was better than force, and having his people instructed in the way of truth the surest way to have peace, and freedom from rebellion. Advised him to excel all in reading and knowledge, and asked if I might come to-morrow (Sunday). He said, 'Come.'

" *May 10th.*—Saw king quite alone. Gate and doors all closed for fear of intrusion. Gave him long lesson on God's purpose in creation and redemption. He listened well, and gave me a fat cow when I was done. Promised to learn to read, but said that he was thwarted by old chiefs. I told him he was king, and powerful when he liked."

About this time Mackay had many interviews with

the king, who professed much friendship. One day he said, " I will never let you leave me ; and while I live, and my son's son, I am determined to have white men in my country." Mackay begged of him not to let his kingdom stink with blood and fire, for God had raised him up to save men and not to kill them, and that no blessing would rest on the country while murder and cruelty and oppression lasted. He also gave his Majesty advice on several sanitary measures necessary to drive off the plague and small-pox, which were causing men to die off like flies ; and last, but not least, to cease to trust in charms, which were valueless, but to give God the honour due to Him, and a blessing instead of a curse would rest on the land.

Meantime, the katikiro was building a shrine to Mtesa, and he sent for Mackay to go to see it. Mackay was glad of the opportunity to talk seriously to him. He told him that he hoped the day would soon come when he would build a church to the living God, who would help him more than the spirit of a dead king, and that God would call him one day to account for despising Him and His word and His Son.

The katikiro answered, " I have the Book, and I do not believe in charms made by men. I will send for you privately to teach me to read, and then you can explain to me your religion!" But, alas! as in the case of Felix, the convenient season was never found.

Mackay knew this would be so, and he embraced the opportunity of showing him the folly of raids and robbery, by which no blessing nor even profit came to him. He told him that instead of selling his children (slaves), he ought to keep them, and make them till the ground, and rear cattle, and work like Europeans, and he would become far richer, and in a more righteous way, than by his robbing system.*

* Mackay drew out the following ten rules to assist the boy-king in protecting the life and liberty of his subjects, and their property from arbitrary spoliation :—

1. King to receive all honour, and regulated tribute settled in council.

2. All matters of importance—peace or war—to be settled by king and chiefs in council.

3. No sentence of death to be passed on any man—free or bond—except in public court, and by consent of the whole court.

4. Justice not to be sold. Capital punishment to be restricted to cases of murder only.

5. Executioners to be abolished. No cruelties or tortures to be tolerated—*e.g.*, roasting alive, taking out eyes, cutting off ears, hands, lips, teeth, or other mutilation.

6. No chief to be deprived of office except by common consent of council, and then only for grave offences. No poor man to be robbed, or apprehended but by law.

7. Selling of slaves to be absolutely forbidden. Any trader found taking any women or slaves out of the country to have all his goods confiscated.

8. Raids for plunder either in country or against other tribes to cease. Wars to be waged only for just cause. On such expeditions only cattle to be taken. Men, women, and children not to be taken out of their country.

9. No wounded or live prisoner of war to be put to death.

10. Perfect freedom of religion to be granted to all creeds. No one to be arrested for his belief, nor liberty of worship to be interfered with, either by king or chiefs.

In August of this year the king took a trip on the lake, and ordered Père Lourdel * and Mackay to accompany him. The very first day twenty poor natives whom they met were killed. Mackay writes in his diary : "This bloody work must stop. I hope to try, by God's help, to show the evil of such murder, and if it continue I must enter my protest and return to the capital."

There were eighty canoes in the Royal fleet ; but, instead of enjoyment, there was terror on all hands of the head man-killer, Mukajanga, whom the king had authorised to kill whomsoever he pleased, without reporting !

The king had a strange idea of the way of spending a holiday. Every night he encamped at some part of the mainland, and before dawn he set off with reed lights, on a walking expedition, or rather a *running* one, over hill and down dale and through swamps (some of which were most objectionable), as fast as he could, and his multitude of women rushing after him ! Many things transpired which Mackay did not like, and he was most thankful when the king returned to Mengo, to which he was escorted with great gun-firing and flourish of trumpets. He entered the palace courts with shield and spears, taking his own capital by storm !

* The French priests, having heard of the success of the C.M.S. missionaries, had returned to Uganda.

CHAPTER XIX.

DEEDS OF BLOOD.

> "Yet, yet their deeds,
> Their constancy in torture and in death—
> These on tradition's tongue still live, these shall
> On history's honest page be pictured bright
> To latest times.
>
>   *   *   *   *   *
>
> With them each day was holy, every hour
> They stood prepared to die, a people doomed
> To death—old men, and youths, and simple maids."
>
> JAMES GRAHAME.

OCTOBER of 1885 brought great trouble to the missionaries, and for a long time subsequently they lived in daily expectation of being put to death. The future was ominous and dark, but, as the sequel will show, God was better to them than they feared.

A Baganda army had gone raiding in Busoga, and sent word to the king that "there were two white men there, and some more behind with a great caravan." The missionaries at once suspected that the strangers were Bishop Hannington and party, although they had never dreamed that they would venture to enter the country by the Masai route, which the king considered his "back door." Mackay and Ashe were sorely perplexed, and after praying together they went to court at once, but failed in getting an audience. While waiting, they heard definitely that it was really the bishop, and that he had been put in the stocks; that Mwanga had held a great Baraza with his chiefs, after which he had sent messengers to kill the bishop and the whole party, servants and all, and fetch their goods to the capital. But the crafty king would not see the missionaries; he sent word that "if they had any reason to suppose that their brethren were prisoners they should tell the katikiro." Mackay and Ashe next tried to bribe Koluji (a chief) to send after the man deputed to commit the murder, and tell him to wait for fresh orders from court. Koluji professed to agree. The following entries in Mackay's note-book tell the course of events:—

"*Oct.* 26*th.*—Too nervous to sleep. Up long before dawn. Ashe and I wrote note to king, craving an interview, but we did not succeed in seeing him. The good Lord save our bishop and the brethren from the hands of these assassins!

"Got Père Lourdel to go to court and read our letter to the king, but the latter merely replied, 'Let Mackay come and write a letter, and I shall send a message to have the bishop *sent back.*' Lourdel came down in haste to tell us. Wrote letter and Ashe went with it, as I felt unwell. But fearing Ashe would not see king, on the pretext that *he* had not been ordered to write the letter, I hastened after him on the donkey. Got ourselves reported, but the king set off at once to the pond, in case we should see him!

"*Oct. 29th.*—Hear that the king goes to-morrow to the lake, to shoot. He has given the executioner orders to catch people *here*. It may be ourselves, or our boys, or mayhap readers, or pages coming to tell us news.

"At once we sent away all our boys to hide among our Christian friends. Writing out revision of St. Matthew's Gospel. Ashe busy setting it up. Time of persecution has always been a printing time.

"*Oct. 30th.*—After dark one of our friends came to tell us that messengers had returned from Busoga with the tidings that the white men had been killed and all their Wangwana. It appears that a great army had gone from the katikiro's country to murder our brethren.

"Oh, night of sorrow! What an unheard-of deed of blood!

"God alone knows the cause, and He alone knows what the consequences will be."

"*Nov. 1st.*—This day last week we heard of the arrival of our dear brethren in Busoga. What a week of dreadful anxiety and sorrow this last week of October has been!

"Now is the time to actually carry out our former plan,—viz., to get our elders to assemble their friends in each neighbourhood and have worship in their house. We have now ten elders, and they could hold half as many meetings simultaneously. While the present suspicion lasts we only increase it by collecting caowds on our premises.

Nov. 5th.—Nine lads baptised to-day. Had letters from ——, assuring us that bishop and party are killed outright. Musoke has got orders to go and fetch the white men's goods* *by night*, that the news might not get out.

"We have no hope now. The worst seems over. Our dear brethren are happy, while we remain in the midst of death. Lord, Thy will be done! For me the bitterness of death is past. I have become at times almost unconscious to the most terrible realities.

"*Nov. 9th.*—Père Lourdel sent a note to say that he has been told that the katikiro allows that the bishop and party are all murdered, and that the court is only waiting for the Church Missionary Society's boat to come back ; and when they know that the men they have killed are the very men we have sent the boat for, they then mean to kill us all ! This is probably in the fear that we have power to punish them for their dreadful deed."

Some of the Christians sent word to the missionaries that a gift to the authorities was necessary in order to remove suspicion of any desire to take vengeance. One of the princesses, a daughter of the late king,

---

* The goods arrived, and Mwanga dressed himself in the bishop's robes, but could not understand how there were no sleeves !

also sent them a message, telling them to make friends with the king without delay. Accordingly Ashe and Mackay made up a large present for his Majesty, another for the chief judge, and smaller ones for two of the chiefs, who had been instigators in the plot to kill the bishop. Seventeen loads in all! It was a great loss to the mission; but what was the use of hoarding barter goods, when the very existence of the cause, and their own lives, were in imminent danger?

The avaricious judge was in high glee, accepted the gift, and swore by the ghost of Mtesa that while he was in power he would never do the white men any harm. The king, however, was in a great rage, and demanded to know "why the present had been sent? Why should they rob themselves to give him what they lived upon? Had he come to the throne yesterday? or had the Church Missionary Society's boat come? Let Mackay and Ashe come up at once, and explain the meaning of their gift." They went, never expecting to return alive. All the wrath was because they had been informed of his wicked intention to kill them; and he tried hard, by threats and entreaties, to get them to tell the names of those who had revealed the plot. This the missionaries declined to do; and their punishment was that no one was to visit them, and they would both be arrested and killed if a single Muganda was found in their premises, whether by their knowledge or not. Then he insolently asked, "If I kill you, where shall I put your bodies?" They told him they were not afraid of him, as they relied on protection from God. At this the whole court made merriment. After a tedious interview, lasting over two hours, he let them go, ordering two cows to be given them, "to pacify their minds"! They returned home, weary, but grateful to their Heavenly Father for preserving them in so great a danger.

As it has ever been, in all lands, from the early centuries downwards, so it was in Uganda. In the times of greatest trouble and trial, many pressed into the kingdom.

The missionaries set a watch at the gate to warn off all natives; nevertheless many lads pushed in, and their friends could only commend them to God, and send them off with a portion of the Scriptures. Gabunga (the young lord of the lake, and admiral of the fleet) sent at midnight to ask when he could be baptised. Two days afterwards Mr. Ashe performed the rite (see p. 237).

Meantime Mwanga did not prosper. First he had bad eyes, and he believed the missionaries had bewitched him; next his palace at Mengo was burnt down, and all his goods lost. His gunpowder kegs, which he kept in a straw hut, where a fire was continually burning, blew up, and caused terrible damage; while many of his people were killed, and others terribly injured. His Majesty took refuge at the katikiro's, but he was not there long before his host's store was struck by lightning and the powder exploded

The king was now absolutely certain that Mackay and Ashe were bewitching him, and fled, in great alarm, with only one or two lads, to Rubaga, with his drawn sword. He declared that "he felt sure he would be the last black king of Uganda, for white men were appearing on every side, and would soon take his country from him!" Still he continued his evil practices, burning converts now and again, sending out large raiding armies, and anon making plots to kill the missionaries. They, however, led a charmed life; something always occurred to frustrate his designs, when evidently he had some pangs of conscience, for on these occasions he sent Mackay presents of eight thousand or ten thousand cowries, with the message that he "remembered him and liked him." Once, after plotting to entrap and kill him, he had the effrontery to say, "A great king like me should never be without a man of skill to do work for him. I will not let you go away, not even if they send seventy letters for you!"

But more troubles were looming in the distance, which are best explained by jottings from Mackay's own journal :—

"*Sunday, May* 23*rd*, 1886.—Very wet, and we expected few people, but by ten a.m. it faired, and a large congregation gathered. Little did we think that many of these faces we should never see again in this world. Service in our former chapel. Mattayo married. Last Sunday several couples were also joined together by the rites of the Church.   After the Litany, Nua unexpectedly gave utterance to an earnest and impressive prayer, in which all joined audibly. Our lesson was upon the marriage at Cana of Galilee. How soon have the waters of the bitter river of death been crossed by most present, and now they drink freely of the glad wine in the kingdom above, where no more sorrow can ever be mingled with the cup!

" *May 25th.*—What we have been in daily expectation of for a long time has now taken place—an order for the arrest of all the Christians.   The katikiro ordered one of his own lads to be killed at once, while almost every one of the pages were immediately seized and carried off for execution.   Eleven of our friends were thus killed the first day, and some of our old favourites condemned.   May the Lord and Saviour whom they have learned to trust, be with the poor lads in this hour of horror and death, and give them a joyful entrance into the happy land !   Armed bands were sent out in all directions, and a host of our best people arrested, and an effort made to get them to inform on others.   Bilali arrived here with an armed band to seize people.   Happily there were none about our place, at the time, as we had got warning a few minutes before.   Even at Rusaka, the queen-mother's place, many boys have been put to death.

" Many of our pupils we know nothing of, but hope they have escaped.

" The Lord mercifully look on the agony of these

poor black children, who are laying down their lives for His name's sake!

"Six of our boys we sent a few days ago to live with the Arabs. We gave Mahommed (Tripoli) a letter authorising him to receive an honorarium from any of our brethren between this and Zanzibar, or from the Consul, should he deliver them up, in case of our being evilly handled by this king."

It was a terrible time for Mackay and Ashe, and sorely perplexed they were as to the best course to take. When they saw the dear people, who had been taught by them, murdered in cold blood for the acceptance of their religion, they were at times driven to desperation. They then believed that they should insist on leaving the country, feeling sure that they would soon be asked back, if indeed they were allowed to go. Again, should they manage to get away, some of the Frenchmen would consider it their *devoir* to remain, in the hope of reaping a golden harvest from the neglected Protestant converts. The king was eager for Mackay to stay, for the work he could get out of him ; and both missionaries not only made great progress in translation and printing, but they were able to distribute books and papers in vast numbers. It was the desire of both to remain at their posts, if it was at all possible to do so. Mackay went one day to see the king, and reminded him that he had promised to give him anything he liked to ask, provided the royal gunsmith was shown the way to make cartridge-cases. "Will you give me my reward now?" asked Mackay. "Yes." "Well, I wish the lives of those condemned, but not yet executed." He declared that they were all already executed. Mackay pleaded earnestly, and told the king that he had been toiling hard at making him a loom and a spinning jenny, and that he had been successful in making some cloth for him. This apparently pleased him, and he agreed to spare whoever was left. Mackay pressed the point as far as he thought prudent.

At this time the miserable king was so often under the influence of bangh and beer that he was dangerous, and Mackay had to be very careful lest he irritated him, and thus cause death to more of the poor prisoners.

One day Mr. Ashe went to the capital, but obtained no audience. On the way home he met a ghastly spectacle, viz., a human head, newly cut off; and, farther on, arm and legs.

Two or three days after this the very flower of the Christian community, thirty-two in number, were slowly burnt to death, and that too by Mwanga's express orders, after he had declared to Mackay that "only four or five remained alive, and that he would liberate these."

These martyrs made a noble confession, praying to God in the fire, so that even the head executioner reported to the king that "he had never killed such brave people before, that they died calling on God." This caused Mwanga to laugh and say, " But God did not deliver them from the fire."

Mackay and Ashe made an effort to get the Frenchmen to unite with them in trying to save the poor people, but they absolutely refused to help in presenting a united front to the king's cruelties, either by word or deed. " The C.M.S. men could do as they liked, but *they* would not interfere." They were afraid, just as they were in 1881, when Pearson and Mackay asked them to join in petitioning King Mtesa to countermand an order he had given for a *kiwendo* or massacre of common people to appease the gods. The C.M.S. missionaries based their request on the ground of common humanity, but on both occasions the Frenchmen asserted that it was as much as their lives were worth to interfere. On the occasion of the kiwendo, the C.M.S. missionaries sent in their petition to King Mtesa without the aid of the Romanists, and he granted it.

Very many of the Christians were now in hiding, and appeared after dark at the Mission-house ; there were many inquirers also, and numbers were baptised by Mr. Ashe. On the 25th of July, 1886, the baptismal register read two hundred and twenty-seven names. That night fifty converts assembled at midnight, and two more elders were elected. It was the " Church in the Desert," revived in the heart of Africa ! The missionaries used their endeavours to get the people to meet in the houses of the "elders" on Sundays, especially when they were most watched; but many waxed very bold, and seemed reckless as to their fate. The rulers were quite aware of it, but could not put down the new religion, especially as many powerful chiefs had embraced it!

The king called in his sorcerers, to divine whether or not Mackay should be put to death, as some of the chiefs were complaining that their children were killed for reading what the missionaries taught. But the katikiro would not assent to Mackay being killed. He said, "No! he buried Namasole, and he buried Mtesa, and I shall take no part in such a plan; besides, if you do, no Arabs will come near us." Mwanga replied, "I will go with my soldiers to their place at night and fight them, and if I prevail I will kill them both, before the katikiro knows anything about it." The katikiro sent the king a handsome present for opposing his scheme.

In August, 1886, permission was obtained for Mr. Ashe to leave Uganda,* and Mackay was once more alone. Sad enough he felt at times, for it was given out that the king intended to have another grand massacre of the Christians. The queen-mother, however, sent the king a message to tell him not to kill his lads, but to make them chiefs. "What harm are they doing?" she asked; "you are only being laughed at!"

---

* Mr. O'Flaherty had left some eight months previously.

At this time Mackay writes home: " I am plodding on, teaching, translating, printing, doctoring, and carpentering. Strange medley, you will say. That cannot be helped. Man was made to be like his Maker, who made not one kind of thing, but all things. There is no doubt but that your prayers on our behalf have been heard, and will be answered more and more. We have the assurance that the Lord's people will be ' brought out of great tribulation '; we therefore cannot take it to be His will that they will be for ever left in trouble.

" The king has sacrifice killed to bewitch the Christians ! If he never goes farther than that, he will do them little harm. But there is trouble brewing, which only our loving Lord can save us all from."

The Arabs were now very hostile, and were constantly accusing Mackay to the king, with a view to get him driven out of the country. They were most unscrupulous as to the means they used to gain this end. Their race and religion led them to calumniate all Europeans. Mackay's exposure of the slave trade had made him obnoxious in their eyes for many years, and now he had manufactured weaving and spinning apparatus, and was actually teaching the Baganda how to make cloth out of fibre. Why, their trade would be stopped. No slaves to be got, and no demand for cloth ! If Mackay could be killed, not only would he be out of the way, but other white men would be frightened to come !

So they reasoned. One of them reported to the king that crowds collected at Mackay's place every Sunday, and that he said, " I came to *teach*, and mean to teach, while I remain in the country, or am alive ; I will go and teach publicly in the market-place, if people are afraid to come to the mission-house."

Next they declared that "all Europeans were evil, and land-eaters." Mackay used the globe, to show the absurdity of thinking that all the world of white men were concentrating their thoughts on eating up a little patch in the centre of Africa !

But Mwanga still withheld permission for Mackay to go, and the katikiro and chiefs (many of them heathens) would not hear of his leaving them. Mackay says : " I was astonished to hear Wakili explaining to some other chiefs that ' we Europeans are striving only for the good and peace of Africa, and that our religion led us to spread ideas of mutual love and friendship among men and nations.' This from a heathen is wonderful, and far more divine than the Arab creed of enmity and malice.

" By all accounts Mwanga seems to be meditating another massacre of the Christians, which our dear and ever-present Lord keeps his hands from doing. ' God is our refuge and strength, in straits a present aid.' Yesterday he was growling that he would not have me teach his people. He took an Arab dirk, and brandishing it, said, ' Thus will I kill any Muzungu ! '

(white man). The Arabs said, *Amen!* They are making a desperate effort just now to establish their creed, and have Christianity crushed. Good Lord, this cause is Thine, and will triumph! Why do the kings of the earth set themselves against the Lord and His anointed? 'He that sits in the heavens shall laugh.'

"Strange to say, the queen-mother sent me the present of a large fat cow very early to-day, without begging for anything. She must have heard of Mwanga's words of fury yesterday.

" Praise God! St. Matthew's Gospel is now published complete in Luganda, and rapidly being bought. I merely stitch it, with title-page, and supply a loose cover. Binding, by-and-by. This work, with the packing and giving medicine to the Christians ordered off to war, and sitting up to all hours, teaching housefuls, has thoroughly exhausted me. I am almost entirely broken down with fatigue, and anxiety, and want of sleep.

"*June* 19*th*, 1887.—Read three chapters of Romans, vii., viii., ix., with good class this evening. The argument they seem to comprehend. Where is Thomson, with his feeble scheme of Islam for Africa? or Reichard, with his charge of extreme poverty of mental power in the negro?

"*July* 12*th.*—Since the last entry I have had a month of trouble and anxiety. The existence of the mission has been wavering in the balance, and even yet is undecided. Our enemies have tried their very utmost to prevail. Even Père Lourdel seems, partly too by his own confession, to have helped to seriously bring increased suspicion on our objects, and therefore to lend a hand to our overthrow. The whole case I have given into the hands of our Master, whose we are. Whatever way He will lead, I am prepared to follow.

" Père Lourdel, I hear, told the king that ' it was not well for me to meet Stanley here, as we would lay our heads together to eat the country.' The king, at any rate, told the katikiro and Pokino, in court, that Lourdel had made this statement, whereupon the chief judge accused the Frenchman of jealousy. I wrote and asked Lourdel if he had given this advice? He denies having done so ; but, from his own confession, there is some ground for the king's statement. He (Lourdel) allows to having said to the katikiro that ' white men do not intend *meantime* to take the country ; but *by-and-by*, he did not know !' This imprudent remark will take us much pains to controvert in the days to come, as the king himself said that had the Arabs told him ' not to let Stanley and Mackay meet,' he would have looked on their words as merely enmity, but when a *white* man said this, it must be true !"

The katikiro again gave out that he was unwilling Mackay should leave, and the king also expressed great regret. On all sides much sorrow was expressed,

and no one would hardly believe that he really meant
to go.   Mackay says :—

" I am at times sorely perplexed, but I think it
well to bend before the storm till it breaks, and when
a reaction comes we may lift up our heads.   If their
regrets are sincere, they will agree to another missionary coming on with the boat.   I have gained one
important point in getting permission to leave the
C.M.S. station in possession of some of our pupils,
and not to abandon it entirely, as the Arabs * were
determined should be done.   I have resolved, however, not to go unless they send a mubaka with me
to fetch Gordon to take my place.   I mean to make
this point a test of their sincerity in asserting that
they wish friendship."

After many tedious discussions at Court, a mubaka
was at length granted.

Many chiefs begged parting gifts, and gave him
others in return.   The king also sent farewell presents,
with a message that he was to " return very soon."

Finally, on the 21st July, he started for the port.
He says: " I called on the Frenchmen on my way,
and gave the keys to Père Lourdel—Simeon Lourdel
—Peter should have the *keys!* "

* They went to the katikiro and did their best to persuade that
dignitary not to allow him to leave any one in charge, nor a single
article in the country, as he would (they said) be sure to write to
England that he had been robbed, and much trouble would ensue.

CHAPTER XX.

THE NIGHT IS GONE.

" So long Thy power hath blest me, sure it still
Will lead me on
O'er moor and fen, o'er crag and torrent, till
The night is gone ;
And with the morn those angel-faces smile
Which I have loved long since, and lost awhile."

J. H. NEWMAN.

IT must be distinctly understood that Mackay did
not leave Uganda out of fear. He would have
greatly preferred to remain, but he believed it was
for the good of the mission that he should retire for
a time, and the king and katikiro ultimately agreed
to this. But when his eyes were opened to the
fact that the Roman Catholics were looking eagerly
forward to having the fort to themselves as soon as he
had quitted it, he resolved that he would not go until
a messenger was sent with him to take back one of
his brethron. He felt quite certain that, notwithstanding all that had happened, there was not one
among them but would be quite ready to occupy
the post. Had Mackay believed that any evil would
befall any of his brethren he would not have advised

THE WONDERFUL CART.

[p. 219.

them to go on to Uganda, but he rightly felt that the hostility of the Arabs was due to *his* influence with the authorities, and that, as soon as he left, that would cool down.

The Christians were in great alarm, lest another general massacre should take place immediately on his departure, but he comforted them with the promise that another missionary would speedily come to help them ; and that he had no intention of returning to Europe, but would remain somewhere on the south coast of the lake, where he would watch over their interests to the best of his ability, and be ready to return should God open the way.

Many sad good-byes to this and that dark friend, and he was once more on board the *Eleanor.*

> " All had been dimly star-lit ; but the moon
>   Late rising, silvered o'er the tossing sea,
>   And lighted up its foam-wreaths, and just threw
>   One parting glance upon the distant shores.
>   They meet his eye ; the sinking rocks were bright,
>   And a clear line of silver marked the hills,
>   Where he had said farewell.   A sudden tear
>   Gushed, and his heart was melted ; but he soon
>   Repressed the weakness, and he calmly watched
>   The fading vision."

Mackay reached the south shore of the lake on August 1st, 1887 ; and, as he expected, a few days afterwards the Rev. E. C. Gordon nobly went to hold the fort in Uganda.

After various futile endeavours to form a station at

Msalala, he pitched his tent at Usambiro. He writes : "You ask me where Usambiro is—I may define it as the whole region immediately north of the wide country called Msalala. This station is six miles north of the old Msalala station, and only about three miles from the extreme south end of Smith Sound.

" On the maps you will see a place marked *Makolo*, which is our position. From our front verandah we have a view of the extreme end of the creek, which, being closed in by hills, looks like an independent lake. Although the water is only about three miles off, it is quite inaccessible on this side, on account of a broad belt of papyrus and bamboo. Hence we have to walk about six miles before getting to our port. This papyrus fringe breeds myriads of mosquitoes, which infest the country for many miles. These pests are most numerous in the rainy season, and were it not for the fact that they come out only at night, existence would be nearly impossible. But I am at home anywhere on the shore of my beloved Nyanza, despite the strange mystery which still hangs round its coast—east and west. All along the shore of the lake, every half mile or so, are studded tiny hamlets, consisting of about a score of round huts in a paling of coarse logs, and of course a cattle kraal in the centre. These many villages, besides their geographical interest, offer a peculiar interest to the missionary, as being so many fields—I shall not say ripe for harvest, rather acres—where ploughing and sowing must be done, and a patient waiting for the reaping diligently practised. Unfortunately, every day's march generally finds one in another tribe, with another language new to the preacher, and therefore presenting obstacles to its ready acquisition."

He had brought with him his engines and machinery, together with the printing press, heavy boxes of type, ink and paper. At a new station, building and other work had to be carried on vigorously, as he was daily expecting Bishop Parker, the second bishop of East Equatorial Africa ; Mr. Ashe, back from England, and some others, and there was no accommodation for them. The work of printing and translation also went on apace, and he was able to send on many books and portions of Scripture to Uganda.

Before Christmas the new reinforcements had arrived, and as there were now six missionaries at the little station, they held a many days' conference.

Mackay had been so long in the midst of barbarism and degradation and persecution, with no educated brother to exchange sentiments with, that to enjoy the society of the Bishop he had so long pleaded for, and of four other Englishmen, among whom was his dear old friend Ashe, was indeed a rare treat. He says : " Coals of fire, however hot at first, if scattered by ones or twos, here and there through the room, are likely soon to die out ; but if gathered together in one grate, speedily burst into flame and contribute more warmth, even in the remotest corners, than when lying about singly in all directions. So it is here. So down-sunk are the people of East Africa in the scale of religious and intellectual existence,[*] and so little encouragement does the missionary find in endeavouring to elevate them by the power of the glad tidings of grace, that one or two most earnest men, stationed in isolated positions, are apt to find their ardour cooled and their courage gone. But three or four men in one spot, living together, working together, encouraging one another, loving one another, form in themselves an element of strength which, by the blessing of God, soon makes itself felt in all the country round."

About this time he wrote to his old friend Dr. Baur, asking him to enter into communication with the Moravian brethren, with a view to their sending missionaries to Central Africa, and to let Bishop Parker know the success of the negotiations. This was done, first because the Bishop found that East Equatorial Africa alone could easily absorb a hundred new men every year, for always half of them would be either sick, or otherwise *hors de combat*; and secondly, because schism and self-content so occupy the minds of Christians in England and Scotland, that really only a very small fraction of them have ever come to realise that the extension of Christ's kingdom is their DUTY AND PRIVILEGE ; and consequently

---

[*] Mackay was referring here to the tribes at the south of the lake, and not to the *Baganda*, who are vastly superior to the surrounding nations, and hundreds of whom have been brought to Christ.

the Church Missionary Society never succeeded in supplying even the vacancies at the existing stations.

The Moravians entered heartily into the undertaking ; but, alas ! the letters to Bishop Parker were returned, as he had already "gone home"; and Dr. Baur says : "When the Moravians again inquired of me if it would be advisable to commence a correspondence with Mackay on the matter, the sad news arrived that he also had entered into rest."

The station at Usambiro was very unhealthy, and several of the party suffered much from fever. Soon it became a diminished band, for within a fortnight the Bishop and Mr. Blackburn were called to higher service. There was no time to make coffins, as the natives objected to burial, so graves were hastily made, and the blessed dead were reverently wrapped in some beautiful bark cloth of Uganda manufacture. Necessity knows no law, and in order that the Christian porters, who had accompanied the Bishop from Freretown, might understand, Mackay, who alone of the mission band could speak their language, read the burial service, on both occasions, by the wish of his clerical brethren.

One day, Mackay received a letter from the King of Uganda, requesting him to "send on, at once, the new Muzungu who had accompanied Mr. Ashe from England." The gentleman in question was the Rev. R. H. Walker. The first day that the *Eleanor* was in port Mr. Walker bravely set out, and on arrival was received by Mwanga with great pomp, the petty tyrant believing he would thus inspire his guest with fear of the gigantic power of Uganda.

Mr. Ashe also was compelled to leave and to return to England, on account of his health, and once more Mackay was alone ; but he did not feel lonely, for he had more than enough to do, and hosts of natives were always crowding about him.

While in Uganda the missionaries were always more or less in fear of the authorities, but at the south end of the lake the great trial was inter-tribal wars. About this time there was a war scare at Usambiro, and Mackay had an anxious time, as the fighting lasted three days, and he had to arm himself and his men and prepare for being attacked, although he would willingly have paid an indemnity, if at all possible, to avert bloodshed. Happily the enemy, after a great blazing of gunpowder, were defeated by the chief of the place, and left. All Stanley's bales and boxes, which had been sent up country to Mackay's care, he had to secrete ; while the multitudes of bundles of beads, belonging to the Emin Relief Expedition, he stored high up among some rocks. The foe actually burnt the villages, and several were killed on both sides. Had the chief been defeated, who knows what would have become of the mission station ?

Meantime, strange events had happened in Uganda. Mwanga's robberies had raised general discontent, and matters came to a climax when his wicked plot was discovered, of trying to ship all his body-guard to a desert island in the Nyanza, and leave them there to die of starvation.

A new king was elected, and Mwanga fled to the lake, and all his women, of course, after him. Arriving there he found only five canoes, so that most of his harem had to be left behind. Soon, however, four canoes deserted, and there was only one left. Mwanga, with his thirty boys and six women, held on until they reached the Arab settlement of Magu, on the south coast of Speke Gulf. Thence he sent a letter to Mackay, imploring him " to come and take him away from the Arabs, who were fleecing him." Mackay felt very sorry for him, notwithstanding all his murders and persecutions, and sent him, on three occasions, cloth to buy food, and to wear. Mwanga begged Mackay to " forget bygone matters, and to restore him to his kingdom, and he would never be bad again ! " Again he sent urging Mackay to " take him to Europe, or anywhere he liked, or kill him if he chose." However, ultimately he managed to escape from Magu to the station of the French priests, who *baptised* him ; and by-and-by, after many humiliations, he was, "with loud and real rejoicing, carried shoulder-high from the lake to his former capital, and made kabaka once more ; only he was no longer the despotic master and murderer of the Christians, but a helpless instrument in their hands, or *they* occupied all the posts of authority."

But how had the noble missionaries Gordon and Walker been faring in Uganda? Mackay was most anxious about them, as he heard there had been another revolution, caused by the Mohammedans (who were determined to have no Christianity in the country), and was just starting to the French mission station for news of them, when he sighted the *Eleanor*; and, sure enough, his dear brethren were on board, but in strange plight, for, as Mr. Walker expressed it, "they had just been taken by the scruff of the neck and bundled out, but without their bundles!"

They had been imprisoned for a week in a wretched hut, where they had almost no food, and only a blanket each, and had to lie amid filth and vermin, while more than once they had reason to believe that they were about to be murdered. Writing to Mr. Ashe, Mackay says: "You know how we were often in the same state, and how it makes the hair turn grey."

Both missions (French and English) were sacked and plundered of everything by the authorities and the mob. Every book was torn from its back, every bottle emptied of medicine, everything else taken, struggled for, and destroyed, the doors wrenched off their hinges, and the C.M.S. house left a fearful wreck. Ultimately, they were all (French and English missionaries) pushed on board the *Eleanor*, with no food, and almost no clothing, and no bedding or tents, or

any protection from sun or rain. The evening they
set out they were shipwrecked, and five boys drowned,
but after much difficulty the boat was recovered and
patched by Mr. Walker, and the voyage continued.
The C.M.S. brethren had absolutely nothing with
which to buy food on the way; but the Frenchmen,
finding themselves, in more senses than one, "in the
same boat," showed them the greatest kindness and
shared everything with them.

Mr. Walker had been stripped of his coat, trousers,
and hat, before embarking, but he contrived to save
a blanket. Such is the fanaticism of Islam, that the
only two books he had saved, his Testament and
Prayer-Book, were snatched from him and thrown
into the lake.

After a little while, a great many Christians, who
had escaped from Uganda at the time of the revolution, found their way to the mission station at Usambiro. The Baganda are naturally lazy, but Mackay
made them work for their food and clothes. He ever
strove to instil into their minds, by his own example,
the importance and dignity of labour, and that idleness is quite inconsistent with the Christian life.

They were very eager to acquire mental knowledge,
while some of them were capital readers and of great
assistance in translation work. Mackay was also
teaching two of them to help in the printing office,
as he found there was no want of intelligence to
enable them to become rapid compositors in time.

While Mr. Gordon was with him, he was relieved of much teaching, and spent a good deal of time in the workshop. The *Eleanor* was becoming almost unseaworthy, and it was absolutely necessary to get another boat; but first a month had to be spent in the dripping forest (among long grass, taller than himself), felling and dressing trees for sawing, etc. On returning to the station, he found that a leopard had visited the goats' house every night for his supper, until thirty goats and calves had disappeared. So he made a strong stockade all round the mission premises, and built a huge trap by which he captured the animal.

But a day came when a reaction took place in Uganda; and at the urgent request of Mackay, Messrs. Gordon and Walker immediately started in canoes for the country whence they had been so summarily ejected a few months previously. Writing to Ashe, he says: "I have great hopes of them. They are good men and true, and we may be proud of them as our successors."

But what could have happened? A few hours after they left, Mackay despatched two men after them to fetch them back with all speed, but they failed to catch them up.

Something unusual must have taken place, for by dawn next morning all were early astir at the station, and great preparations were being made. A fat goat was killed and fresh bread baked, and every now and

again some one was sent to a point of vision to look.
At last Mackay went himself, and behold, in the
distance a great caravan!   On went a white linen suit
and white felt hat, and off he set to welcome the
Emin Relief Expedition, including Mr. Stanley,
Emin Pasha and daughter, Signor Casati, Signor
Marco (a Greek), Signor Vita Hassan (from Tunis),
Lieut. Stairs, Captain Nelson, Dr. Parke, Mr. Jephson,
and Mr. W. Bonny; together with four hundred
Soudanese, three hundred and fifty Zanzibaris, and
a hundred *Manyuema*, who were, however, no longer
cannibals.

Writing to Sir Francis De Winton, Mr. Stanley
says :—

"C.M.S. Station at Msalala, South end of Lake Victoria,
East Central Africa.

"*August* 31*st*, 1889.

" My dear De Winton,—We arrived here on the
28th inst., and found the modern Livingstone, Mr.
A. M. Mackay, safely and comfortably established at
this mission station.   I had always admired Mackay.
He had never joined in the missionaries' attacks on
me, and every fact I had heard about him indicated
that I should find him an able and reliable man.
When I saw him and some of his work, about here,
then I recognised the man I had pleaded, in the name
of Mtesa, should be sent to him in 1875, the very
type of man I had described as necessary to confirm
Mtesa in his growing love for the white man's creed."

Dr. Baur, referring to the testimony of some other members of the Expedition, says : " I remember also with great pleasure hearing Casati say : ' When I shook hands with Mackay he appeared to me to be the man my imagination had pictured : gentlemanly in his bearing, outspoken, but without harshness ; clever-looking, high-minded, scanty of words. Death took away in him, soon after our arrival at the coast, a life which, with noble greatness of soul, was devoted to the salvation and civilisation of his fellow-men.' "

Twenty days the Expedition rested from their long and arduous journey, and the society of so many gentlemen was a great enjoyment to Mackay.

On the 17th of September they all departed, and he walked part of the way with them and wished them God-speed, waving his hat till they were out of sight.   As one has said, " Stanley and his party came home to European platforms and royal receptions ; the lonely missionary went to the Palace of the King of kings ! "

Stanley and his officers all urged Mackay to accompany them to Europe ; the Church Missionary Society had invited him, time after time ; his friends continued to plead with him to return home to recruit, but in vain. He would not quit his post until re-inforcements arrived. Whether he had any presenti-ment that a call would soon come which he could not disobey, is not clear ; but during the next four months, amidst his multitudinous duties of teaching the Baganda refugees, drugging, printing, translating, together with the laborious work of the new steam launch he had on hand, his spirit seems to have been greatly exercised about the half-heartedness of Christians at home, towards the claims of missions, especially of African missions, which are languishing for lack of aid.

His heart was gladdened by the news that Christianity was again established in Uganda, and he sent home a ringing appeal to Christian England, saying that the Continental idea of *" every citizen a soldier "* is the true watchword for Christian missions, for that the King's command is " GO YE," not *Send !*

He says : " Eagerly I long for a strong batch of good men for the work, and, Oh for a bishop !

" Our people are most urgent that we should plant stations all over Uganda, not merely at the capital, and no one will hinder us *if we only had the men.* The Roman Catholics have already sent five men in, and many more will follow. Where is the great Church of England, and the greatest of Missionary Societies ? "

About this time he writes : " I have been toiling at the forge and lathe, and have got our steam arrangements far on to completion. The three-cylinder engine and two steam pumps and injector stand all ready fitted for the boiler. The main boiler-shell is also carefully jointed and riveted together, and so is the fire-box. But that has been a most serious job, as all these years of knocking about have thrown all the shells terribly out of shape, as well as rendering them *steely* and brittle. Many new parts had to be made, and rivets also by the hundred, as these were mostly lost ; but the most of that work is now done, although a good deal remains to complete it to my satisfaction. High-pressure steam is not a thing to play with, and unless every part is carefully calculated for strength, and exactly fitted, there may be accidents, for which I would be responsible."

But one morning, early in February 1890, " the din of the iron hammer was hushed, the glare of the furnace faded, the last blast of the bellows was blown," and all was still within the little stockade, save for the silent footsteps of his Baganda pupils, flitting in and out with awe-stricken faces. Why is this? Where is Mackay? But yesterday he was busy packing for, and assisting his colleague, Mr. Deekes, to go home to England ; and now he himself lies delirious on the bed where Bishop Parker breathed his last. The worst was feared, but no help could be obtained. No more dangers, or trials, or sorrows, or hopes deferred, or fitful fevers for the faithful missionary. Four days more of delirium, and on the 8th of the month the summons came, " Enter thou into the joy of thy Lord."

May his life and example stimulate and inspire many to live unselfish lives in the same living faith of a living Saviour !

Letter from Mr. David Deckes.

"USAMBIRO, CENTRAL AFRICA, *Oct.* 14*th*, 1890.

"DEAR DR. MACKAY,—Your letter dated June 4th reached me a few days ago. I am sorry I was not able to give you a more detailed account of your son's death, but I was so ill at the time of writing that what I did write was written with great difficulty. Thank God, my health has improved, and I now feel better able to write you the particulars of that sad event.

"From the time I first met Mr. Mackay, which was about two years previous to his death, he has invariably enjoyed good health ; he would occasionally have an attack of fever, generally preceded by a cold, but never any bad attack.

"At the time Mr. Stanley and his party passed here, and for some time after, in fact right up to within a few days of his death, he was as jovial and well as I have ever known him to be. He thoroughly enjoyed Mr. Stanley's visit, and was always referring to it ; even when delirious he would again and again ask me if Mr. Stanley and his party were being properly entertained and made comfortable.

"The first symptom of fever was an ordinary cold in the head, which he got, I think, when working down in the workshed on the boiler of the steamer he was making for the Nyanza. From early morning right up to sunset he would be at work, and after the

evening meal he would sit with the Baganda Christians (there were several here at that time), and
translate the Scriptures.　He was then doing St.
John's Gospel, which I think Mr. Gordon has since
finished; he also held a reading-class at midday,
whilst the workmen were having their dinner.　I have
often advised him to give up something and rest
a little (I was not able to do any part of his work
myself, not having the mechanical skill, and not
knowing the Luganda language); but he would say
' the great secret of health in Africa was keeping
oneself fully employed.'

"I agree with him; but I cannot help thinking
he overdid it, and that the heavy, laborious work in
which he was engaged in a draughty workshed was
to a great extent the cause of his last illness.　He had
been unwell with a cold, as I have said before, but
this did not hinder him from making arrangements
for me to leave for England.　The day had come
for my departure, and I was ready to say good-bye,
when on entering his room I found him on the bed
in the hot stage of fever.　I could not leave my
brother missionary alone in this condition, therefore
at once I dismissed the men who were engaged to
carry my loads, and decided to wait a few days
longer.　On the morrow, however, he became delirious,
and continued so for four days, when he expired.
Strange to say, all his remarks during the time of
unconsciousness were made in English.　At times

he was somewhat violent, and threatened to leave the house and go and sleep in the forest.

"I had a coffin made of the wood he had cut for the boat, and at 2 p.m. on the Sunday I buried him by the side of the late Bishop Parker. The Baganda Christians and the boys of the village stood around the grave, and I began to read the burial service, but broke down with grief and weakness. The boys and Baganda Christians sang the hymn, 'All hail the power of Jesus' name,' in Luganda, and we returned to the house. Never shall I forget that day, and many others that followed it. I did miss my friend so much; tears come to my eyes when I think of those sad days. I prayed that God would spare me that I might hold the post till others came, and this He has been pleased to do, inasmuch as Bishop Tucker and his party are now within three weeks' march of this place, and my health remains good.

"A few days ago his Excellency Dr. Emin passed here. Mr. Walker, who was here at that time, accompanied him to the grave of our dear brother. His Excellency did not leave the grave without shedding a tear and taking away a small piece of stone on the grave. He said 'he had lost a great friend, but he rejoiced that there was a hope of meeting him again.'

"It is hard for us to realise God's purpose in taking away such a valuable servant, when by us he was so much needed, but God knows best and doeth all things well.

" May we who are left follow the example of those who have gone before, in using our time well in the service of our Lord. His Excellency Dr. Emin has taken three things belonging to the late Mr. Mackay, for which he has given me a receipt, which I enclose in this letter.

" With kind regards to the members of your family,

" I remain, dear sir, yours very sincerely,

" DAVID DEEKES, C.M.S."

On April 2nd, 1890, a messenger arrived at the mission station in Uganda, with the news :—" Mackay is dead, and Deekes is dying." Next morning the Rev. R. H. Walker started for Usambiro, but, owing to vexatious delays in getting canoes, and rough weather on the voyage, he did not reach the south end of the lake till the 18th of May. He writes :— " Deekes is much better, I am thankful to say. Poor dear Mackay! I wish I could have been here to nurse him a bit. Deekes was helplessly ill himself, and sent off to Bukumbi to the French priests to help him, but ere the good Samaritan came our dear friend had died. Unavoidably, he was a bit neglected. I do not know what could have done him good, but I should have liked to have tried."

CHAPTER XXI.

THE IRON HORSE.

"When the Indian trail gets widened, graded, and bridged to a good road, there is a benefactor, there is a missionary, a pacificator, a wealth-bringer, a maker of markets, a vent for industry."

R. W. EMERSON.

MACKAY believed that a railway from the coast to the lake would prove a mighty power in opening up the great interior, as it would benefit the natives, in a just way, at every step, and enable missions to be worked at an enormous reduction of life and expenditure.

The following article, under a different heading, was written nearly three years ago, but was mislaid, and consequently never published. His views about a railway, of very light construction, were quite assented to by Stanley, who promised to do all in his power to persuade Sir William Mackinnon, of the " Imperial British East African Company," of the necessity of it. This railway is now commenced, and will do much to develop not only missionary enterprise, but legitimate trade. The fame of honest Christian traders will soon spread far and wide among the natives, and white men will rapidly gain a footing, firm and sure and friendly, to the exclusion of dishonest Mohammedan dealers.

By the formation of a railway the slave trade will cease, and merchants will be able to forward their ivory and native produce very quickly to the coast, and at a far cheaper rate than by the old barbarous system of porterage. Arabs have never learned, and probably never will learn, to adopt even wheeled vehicles; hence it will be an easy matter to outwit them, by selling cloth and other European goods, in the far interior, at a price far below what they can afford to do it for.

A regular mail service, which the railway will inaugurate, will be an indescribable boon to the isolated missionaries. The climate, and the everlasting sameness in food, help to bring on anæmia, and its many evil consequences. Two meals a day—plantains and boiled goat's flesh, frequently without the goat's flesh—tend to monotony and loss of appetite. At such times a fresh mail, bringing good news of loved ones at home, a newspaper, or a new book, acts like a tonic; hope returns, and the Lord's work is carried on with renewed vigour.

The merchants, too, will be kept constantly aware of the market value of ivory, etc., and thereby save themselves from loss.

Mackay says : " Unquestionably it is now high time to introduce a radical change in the present method of trying to penetrate into the interior of this continent. Probably the English public is little aware of the appalling number of failures which have occurred from the rough-and-ready system of employing human beings as beasts of burden, or of the efforts already made to introduce a more rational means of transport. A brief enumeration of some of the most lamentable instances of failure in East African expeditions may serve to deter others from continuing the old method, while a knowledge of experiments already tried to use animal power in the same region, may help to prevent useless waste of money in making fresh trials of the same kind.

"It is now fully a dozen years since, on my first journey into the interior from the Zanzibar coast, I pointed out that *the* difficulty of African travel arose, not from the physical nature of the country, nor from the character of the natives, but from the barbarous and inhuman method of employing porters. In Africa a hill is no more to climb than one in England, nor are the forests harder to penetrate than is the Schwartzwald. Along the well-watered banks of the Upper Congo dense ' black forests ' undoubtedly exist, and would prove a sore hindrance to land transit, but these regions are, on the other hand, accessible by water. Generally, however, the vast area of East Africa, from Nyassa to the Nyanza, presents one unbroken piece of open jungle, sparsely wooded with dwarf trees and bushes, presenting little difficulty, except in the wet season, to the passage of pack animals or vehicles. The natives everywhere carry on their own shoulders any articles they wish to transport from place to place ; the Arabs, ignorant of wheels, have only too readily adopted the same method ; but that can be no excuse for Europeans casting aside all the resources of civilisation at the coast, and adopting native or Arab barbarity the moment they enter the interior. Explorers penetrating the region of the unknown, and eager only to cover long distances, may be excused for declining to hamper themselves with heavy wagons, or animals the life of which they are not sure of. Now the case is entirely changed. The physical features of the whole continent are to-day pretty well known. Only limited portions require mapping in detail. Travellers now demand means of transporting goods, in large quantities, for consumption at stations in the far interior. This renders quite inexcusable the continued adoption of a method ever fraught with enormous inconveniences to even the lightly-equipped explorer.

"Early in the year 1876 the two great missionary bodies, the Church Missionary Society and the London Missionary Society, undertook the task of planting stations in the centre of the continent; the former on the Victoria Lake, the latter on the Tanganyika. The directors of both Societies, fully conscious of the cruelty attending the use of porters, at once resolved to try bullock-wagons, which are widely used in South Africa. But, as in most undertakings by white men in Africa, the desire for haste overcame other considerations. The Church Missionary Society sent up their first parties with the goods on men's shoulders. Only two hundred miles from the coast all the porters mutinied and left, but were subsequently persuaded to return ; four hundred miles farther on they again threw down their loads and departed finally. The leader, Lieut. Shergold Smith, after spending months collecting fresh porters, was able to make another start, but only with worse result. 'The porters deserted by fifties daily,' he wrote, 'and after a stormy passage, our expedition arrived at the lake *a perfect wreck.'* Shortly afterwards, a caravan of supplies was sent up to the relief of the men, all but starving at Kagei, under an Englishman of many years' experience with natives ; but he too was deserted by all his carriers about half-way to the lake. Year after year renewed efforts were made to forward men and supplies to the Nyanza, generally with similar results. One leader of a Church Missionary Society caravan, an Englishman named Penrose, was attacked by robbers in the jungle ; his two hundred porters threw down their loads and fled, leaving their leader to be butchered and all the property to be destroyed.

"The London Missionary Society suffered similar losses through the mutiny and desertion of their porters, although subsequently some of their caravans,

as also some of the Church Missionary Society, were
fortunate in reaching their destination, but in no case
that I am aware of without serious losses.

" The case of the Abbé De Baize was particularly
painful. Subsidised by the French Government, he
started from Zanzibar with about a thousand followers,
intending to cross Africa ; but by the time he reached
Ujiji, his great company had melted away, and there
the Abbé died of disappointment. Little better
success attended the numerous expeditions of the
African International Association, mostly led by Bel-
gian officers. Their losses, by mutiny and desertion,
were even greater than those experienced by the other
Europeans. I need not detail more instances. The
story of the trials of the Romish missionaries, of
travellers like Reichard and Giraud, and others, reveals
only the same tale of disaster and failure—all owing
to the barbarous employment of a mob of more or
less savage blacks as burden-bearers.

" Meantime, the missionary societies were active
with experiments in a different direction. One agent
of the Church Missionary Society was appointed, early
in 1877, to clear a track through the bush as far as
Mpwapwa, with only a force of fifty axes ; this was
accomplished without difficulty. The line followed
was the valley of the Wami river, and its tributary
the Mkondokwa. The length cut was two hundred
and thirty miles, and the time occupied only three
months. The London Missionary Society soon after-

wards landed at Sadani about a dozen strong English wagons, and teams of draught oxen and skilled bullock-drivers from Natal. Scores and scores of oxen were purchased on the spot and trained to *trek*. A Swiss trader—Philip Broyon—followed with heavy teams and tire-wheeled vehicles. The Church Missionary Society brought teak carts from Bombay, and got others made in Zanzibar. Oxen were purchased and trained, and what was more difficult still, Zanzibaris were trained to manage the teams. For a while all worked well. The caravans of wheeled vehicles followed each other up country in quick succession. But before one hundred miles of way were covered, the whole four hundred oxen, bought at $20 per head, and broken in with much labour, succumbed to the bite of the *tsetse* fly, and the wagons had to be abandoned. Thus terminated for the time all experiments to introduce the use of oxen in place of human porters. Yet, all the way along, in most of the villages, large herds of cattle are to be found. It is the reach of jungle between the native clearings that is full of the fatal fly.

"The next effort to use animal power was made by his Majesty the King of the Belgians. His expedition, under the leadership of Captains Carter and Cadenhead, left Dar es Salaam for Tanganyika with three fine Indian elephants. The baggage of the party was far in excess of what the elephants could carry, and porters were sought in addition. As these were

not speedily* forthcoming, the Englishmen, with characteristic impatience of delay, piled on the elephants
double their customary load.   As was to be expected,
the animals broke down, and ultimately all died.
The white men themselves were subsequently killed
in a native war, and no further trials were made with
Indian elephants ; although I feel safe in saying that,
had the animals got justice, the experiment with
them would have proved a clear success.

" *Mules* have been tried, by both the French and
English missions ; but, for some reason or other, they,
as well as native donkeys, have always died on the
road.   The Church Missionary Society has also tried
to use *camels* in the coast region, but the result was
failure—probably owing to the dampness of the
climate.   It will be remembered that Livingstone
(ever harassed by the 'intrigues of deserters') took
with him, on his last journey inland, camels, buffaloes,
mules and donkeys, almost all of which died, unmis-
takably of *tsetse* bite, although their end was hastened
by overloading, bad treatment, and bad weather.

" The question will readily be asked, ' Is there no
specific against the *tsetse ?* '   The natives have preventives of their own, but to what extent they succeed
I cannot say.   Certain it is that cattle are constantly
driven from village to village with apparent impunity,
although realms of the 'fly' lie between, while every
year herds of cattle are taken by the Wanyamwesi to
the coast : but these are purchased there chiefly for

A MASAI WARRIOR

[*p.* 273

slaughter. I am not aware that any survive the journey more than a few months. As to remedies or preventives, Livingstone tells of lion's fat being rubbed on the root of the tail of the cattle, while some have made the amusing suggestion of daubing the horses' nostrils with nitrate of silver, not knowing that it is not the nostrils only, but the whole body of the animal which is bitten!

"Our party tried petroleum, which seemed to be effective, for a time at least. Failure in the supply of that article prevented its continued application ; and as all our oxen subsequently died, I cannot say how far the oil was of real service at all.

"Almost any animal will draw twice as great a load as it will carry ; hence vehicles should be used wherever possible. Oxen, mules, camels and donkeys will, I fear, never succeed, except about a station, or in particularly favourable and limited regions. Camels might be used for crossing the desert between Mombasa and Kilimanjaro, or on the sandy plains of Ugogo, but certainly not in damp regions. Donkeys might do well in the Masai country, especially if procured there, and not imported from a district where they have been accustomed to different conditions. There seems also to be no reason why African buffaloes should not be proof against the *tsetse.* The failure of the three *imported* by Livingstone affords no proof to the contrary. The African jungles are swarming with buffaloes, and skill and patience seem alone to be needed to turn these animals to the service of man. But on all soils and in all seasons *elephants* will, I believe, prove the most reliable for either burden or draught. If brought from India their cost will be considerable, but that will be to some extent compensated for by their marvellous longevity. They are said not to breed in confinement, yet one of the three elephants of Captain Carter's Expedition bore a young one in Unyamwesi. Skilful hands will know how to use their Indian elephants to decoy and tame those of Africa itself. General Gordon foresaw the value of the African elephant, if trained, and actually had four Indian ones taken up to the Equatorial province, with a view to having others. What became of these when the Soudan was abandoned to barbarism, I do not know. Perhaps the best way to check the rapid extinction of the elephant in Africa, and at the same time to lessen the ivory trade, which is the *root* of all the ills of this Dark Continent, will be to encourage the natives to capture the animals alive. These will fetch an enormously greater price than the bare tusks, and I have generally found the African ready to turn to that by which he will get most money. It seems ridiculous to go on extirpating such useful animals merely for their teeth.

" But elephant, buffalo, or whatever animal power is found most suitable, the use of them can never be regarded as more than *auxiliary* to the only power which will ever effectually bring the light ot civilisation into the heart of Africa—the iron horse. Let the British and German East African Companies pursue a daring and persistent policy, as the Russians are doing in Central Asia, and carry a skeleton line of rail to the Nyanza and Tanganyika, respectively. A dash to Wadelai by either party will never amount to much. Treaties made by a flying brigade are a farce; but a policy of 'governing as they go,' and establishing cheap and fairly rapid communication with their remotest stations, will well repay any initial outlay. No finely measured gradients nor even much solidity will be needed in the first instance. The roughest conceivable track, with light pit rails, and only temporary bridges, would prove an inestimable boon to Central Africa, and develop the resources of this continent far beyond the most sanguine expectations of its well-wishers.

" A. M. MACKAY,
" *C.M.S. Missionary.*

"USAMBIRO, VICTORIA NYANZA,
"*January* 1889."

CHAPTER XXII.

BISHOP TUCKER IN UGANDA.

"Onward, ye men of prayer!
Scatter in rich exuberance the seed,
Whose fruit is living bread, and all your need
    Will God supply; His harvest ye shall share.
        *   *   *   *   *
"And thou, O Church, betake
Thyself to watching, labour—help these men :
God shall thee visit of a surety, when
    Thou'rt faithful : Church that Jesus bought awake, awake !"
                        W. B. TAPPAN.

WHEN the telegram reached England announcing that Mackay had gone to his rest, Bishop Tucker, the third bishop of East Equatorial Africa, was just setting out with six earnest young men for Uganda.   Through the goodness of God, he has been spared, after encountering many perils, to return again to England ; and as his speech, at his reception at Exeter Hall, is a wonderful picture of what God hath wrought in Uganda, it is given below.

The six lay evangelists whom the Bishop set apart for Christ's service are : Sembera Mackay, Henry Wright Duta, Mika Sematimba, Paulo Bakunga, Zachariah Kizito, and Yohana Mwira.

The three first refused chieftainships from Mwanga, after his restoration to his kingdom, in order that they might be free to become teachers and preachers of the Gospel.

Sembera was Mackay's first convert in Uganda, and was the first native baptised in that country, nearly ten years ago (see p. 223). One day he brought Mackay a note, written by himself with a " pointed piece of spear-grass and some ink of dubious manufacture." It ran thus—" Bwana (Mr.) Mackay : Sembera has come with compliments and to give you great news. Will you baptise him, because he believes the words of Jesus Christ ? " He was a most diligent pupil, and not only did he read everything Mackay put into his hand, but he taught his master, who was one of Mtesa's great chiefs, to read also. His master received the truth, and was also afterwards baptised.

Sembera was a member of the Church Council, and presided over a little congregation in the country during the reign of terror, when it was unsafe to assemble at the mission-house.

He and Mika Sematimba have led all along most exemplary lives, and Mr. Walker describes them as " thorough gentlemen." Sembera was sent for by Mackay to Usambiro to assist him in translating the gospels ; and, after the death of the latter, he sent a most touching appeal to Mr. Ashe, imploring him to go back to Uganda.

Mr. Ashe responded by taking a hasty farewell of his friends, and starting with a party of zealous men, in May of this year.

Regarding Zachariah, Mackay, writing in April 1887, says: "I have advised him to escape also, as Mwanga is watching for him. Much I would like him to get to Mombasa, for instruction and ordination. He would make a good native pastor. Possibly he may get to Wadelai, and thence find his way to the coast by another route."

SPEECH OF BISHOP TUCKER.

"Dear Sir John Kennaway, and my very dear friends: I am simply overwhelmed with the warm and hearty welcome which you have given me on my return from Uganda. To say 'Thank you' seems such a cold way of expressing the depth of gratitude which I feel; but still it is all that I can say, and I do say it from the very depths of my heart. I thank you, Sir John, for those very kind and loving words spoken in regard to myself; I thank you, Mr. Wigram, for those equally kind words to which you have given utterance; and I thank you, dear friends, for the hearty endorsement given to them. But I desire above everything, in returning thanks to you, to remember the great fact that thanks are due to our Heavenly Father for having brought me back in health and strength. I ask you to believe that in all that I shall say to-night—and I may have to speak a good deal about myself—I do not wish to magnify myself; I desire above everything the glory of God. Permit me to say, in the first place, that I stand here in a certain sense in a threefold character. First of all, as a living monument of God's protecting and preserving love ; secondly, as a witness for Christ ; and thirdly, as an advocate for those who cannot speak for themselves. In other words, I stand here to-night as one delivered on more than one occasion from what seemed to be impending death ; in the second place, as one who has to tell of the marvellous acts of the Lord, and of the great things that He has done for the children of men in the heart of Darkest Africa ; and thirdly, as one who has to plead with man for God and for those for whom Christ died in that far-off land.

"First of all, I cannot do better than commence at that part of our journey when we reached the south end of the lake. On October 17th last, I first saw the Victoria Nyanza. There, gleaming in the full blaze of an African sun, lay the waters of the lake. Seen under such an aspect it can never be forgotten ; stretching from east to west as far as the eye can reach, like a shield of burnished silver. As I stood there, I thought of those who had gone before, to whom reference has been made to-night. I thought of the lion-hearted Hannington, and of the meek and lowly Parker. There they lay, one by the side of

the noble Mackay, and the other low in his grave in
the east. And irresistibly the thought rushed into
my mind—Will it ever be mine to cross that vast
expanse of water, and to do that work in Uganda
which they so longed to do, and for which they were
so pre-eminently fitted? Then came the words of
him who has lately passed to his rest :—

> " 'Keep thou my feet : I do not ask to see
> The distant scene, one step enough for me.

" My first experience of a canoe was not a pleasant
one. The water came in, and continued to come in
almost as fast as we could bale it out. However,
' all's well that ends well,' and by putting an extra
hand at baling we reached the opposite shore in
safety. In an hour we were at the mission station at
Usambiro, and received a hearty welcome from our
friend in charge there. It was then that I learnt, to
my intense disappointment, that the mission boat
had started some ten days previously for Uganda.
To say I was disappointed does but express very
inadequately the depth of regret I felt, when I saw
that in all probability for something like two months
we should have to stay at Usambiro ; but the delay
was unavoidable, and Mr. Hooper and I started off
to visit Nassa, a place some hundred miles away, to
inspect the work there. After spending about three
weeks in this way, interrupted by two attacks of
fever, we returned.

"On approaching the mission station at Usambiro, after having lost our way in a wood at dead of night, and wandering for hours we knew not whither, I was startled on being told by a native, whom we had taken as our guide, that one of the white men had died that day. Who was it? Was it Pilkington? No; dear Hunt had passed to his eternal rest. Verily, the clouds had commenced to lower. Dunn and Baskerville were down with fever ; and while I lay in one room suffering from fever, dear Dunn—one of the most devoted, earnest Christian men I had ever met —passed away. How can I tell you of the grief that possessed my soul, as one blow after another thus came down upon us ? As I lay there in the early morning of the day when dear Dunn was laid to rest, there came the words to my comfort, ' For ever with the Lord.' In a little while Hooper became very ill —he had never been so ill ; and with myself, one attack of fever succeeded another, until at last I was reduced to a state of much weakness and debility. At length hope commenced to fail, and despair—no, I won't say that, I don't think despair ever possessed the hearts of any one of us ; we remembered the word specially given to us, ' Lo, I am with you alway,' and despair never took possession of our souls. But most providentially, at that moment a cry was raised, ' The boat has come ! ' Oh, how our hearts leapt for joy, and how we thanked and praised God ; for I verily believe, had it been delayed for any considerable period, that it would hardly have found one of us left to tell the tale in Uganda. At length, on December 4th, we started. I was carried to the boat in a state of blindness and weakness. Baskerville and Pilkington were only just able to walk to the place of embarkation ; but in the course of a few days we picked up wonderfully—the fresh air revived us. Our strength was renewed, and our spirits quickly rose.

"There came next a very wonderful deliverance. Shall I tell you of it ? Yes, because I am to tell you, for one thing, of God's preserving love. We were sailing with a fair wind, but there were signs of a coming storm. The thunder was behind us, and dark clouds were crowding up ; the water was becoming disturbed. The boatmen thought it a good thing to spread the awning, a most dangerous thing to do under the circumstances. The mainsail, instead of being held loosely in the hand, was tied to the side of the boat. Hooper shouted, 'Loose the sheet !' but before the words were out of his mouth the storm struck us. The boat heeled over in such a manner that it seemed utterly impossible she could right herself again ; but just at that moment, most providentially, the sail gave way, it split, and we were saved. Had it not done so, it is almost a matter of absolute certainty we should all have gone down like a stone. I wish to say here, with a very great deal of emphasis, that if you wish to preserve your missionaries—and from what I know of your missionaries in Eastern Equatorial Africa, I may tell you they are worth preserving,—I say if you would save your missionaries from such perils as this, you must first of all give us something like safe navigation on the lake. I am thankful to know that, until a steamer is there, the Committee have done the next best thing, in providing a steel boat. In a few weeks she will set out for the East Coast of Africa. Let me also impress upon you another matter which concerns the safety of the missionaries, and that is the construction of the railway. Do your utmost to assist that scheme, for by so doing you will not only preserve your missionaries from great dangers, such as we encountered in Ugogo, to which I have not time to make further reference, but you will be doing a great work in opening up that vast country, in developing its great resources, while you will also be assisting towards the evangelisation of the natives and the extension of Christ's kingdom.

" Let me turn to my second point, and that is, to tell you of God's work of grace in the hearts of the people of Uganda. After paying a visit to Emin Pasha on the western shore, we approached the confines of the country of Uganda, and it was truly wonderful the evidence we saw from day to day, as we camped, of the intense desire of the people for Christian instruction. Within a few minutes of our landing, quite a crowd came about, and those who had books would bring them and ask to be further instructed, whilst those who had none begged and implored us to give them some. Mr. Pilkington, who was the only one able to speak the language of Uganda, would frequently have within a few minutes quite a crowd round about him, who would be engaged in learning and repeating texts of Scripture ; and by simply giving notice that in an hour or so a service would be held, some fifty or more would come together for prayer, etc. Of course all this filled us with great hope, and increased our impatience to reach the capital. At length, after many delays caused by light and variable winds, on the twenty-third day of sailing, and on December 27th, we reached the capital. And how shall I tell of that warm welcome given to us by the natives of the Church and by brethren Walker and Gordon, who for so long have so nobly held the fort ? The natives came in crowds to see us day by day. The day after our arrival was Sunday, and on that day it was my great and glorious privilege to stand up in the midst of a congregation, which Mr. Gordon assured me numbered something like a thousand souls, to speak to them of God's great redeeming and sanctifying love. This congregation was not an unusual one. Every Sunday a church, built by themselves, is simply crowded from end to end. A little after sunrise you hear the tramp of many feet. What can it be ? Why, the people are coming in crowds to the house of God ; and there they sit, either singly or in groups, reading their Testaments and Prayer-books, and being taught by the better-instructed among themselves. It is a great feature of the work in Uganda that the people teach one another. There are numbers of Christians in the country who have learned to read and have learned to know Christ, who have never been taught by any white man at all. And there these informal Bible-classes are held until nine o'clock, and then the time for native service in Luganda arrives : a drum is beaten, instead of a bell being rung, and the service commences. A hymn is sung, with remarkable accuracy and power. How shall I describe the fervour and heartiness of the responses? Surely they approach more nearly the description given of the responses of the Primitive Church than anything I have ever heard either in Africa or England. The people disperse until three in the afternoon, when another service is held. The congregation at that service is not so large as in the morning, but still from five hundred to eight hundred people come together for prayer and praise.

"On my arrival in Uganda, I arranged for a confirmation. The classes were held daily, and it was very wonderful indeed to note how, as time went on, hearts were touched and consciences moved. First one man and then another would come to his teacher, and say they could not wish for confirmation with sin unconfessed and wrong not set right. One of the

most touching incidents was that of a man standing
up in the midst of the congregation, and professing
sorrow for sin, praying to be received back into
Christian fellowship and privileges ; also begging the
prayers of the brethren that he might be kept faithful
for the future.   I shall never to my dying day forget,
in the name of the congregation, receiving that man
back again into Christian fellowship and privileges.
He was one of seventy who, on January 18th, received
the rite of confirmation at my hands.

"I now come to an event fraught, I trust, with
great hope for the future in the development of the
work in Uganda—the setting apart of six earnest
Christians as lay evangelists. Some of these men
had passed through the scorching fires of persecution.
Some confessed Christ at the peril of their lives. One
or two, like Henry Wright Duta, had turned their
backs on such worldly advancement as a chieftainship
offered to them, esteeming, like Moses, ' the reproach
of Christ to be greater riches than the treasures of
Egypt.' On January 20th these men were set apart,
in the presence of a large congregation, for the work
of lay evangelists. They will be supported entirely
by the native Church ; and they will I trust, be
trained in such a way that in God's own time they
may become ordained ministers of Christ's Church.
I am bound to say that I look on this band of earnest
men with the greatest possible hope. I know the peculiar aptitude of the people of Uganda for teaching,

and it is the greatest desire of the most intelligent among them to be teachers. And so, in looking forward to the future, I seem to see in these men the messengers, not only to their own country, but to 'regions beyond,' spreading the glad tidings of salvation north and south, east and west, labouring and striving for the extension of Christ's kingdom in the countries of Africa now lying in darkness and in the shadow of death. On that memorable 20th of January those six lay evangelists, together with the seventy who had been confirmed on the 18th, and the European missionaries, all gathered round the Table of the Lord, to commemorate His dying love, by partaking of the elements of His body broken and His blood shed. That was a happy day, although I was down with fever before it was over. What joy to kneel with those dusky brethren and sisters, and with heart and soul repeat that wonderful prayer of self-consecration, ' Here we offer and present unto Thee, O Lord, ourselves, our souls and bodies, to be a reasonable, holy, and lively sacrifice ; humbly beseeching Thee, that we who are partakers of this Holy Communion may be filled with Thy heavenly benediction '! And then, what joy to rise up and say, ' Glory be to God on high, on earth peace, good will to men ! '

" In letters I have alluded to the great love of reading possessed by the people of Uganda. A man will very readily do three months' work for a New

Testament. 'A sister of the late king Mtesa for
several days came to see me, but sat in my room
almost in silence. She was naturally a very taciturn
woman, but at last she summoned up courage enough
to ask if she could have a New Testament. Happily
we had one, and she purchased it—for we believe in
selling our books ; we believe the people value them
when they buy them—and it was remarkable the
change that came over that woman as she got her
new possession. She smiled, she laughed, she clapped
her hands, and I almost thought she would sing ; but,
at any rate, she told us that her spirit was singing
within her for joy. On another occasion a man
named Benjamin came to me with a Testament in
his hand, but he asked if I would give him another.
I said, ' You have one.' ' Ah ! ' he said, ' this one is so
injured that I can only read a part of it.' I asked to
be allowed to see it ; and, true enough, it was greatly
injured. I asked how this had happened. ' Well,'
he said, ' when I went to war against the Mohammedans, I took my book with me, and I wrapped it
in my cloth here. In the fight a bullet struck it, and
it has pierced it nearly through. It saved my life.
I love it very much ; but can you give me another ? '
I told him, ' I have only one, and that is my own ;
but,' I said, ' if you will give me your book, I will give
you mine.' The exchange was made ; I received the
shattered book, and here it is, and I need not say that
I look on that book as one of my greatest treasures.

Verily it is the sign of God's preserving love, as well as of that man's love for the Word of the living God.

"At length, after a conference with the French priests as to the unhappy differences existing between the two parties, Catholics and Protestants—a difference, I hope, that is happily arranged—the time came for leaving Uganda. It was with a very deep sigh that I said good-bye to those warm-hearted Christian men and women. They accompanied us in large numbers along the road, the last good-bye was said, the last ' God be with you, God bless you ! ' was uttered, and Hooper and I were alone to face the journey to the coast. We marched down to the place of embarkation, where we had our luggage. We were astir before sunrise. The purple blush of the dawn was brightening when there came, on the stillness of the morning air, a sound which stirred our souls to the very depth. What was it ? From some little distance, from a native hut which we could see but dimly in the half-light, there came a voice from one pleading with God in prayer, and then, after awhile, came the responsive ' Amen ' of several voices, then a single voice was heard again, then another response ; then all was still and silent. In a few minutes, from the other side, from another hut, there was heard a voice engaged in pleading prayer ; then came the response, then once more all was still. What was the meaning of it ? Why, these were the voices of men and women—and, mark it, Christian men and women—engaged before sunrise in family worship. (Applause.) They were men and women who only a few years ago were living in all the darkness of heathendom. Could we, I ask, as we stood there on the Uganda shore for the last time, could we have had a more touching proof of God's work of grace in the hearts of the people, and of the power of the everlasting Gospel to change men's minds, turning them from darkness to light, and from the power of sin and Satan unto God?

" And now I come to my third point—*my plea.* I am told that certain critics are asking why I have come home. I might plead, and I think not unfairly, the great physical, but particularly the great mental, strain of the last twelve months, a mental strain which I pray that none of my critics may be called upon to bear. But I will not plead it. Thank God, I have no need to plead it. I have come to plead for those who cannot plead for themselves. I have come to plead for millions of souls in East Africa, committed to my charge, who are living without God and without hope in the world. I have not come to plead, as I might, I think, in all modesty do, for a thousand missionaries ; I have not come to plead for a hundred ; I only plead for forty, and I pledge my word to those critics who ask why I have come home that, if they will only give me these forty missionaries to-night, I will go home to Mombasa to-morrow.

(Loud applause.) My brother, may I plead with you? Your work is what? To glorify God. You are called upon to glorify God in your spirit, and you must, in fact, glorify Him there before you can glorify Him elsewhere. What God requires is nothing less than entire consecration to Himself of all you are. He says, ' My son, give Me thy heart,' and by the heart He means all the powers, all the affections of your manhood. Therefore, I say, He calls upon you to consecrate to Him all the powers of your nature—your mental faculties, your understanding, your memory, your imagination, your physical power, your strength, your manliness, your every talent, time, property, friends. He demands a complete renunciation of self in the use you make of all these, and the complete consecration of all to the glory of His own great Name. What follows upon that? My words to-night, 'Yield yourselves unto Him.' At the feet of your God lie down ; confess the unbelief and the unfaithfulness that have disgraced the past, and then, trusting in His mighty power, lean by faith—yes, by faith, remember—on His strong right arm ; boldly and earnestly take your place as the redeemed of the Lord, claiming your glorious privileges, and not shrinking—this is my point—from your *responsibilities and duties.* Will you do it—will you do it, my brother? I know the Holy Spirit is prompting ; will you not obey His impulse? I know that the Lord Jesus is beckoning to you : will you not respond? I know

that the Father is waiting to pour out upon you
all needful grace : will you not accept it? Will you
not come to Him even now, and say, So far as this
missionary work is concerned, so far as East Africa
is concerned—

'Take my life and let it be
Consecrated, Lord, to Thee!'

But you say, ' What can I do? ' Well, it is not for
me to say what you can do; that is a matter of
detail. But what I do insist upon is this, that it is
the duty of every one calling himself a Christian to
do something. It seems to me that no one who
acknowledges himself to be redeemed by the blood of
Christ, no one who has felt the bitterness of his own
sin, no one who knows the joy of his own salvation,
no one who has come practically to Him who loved
him and gave Himself for him, no such one can do
other than feel in every impulse of his heart that he
is spurred on to the conflict, to labour, to live, and to
die for the King. Will you not do something? Oh,
shall we pause for a moment in solemn silence, and
let each one ask himself, as in the presence of God,
Has the call come to me? It may be that God is
speaking even now to you, and in the solemn stillness
of your heart you have resolved to offer yourself. If
it be so, very lovingly and very earnestly I invite you
to meet me in the Committee-room at the close of
this evening's meeting, or, if that is not possible, to
communicate with me at the rooms of the Society

If the Spirit of God is moving in your heart, do not
hesitate ; do not ask, 'Will this step be pleasing or
praiseworthy in the eyes of men?' Go right on. Do
not flinch ; turn neither to the right hand nor to the
left, but, confident in the power that worketh within
you, believing that He who calls you will stand by
you in every time of need, in sickness, in health, in
life, in death ; go right on, and do the Master's will.
It was not by tarrying at home, or lingering by the
shores of the lake, that the disciples followed Christ
of Galilee.   They did it—*they did it.*   Religion is not
mere contemplation—it is action ; it is not a mere
sentiment, demurely praying—it is launching out into
the deep of the world's great necessity, and letting
down our nets for a draught, then following the
example, the footsteps, the word and the will of
Jesus.   Think of the world's great necessity !   It is
computed that, living and dying unchristianised
and unevangelised, there are something like twenty
millions of souls in Eastern Equatorial Africa !   It
seems to me, as I think of it, that I can hear their
cry coming across the Dark Continent, and over the
deep sea, like the pitiful, earnest, and entreating cry
that came to Jesus long ago, 'Carest thou not that
we perish?'   And Jesus Christ has given *His* answer
to that question : 'I lay down My life for the sheep.'
We who belong to Jesus, you and I, what answer
shall we give?   Shall we not follow Him in service,
in sacrifice, in life, and in labour?   Shall we not lay

down our lives day by day that we may faithfully do our part in bringing these perishing souls unto God? Oh, let us join together, let us in heart and soul say together that 'we will carry the Gospel of Jesus Christ to Eastern Equatorial Africa.'"